HOME

JENN ALEXANDER

Bywater
BOOKS

Ann Arbor

Bywater Books

Copyright © 2020 Jenn Alexander

Print ISBN: 978-1-61294-169-1

Bywater Books First Edition: May 2020

Printed in the United States of America on acid-free paper.

Cover designer: Ann McMan, TreeHouse Studio

Bywater Books
PO Box 3671
Ann Arbor MI 48106-3671
www.bywaterbooks.com

This novel is a work of fiction.

To Addie and Sandra—you two are my home.

Chapter One

Rowan Barnes couldn't figure out why Texans were so scared of hellfire when they seemed to already live and thrive in it. *How is it so damn hot outside?* She wiped the sweat from her brow with the back of her arm, and then continued pushing the shopping cart across the parking lot. The inhospitable heat reflected off the pavement, making the air feel like an oven, and she couldn't help but believe the metallic clanging of the cart's wheels were the warning bells of a doomsday harbinger. The walk from the grocery store to her car was a short distance, but even that short walk felt like an unending trek across the desert. The sun beat down relentlessly without even a single puff of cloud to absorb the intense burning glare.

"I'm gonna die," she said to no one in particular. "All these damn little black birds are gonna peck the flesh from my body. They're all gathered up there on those power lines waiting for an outsider like me to keel over from heat exhaustion."

She managed a single bitter laugh. It was official. Her brain was being fried. She'd been in Fort Worth, Texas, barely a week and already she was talking to herself.

By the time she reached her car, her shirt was damp with sweat, clinging to her uncomfortably. She hurriedly tossed her groceries in the trunk, returned her cart, and then slid into the metal broiler of a car that was *at least* fifty degrees hotter than the outside air, by her estimate. She didn't close the driver's side

1

door. She turned on the car and cranked the air conditioning up as high as it would go. The vents only blew more hot air. It would take a while before the engine had cooled enough for AC to have even the slightest hope of counteracting the exterior heat, so she rolled down all the windows, hoping that the drive would at least generate enough of a breeze to prevent heatstroke.

"You're so brave moving to Texas alone." Rowan had lost count of the number of friends who had said that to her. She had thought they were talking about taking the leap to move to a new state. She hadn't known that she'd need bravery for when driving from the grocery store became a survival mission.

By the time she pulled up to her apartment complex, the car-oven had cooled down from deathly "broil" to merely an uncomfortable "keep warm," which she supposed was the best she could ask for in Texas. Cold was clearly not a temperature that existed there.

She parked in front of her building as close to the stairs as possible in an attempt to minimize her time outside. She pulled in next to a truck with a bumper sticker that read, "Pro-God. Pro-Gun. Pro-Life." Her little Civic hybrid was dwarfed by the vehicle which belonged in a monster truck rally, not driving through the city.

At least my car will be out of the sun, she thought. The truck's shadow neatly covered the entirety of her car.

She took a breath of the merely "keep warm" air to brace for the scorching heat. Then she turned off the ignition, went around to the back of her car, and started grabbing her bags of groceries from the trunk. She wanted to spend as little time outside as possible, so she gathered all of the bags at once, attempting to balance the weight evenly for each arm. She strained with the weight of all the bags, but the last thing she wanted was to have to make a second trip.

"Ma'am?"

Rowan was already en route from her car to the stairs when she heard the deep voice, thick with a Southern drawl. She turned.

"Do you need help with those?" An early middle-aged man climbed down from the driver's seat of the truck, tugging his jeans up and over his beer belly with his belt.

"I'm good, thank you," Rowan said, but the man was already making his way over to her.

"I insist."

The next thing she knew, he was pulling a couple of bags of groceries from her hands.

Rowan's tired arms thanked him, but she was fairly certain she didn't want this pro-God, pro-gun, pro-lifer knowing where she lived, on the very good chance that he was anti-feminist, anti-atheist, anti-lesbians. She was too hot and tired to protest, though, so all she said was, "Thank you. I'm up on the third floor."

"My pleasure."

She led the way, rolling her eyes at the situation she found herself in, while uber-Texan followed with her groceries.

"Y'all new 'round here?" uber-Texan asked.

Y'all? She looked around to confirm it was, in fact, just her. There was no *all*.

"Yeah," she said. "I moved here last Tuesday from Portland for work."

"Portland," uber-Texan echoed. "That's quite the change. Well, welcome to Texas. I'm Dave."

"Thanks," she said. "I'm Rowan."

Dave kept talking. "I live down in 2b. Don't hesitate to holler if you need anything. I've been here two years now, since my wife and I split. It's a friendly bunch 'round here."

Too friendly, if you asked Rowan. Apparently incessant small talk was another Texas thing she'd have to adjust to. She reached her apartment and fished for her keys.

"Thanks for helping with the groceries," she said as she unlocked her apartment door.

Dave set the groceries down, but didn't make any move to leave. She hoped he didn't plan on carrying her groceries all the way inside and into the fridge. She tried to think of how to politely tell him that she was good from there, but Dave spoke first.

3

"Have you found a church 'round here yet?"

She wasn't sure if she should laugh at the absurdity of the assumption, or if she should be outraged. Instead, she shook her head and said a simple, "No."

"First Ministry down on Panhandle Street is close," Dave answered, oblivious to the offense Rowan took at his question. "That's where I go. It's a pretty good group there."

"I'll keep that in mind," she lied, feeling the Bible belt tighten constrictively around her.

Dave tipped his hat, told her that he hoped he'd see her there one Sunday, and then wished her a nice day while she tried to recover from the conversation. Finally, she was able to open the door and step into her apartment, where she was greeted with blissfully cool air from the AC which had been running all day. She kicked off her shoes and sank into her couch. Her floor lamp provided a soft light. She had chosen the apartment for its large floor-to-ceiling windows that filled the rooms with natural light, but one of the first things she had bought after the move was a set of blackout shades. The sun was insufferable. She'd pulled the shades tight as soon as they were hung, and hadn't cracked them even slightly since. The cool dark was so very welcome.

She could feel the heat leeching out of her pores. Her skin had a reddish tint, not from sunburn, but from its raised temperature. The back of her neck was sticky with sweat, and she already needed a second shower for the day.

But she didn't move from the couch. Instead she fished her phone out of her pocket and dialed the familiar number.

"Hello?"

Rowan closed her eyes at the sound of her best friend, Alycia's, voice. She'd hardly been gone over a week, and yet it felt like forever.

"Remind me again why I moved here?" she asked.

Alycia laughed.

"I'm serious," Rowan said. "I met my neighbor today. Ultra-conservative uber-Texan with a bumper sticker declaring all of his right-wing world views."

"Well, if I recall, I *did* warn you that Texas comes with Texans."

"You did." She was reluctant to admit that maybe she should have taken that point into more consideration before booking the U-Haul.

"And what did you say to *me?*" Alycia pressed.

Rowan sighed, repeating the mantra she'd said to all her friends and family as she'd packed for the move. "That this was a great opportunity. The type that would launch my career, get me out of being a prep cook cutting potatoes forever, put me on the map." This time, the mantra lacked all of her prior enthusiasm.

"Exactly," Alycia confirmed. "And you were right. You maybe should have prepared yourself more for the whole Texas aspect, but Rowan, this is your dream job. You get to cook with Daniel Stanford. Chances like this don't pop up every day."

Rowan nodded as her friend spoke. Alycia was right. She'd been working as a prep cook for four years, after working as a dishwasher for three. Meanwhile, she'd finished her culinary arts degree and continued to take every cooking class she could. She watched videos online to learn new techniques, spent hours practicing her knife skills, and read cookbooks cover to cover. She wanted to make a name for herself in the culinary world, and landing the job as *grillardin*—the grill chef—at Daniel Stanford's up-and-coming new restaurant opening in Texas was a golden ticket opportunity. It was her *in*.

"But it's a million degrees outside," she complained. "I've had to institute a strict 'no-sunlight' policy in my apartment. I feel like a vampire. Also, I'm pretty certain I'm the only person in this complex who doesn't own a gun. Based on the bumper stickers I've seen, I'm surrounded by a fucking militia. And have I mentioned it's a million degrees outside?"

"Hey, if you can't take the heat . . ."

Rowan felt the small smile that formed on her face. Alycia always had been able to find the perfect mix of empathy and humor to lift her spirits, able to vacillate between the two as needed.

"You'll be fine," Alycia promised, her voice softening around Rowan like a warm hug.

"You mean, '*y'all* will be fine.' Apparently, I'm a *y'all* now."

"Oh God," Alycia said with a laugh.

Rowan laughed as well, the discomfort melting as some of her earlier excitement for this new adventure sank back in.

"When do you start work?" Alycia asked.

"We have a soft opening on Friday, and everything officially kicks off next weekend. But I start tomorrow. We're getting everything ready for this soft launch, so the kitchen staff are meeting in the morning to finalize the details of the menu and then my boss has me scheduled to go out to a cattle ranch. Is that not the most Texan thing you've ever heard?"

"That is officially the most Texan thing ever."

"Right? Talk about farm-to-table. I get to go assess the cuts directly from the ranch."

"You're going to kill it," Alycia said. "The opening. Not the cow I hope."

"Thanks," Rowan said with a laugh. She shifted so that she was lying across the couch with her feet up. She could practically imagine herself sitting in Alycia's apartment, perhaps with their friends Kris and Hannah there as well, making beer flights to taste test their latest craft beer finds and talking about their weeks. She didn't feel a thousand miles away.

"I've got to run, but I expect a phone call Saturday morning to tell me all about how the soft launch went," Alycia said. "And also all the juicy details about this cattle ranch adventure you're going on."

Rowan already looked forward to their next conversation. "Will do. Bye, Aly-cat."

When the call clicked off, Rowan pulled her cell phone into her lap and stared down at it.

"This is a great opportunity," Rowan reminded herself, believing the words more than her earlier tired recital of the phrase. "The type that will launch my career, get me out of being a prep cook cutting potatoes forever, and put me on the map."

It was also the adventure of a lifetime. Before now, she never could have imagined herself visiting a Texas cattle ranch. She didn't have to live in Texas for the rest of her life. A year or two to get some experience working with a high-profile chef was all she needed. When she returned home, she'd have all sorts of stories to tell.

Finally, she got up from the couch. Her skin still felt warm, but it no longer burned. No longer quite so drained from the heat, she began putting her groceries away.

The apartment was littered with boxes, everything but the essentials still packed. She contemplated opening one of the boxes and starting to organize her place, but that made the move too real. She grabbed a beer from the fridge, trying to tell herself that she was too tired and that she'd unpack later.

She could pump herself up to be ready for her Texas adventure, but she wasn't ready to *live* in Texas.

It wasn't home.

"All right, we're going to keep our dinner simple tomorrow. We will be doing a three-course set dinner. The kale and corn fritters for the appetizer, a choice between top sirloin or fried chicken for the entrée, and banana pudding for dessert. For sides, we'll do the cornbread and rajas."

"Got it," Rowan said, listening to the head chef and owner, Daniel Stanford, as he listed the menu for their soft launch, a stripped-down offering from their full menu to get a feel for the kitchen and some feedback from trusted guests. Adrenaline coursed through her. Even with the simplified selection, the menu offerings had nuanced flavors and complexity. There would still be a lot of moving parts in the kitchen to get the meal to come together. The kale and corn fritters would be served with a hatch green chile aioli; the fried chicken was fried with a spicy cactus pear glaze; the cornbread was skillet-cooked and infused with jalapenos and bourbon. Rowan was in charge of grilling the sirloin steaks, and while on paper that was the simplest menu item, it would be no simple feat to get that many steak entrées done perfectly.

There wasn't much of a cushion for her in this soft launch. This was her first chance to prove herself and to show Daniel that he hadn't made a mistake in bringing her on as grill chef. He'd selected her from a large, nationwide pool of applicants all vying for this dream career opportunity. He'd taken a risk in searching for new talent to bring on, and she needed to prove that she was not some inexperienced rookie.

Except, that's exactly what she was.

"We're going to use all local meat and produce where possible," Daniel said. "Over the past few months I've secured deals with a handful of local farms and ranches. We'll pay a bit of a premium, but we can guarantee quality. All of the meat will be ethically raised, grass-fed, and antibiotic free, along with organic and pesticide-free produce."

That was the real reason Rowan had applied for the position at Daniel's new restaurant. He cooked damn good food, but more importantly he cooked ethical and health-wise food. He had recently been listed as one of America's best young chefs and all eyes were on him. His attention to moral standards didn't go unnoticed, and he had the chance to make a real change in the industry. Rowan wanted to be a part of the movement. She wanted it bad enough that as she listened to Daniel describe the menu, excitement swelled within her, and her discomfort with Texas and the relocation that came with the job were all but forgotten.

"Rowan, when you go to Landreth Ranch today, talk to Warren Landreth about *exactly* what we're looking for. Inspect the cuts. We'll need about thirty cuts of sirloin for the soft launch, but make sure he knows that we'll need a far larger amount for our official opening next week and that we'll be needing rib eyes next week as well."

Rowan nodded. "On it."

Daniel gave her the address, and once everyone was set with their preparation instructions for the day, she plugged it into her phone's GPS, ready to go pick up the steaks. As far as she could tell, the ranch was way hell-and-gone in the country, about an hour's drive west.

Guess I'll get some sightseeing in today, Rowan thought to herself with zero enthusiasm. She had driven from Portland to Fort Worth and been surprised at how very un-scenic the drive was. For the most part, the landscape of North Texas alternated between run-down small towns and barren fields. Billboards plastered the length of the interstate that she'd driven during the move, most of which pushed some sort of conservative belief. Pro-God. Pro-Gun. Pro-Life. Her neighbor's bumper sticker pretty much summed up Texas advertising.

Rowan cranked the AC and her stereo and settled in for the drive. She was pleasantly surprised to find that her GPS routed her off of the interstate and onto smaller farm-to-market roads, which were far more scenic. Instead of billboards, she looked out at rolling fields dotted with various livestock. The dense traffic of the Dallas-Fort Worth metroplex dissipated, and she relaxed into the quiet drive.

A large wooden sign with log posts marked the entrance to Landreth Ranch. She turned and drove up the long drive, parking in front of the main office building. She could see a house settled behind the building, nestled amid a patch of trees.

Rowan had never visited a cattle ranch before . . . or any other type of ranch for that matter. She stepped out of the car into the sticky Texas heat, ripe with the scents of cattle, hay, and dust. She could easily recognize the iconic Texas longhorn cattle grazing in the pasture. The other cows looked to be the standard brown and white variety. A loud whinny pulled her attention over to the corral on her right, which contained a handful of horses.

She wished her friends in Portland could see her. She felt a world away.

"Hi there," a woman called as she stepped out of the main office and walked over to where Rowan was standing.

Rowan blinked. She'd admit that she'd expected some middle-aged Texan to step out of that office wearing denim overalls and sporting a thick mustache. Maybe he'd have been chewing on a piece of hay to complete the stereotypical getup. The woman who greeted her was about as far from Rowan's expectations of a cattle rancher as she could get. She looked like she had stepped out of a *Southern Living* magazine, with her rusty red-brown hair tied back in a loose ponytail, her gentle curves, and her denim-clad legs that seemed to go on forever. Rowan particularly liked the woman's legs.

"How can I help you?" the woman asked, and Rowan realized she had yet to say anything.

Great start, Rowan thought. *Ogling makes me look very professional.*

"I'm Rowan Barnes from On the Range," she said. "I'm here to meet with Warren Landreth. Is he available?"

"I'm sorry, he's not. I'm Kate, his daughter. I'll be helping you out today."

Rowan frowned. Daniel had given her explicit instructions about what she needed to discuss with Warren Landreth, *owner* of Landreth Ranch.

"I assure you I'll provide the same quality service," Kate said.

She stood an inch or so taller than Rowan, and gazed down with summer-green eyes. Rowan stood for a moment, held by that gaze. She could see that she was not going to be able to speak with Warren. For a moment she warred with herself, but decided that ultimately Daniel wanted her to return with the beef for their soft launch. She would be sure to pass along the same explicit instructions to Kate.

"We'll need about thirty cuts today. More next week for our official launch. If all goes well, we're hoping to make this an ongoing partnership." Rowan recited the numbers and figures that Daniel sent her with: their anticipated weekly demand and their specifications for type, sizes, and cuts.

Kate nodded and motioned for Rowan to follow her.

Rowan went with Kate into the office. It was a small building with only two rooms. One room had a desk, computer, and filing cabinets, while the other, which Kate led Rowan into, was lined with deep-freeze refrigerators, each marked with a different type of beef: Longhorn, Angus, and Wagyu. A poster on the wall illustrated the various cuts of beef.

Excitement swelled within Rowan as she took it all in. In the kitchen, she considered herself to have more-than-average knowledge of beef. She knew how to cook a steak to desired doneness, and could state the exact internal temperature required for an order. She knew how long to marinate, how to get the best sear, and how long to rest a steak after cooking. In this room, she felt like a novice. This, though, was the real deal. This was the whole idea behind a farm-to-table restaurant. This was the authenticity Rowan craved in her career.

"You'll see that they're all uniform in weight," Kate said, as she pulled individually packaged steaks from the fridge. "Ten ounces, each of them. There's a scale on the far counter. Feel free to weigh each one."

Rowan did, not because she didn't trust Kate, but because she'd been instructed to check each aspect of the steak to ensure perfection. She checked the color and marbling on each, and once she was certain that everything met Daniel's specifications, she said, "Looks good."

Kate smiled, and the smile melted her cool exterior and made her green eyes shine. Rowan found herself drawn to this much warmer Kate. The smile was gone too soon, replaced once more with Kate's distant professionalism.

"I'll get those packaged for you and ring you up."

"Thanks," Rowan said.

She watched as Kate gracefully scanned and packaged the beef into two foam coolers with ice. They each carried a cooler out to Rowan's car, and Rowan found herself sad to be leaving so soon. She wanted to see Kate smile again.

"Your ranch is beautiful," Rowan said as she placed the box in the backseat.

The look of pride was clear on Kate's face. "Thank you. I'm quite fond of it myself."

"Is this where you grew up?" Rowan asked.

Kate nodded. "I moved out for a couple of years for college, but now I'm home again."

She couldn't decipher the wistful look that crossed Kate's face at that sentence.

"How about you?" Kate asked. "Your accent. You're not from Texas."

"No, no I'm not." She realized as she said the words that she might have sounded a bit too happy about that fact. "I only just moved here last week for this job. I'm from Portland."

"Well then, welcome to Texas!" Kate said. "How are you liking it so far?"

She chose her answer carefully. "The heat is killing me."

"Bless your heart." Kate laughed, a warm, rich sound, her green eyes sparkling. "It's not even *really* summer yet."

"I may die." Rowan gave a single resolute nod, nearly certain that death was going to happen.

Kate held her with her gaze. "I hope not."

A spark passed through Rowan.

"Well, assuming I survive, I'll be back next Wednesday for our full order."

"I'm looking forward to it," Kate said. "And I'm looking forward to doing business with y'all."

Rowan slipped into the driver's seat and started her car. As she turned out onto the dusty highway, she realized she was still smiling. She shook her head. She was there on business. It was hardly the time to be all swoony over the pretty country girl.

She laughed out loud as she cranked her stereo and imagined the look on Kate's face if she *were* to flirt with this Southern girl from the Bible Belt. Kate would probably pray for her and run for the hills.

Maybe not the best for business.

So, she could enjoy the view, but she would try to refrain from all swooning, flirting, or related shows of gayness. She could do that.

Surely.

Chapter Two

Kate walked the familiar route through the inpatient wing of the rehabilitation hospital, eager to be out of the sterile building with its stark white walls and lingering smells of disinfectant and disease. Seven weeks ago the hallways were a maze, but now she navigated through them effortlessly.

"Hi, Daddy," she said, stepping into the small private room where her dad lay in his bed. She set her duffel bag down on the chair. "Ready to go home?"

Warren Landreth frowned, a distant look in his eyes as he echoed the word, "Home."

"I know it won't be the same," Kate said. "But it sure as heck beats being here, right? You'll be back on the ranch with your animals. And I'll be there to help you."

"You don't have to do this, Katie."

The words were old and hollow. She'd made up her mind seven weeks ago.

"We'll sell the ranch," he continued. "It's worth a pretty penny. I'll retire, we'll pay off these hospital bills, and your life will keep going as it was."

"Oh, would you hush? This is what I *want*. I love the ranch as much as you."

He huffed. "I don't know about that, but you're certainly as hardheaded as me. Just promise me, you'll sell the place if you need to. I don't want you giving up your dreams for this."

"Let's get you home," she said, not about to promise any such thing.

Warren pushed back the blue hospital bedsheet, and she helped him swing his legs over the side of the bed. Once he was upright, she went to the duffel bag and pulled out a pair of her dad's brown leather cowboy boots. "Let's get these on you," she said, sliding them onto his feet.

"It's not like I'm needing them."

She hated the dejection she heard in her dad's voice. "Yeah, well, you came in here a cowboy and, darn it, you're going to leave here a cowboy."

"Katie," he began, but she cut him off.

"Not another word."

"Hardheaded, I swear," he said under his breath.

Kate got the boots on her dad's feet and then patted his knee. "I'm gonna go get the nurse to help me get you into this chair," she said.

He harrumphed, and she went into the hall to the nurse's station.

"Miss Landreth, are you here to pick up your daddy?" Her favorite nurse, Cynthia, set down a clipboard and gave Kate her full attention.

"Yes, ma'am. Time to go home."

"Well, now it's about damn time, isn't it? We're gonna miss your daddy and his big ol' sense of humor around here, though."

"Uh huh," Kate said with a laugh, "I can just imagine the jokes he's been tellin'." Her dad had always had a knack for making people laugh, but it was usually by ribbing them. And he'd had an even harder edge to his jokes than usual since the accident. His spirit was just not as light and jovial as usual.

Cynthia gave a loud belly laugh. "Yeah, you probably can. But with him gone, who's going to keep Bonnie in line for me? She hasn't worked this hard in the entire time she's been at this hospital."

"Well, we'll just have to come say hello while we're up here for PT," Kate said. "Make sure Bonnie's still doing her job."

"Please do," Cynthia said, this time in full seriousness.

Kate nodded. She wouldn't miss the hospital, but she'd miss

the nurses, Cynthia especially. They'd been good to her dad, and she had to admit she was terrified of getting home and being on her own.

Cynthia headed toward Warren's room. She grabbed his wheelchair from its spot by the window and pushed it over to where he still sat on the edge of his hospital bed.

"Mr. Landreth, I see you're escaping today. I could not be more pleased for you."

"You're just happy to be rid of me," Warren said.

"No, sir. And I'd tell you if I was. You know I'm not about the bullshit."

Warren gave a coarse chuckle, his throat dry and crackly beneath the laugh. "Yeah, you would, too."

Cynthia smiled at him and squeezed his hand. "All right, ready? Time to bust out of here." She motioned for Kate, and they each took a side. Kate grabbed her dad's right arm as Cynthia grabbed his left.

Together the two of them managed to lift Warren down from the hospital bed and into the wheelchair that Kate had purchased five weeks earlier.

"It's going to be an adjustment at first," Cynthia warned. "For both of you."

"We'll be okay," Kate said.

"Oh, I don't doubt that, darling. But I've been around here long enough to know everyone has a hard time adjusting to being home without all of the supports for the first while. The home-care nurses will come out three times a day for the first couple of weeks to give you a hand with getting in and out of the chair, and figuring out ways to maneuver specific tasks. After that they'll only come out as needed. But you have all of the numbers to call if you need any help. Don't hesitate to reach out. Y'all aren't alone in this, got it?"

"Got it," Kate assured her. She knew it wouldn't be easy, but she was beyond ready to have her dad home and out of the hospital. She was done with the chemical sterility; the harsh white walls and lights; and juggling time between the ranch, the hospital, and the drive between the two. Her dad, she knew, was sick of nurses and hospital food, and the 24/7 noise of people and monitors. Home was, well, *home*. Besides, she'd spent the past seven weeks reading up on everything that they would need. Owen and Dean, their two ranch hands, had helped build a ramp up to the front porch so that her dad could wheel in and out. They were working on making the barn and office wheelchair accessible as well. Whatever her dad needed, she was going to make sure they made it happen.

Kate wheeled her dad out of the hospital, Cynthia following behind. It was a bright May afternoon, and she watched as her dad covered his eyes against the sunlight. He used to be outside from sunup to sundown, but she couldn't say if he'd been wheeled out even a handful of times while in the hospital.

She reached the truck without a word, guilt constricting around her. She had wanted to be at the hospital more. She'd wanted to take her dad for strolls outside and help with his physical therapy, but the ranch wasn't going to run itself, and she had to make sure it was still there for him to go home to. That ranch was everything to Warren.

"Let me," he said after she opened the passenger door to the truck.

She had to refrain from stepping in. She knew that her dad wanted his independence, but that didn't make it any easier to watch him struggle. His upper-body strength made it easier for him to haul himself up into things than down currently, but he would get better at both. Soon he'd be getting in and out of the chair on his own.

Warren reached his hands up onto the seat and with a great effort pushed himself into the truck. She refrained from helping as he struggled to pull his full weight into the truck, but she did hold out her hands to spot him.

"I've got it," he said gruffly once he slid into the seat.

Kate raised her hands in apology and stepped back.

"Thank you for everything, Cynthia." She pulled Cynthia into a hug. "You've been a godsend these past seven weeks."

"Oh, believe me, it was my pleasure, darlin'," Cynthia said. "Now you two go and get settled in at home. You must be sick to death of this place."

"Well, now, that's a grim thing to say at a hospital," Kate said, her lips quirking into a half smile.

Cynthia laughed a big warm belly laugh. "Yeah, I suppose it is."

Kate hugged Cynthia again, a final hug for good measure; then she shut her dad's passenger door and climbed into the driver's seat and started the ignition on her truck. The familiar twang of country music came through the speakers, and already life felt halfway normal.

She looked over at her dad who gazed out the window at the hospital.

"Come on, cowboy," she said. "Your ranch awaits."

Her dad didn't look over. "Your ranch now." The grief was heavy in his voice.

Kate wasn't about to let him give up so easily. She pulled out of the parking lot, heading toward the highway. *"Our* ranch."

Rowan pulled the final steaks from the grill and tented them with tinfoil to rest until they were ready to be plated.

I did it. This is real. The steaks were done correctly. She was certain of it. She half felt as if she were in a dream, hardly able to believe her years of hard work had finally landed her the role of *grillardin* in a professional kitchen. *Daniel fucking Stanford's kitchen,* to be precise. She'd followed his quickly rising career in cooking magazines and would never have believed she'd even get the chance to meet him, never mind work for him. But the pleasant ache in her legs and back told her that she was very much awake.

Smoke from the grill wafted through the kitchen. The smell of nicely charred meat was layered with the sweet and spicy scents of the onions and poblano peppers being sautéed a few stations over. The symphony of aromas alone was enough to tell Rowan that their team had killed the soft launch.

Daniel Stanford oversaw the expediting of the final few plates while Rowan and the rest of the kitchen staff began cleaning their stations.

The dishes had been sent out, but even so there was no time to stand back and celebrate.

If you have time to stand, you have time to work.

The night wasn't over until their executive chef said it was over.

Finally, Daniel walked into the kitchen, both hands raised in victory.

"Great job tonight, y'all," he said.

Rowan could practically hear the collective sigh of relief from all of the kitchen staff, and the shift in mood was palpable.

It was only the soft launch, she reminded herself. The kitchen would only get busier and the stress level higher. Still, she felt she had proved herself. As grill chef, in charge of steaks, there had been no room for error. She had been responsible for, arguably, the most important of the proteins. The comment cards from the selected guests had yet to come back—the true measure of how well she'd done—but she was confident in the quality of the steaks she'd sent out. She'd been focused and precise, giving each cut of meat the care and attention it deserved.

Rowan, Daniel, and the rest of the kitchen staff wiped down the counters and moved the dishes into the industrial dishwasher.

"I think we're ready for next week," Daniel said. "We had the stripped-down menu, so it was relatively easy to stay on top of our game, but if we all continue to work together as we did tonight, then I expect everything to go smoothly next week. Our menu will be expanded, but it will still be kept clean and simple. There's no reason things should get too out of hand. Tonight we were a team. Every one of you did the team proud—did *me* proud. This place is going to be a hit."

Rowan knew in her gut that he was right.

"Now go get some rest. Y'all earned it."

Rowan said her good-byes and then picked up her knapsack, which she slung over her shoulder as she pushed her way out the back doors to her car.

It was nearly midnight, but while it had cooled significantly since her arrival, the air outside was still warmer than the air in the kitchen. This time, Rowan barely felt the heat as she skipped across the parking lot. Her first night had been a success!

Once inside of her car, she turned on the AC and pulled off her bandanna, allowing her short, dark hair to fall over her forehead. She turned on her stereo, cranking the volume on her favorite punk album. The energy from the blast beats on the drums and the power chords on the guitar matched the energy she felt coursing through her. She bobbed her head and sang along loudly as she drove back to her place. The roads were quiet, devoid of the traffic that congested the streets during the daytime. The lights of downtown Fort Worth reflected off the Trinity River, and Rowan soaked in the view of her new city.

With the traffic cleared, it was a short drive back to her apartment. She parked in the empty spot next to Dave's giant pickup. She rolled her eyes at his bumper sticker, but refused to let it detract from her good mood. She continued to hum the song that had been playing last as she made her way up to the apartment.

She pushed open the door and was greeted by quiet dark. Too quiet after the buzz of energy that had enveloped her all evening. She turned on the lights and saw her half-unpacked boxes littered around her living room. Disappointment landed square in the center of her chest.

This wasn't home.

Rowan closed the door behind herself and dropped her keys on the end table. She set her bag down and looked around the empty apartment with her still-packed boxes. Then she dropped down onto the couch with a sigh.

A glance at the wall clock told her it was too late to call her parents. She'd have to wait until morning to fill them in on her first shift. Alycia would still be awake, though.

She pulled up Alycia's name in her phone and hit the call button, eager to hear her friend's voice. The apartment was a vacuum, lonely and suffocating. She needed to share her evening with someone she loved.

The phone rang.

Rowan's smile returned to her face as she thought about telling Alycia how incredible her first night as a professional grill chef had been.

Another ring.

The smile slipped away. It hadn't occurred to Rowan that Alycia might not be available to answer.

Another ring.

Please be there.

Voice mail.

Rowan hit "end" and tossed the phone to the far end of the couch, as though the phone itself was responsible for the call going to voice mail. Then she went to the bathroom to get ready for bed, not at all optimistic that she'd be able to climb off of the roller coaster of emotions that she found herself on in order to fall asleep.

She was brushing her teeth when she heard the ding of a text message. She went back out to the living room to pick up her phone from the couch.

Hey, sorry I missed your call. I'm just out at a comedy show with the girls. Will call you tomorrow. Hope everything is going well! XO.

Rowan read the message over once, twice, a third time. Each time, the sting of the words hit her more intensely than the last. She didn't message back.

A part of her felt silly at the strength of her emotional reaction. She hadn't expected her friends to stop everything when she moved and wait for her calls. But a larger part of her couldn't stop imagining her friends out having a good time while she sat in her empty apartment.

She went back to her bathroom, set her toothbrush back in its cradle, and rinsed her mouth. But she was unable to rinse out the taste of loss.

Chapter Three

Kate woke before the sun. Waking early had become a part of her body's natural rhythm, so much so that she no longer needed to use an alarm clock. Even moving away from the ranch for university had not reset her internal clock. She'd never stopped being a rancher.

She stretched lazily, extending each arm and then each leg, before pulling back the sheets and climbing out of bed. She stepped into a pair of slippers and then headed to the kitchen to make her morning pot of coffee. It was her favorite time of day—sitting out on the porch with her coffee and watching the sun rise over the pastures.

As she stepped into the hall, she realized the lights were already on in the kitchen. It shouldn't have surprised her to find her dad already awake as well. He'd been up before dawn since before she was born. Still, the past few mornings, he'd slept in until his home care nurse arrived to help him get up, dressed, and ready for the day.

Kate stepped into the kitchen, and for a moment she just took in the sight. Her dad was at the sink, filling the coffeepot with water, his elderly Australian shepherd, Patch, right beside him. When her dad wheeled over to the coffeemaker, Patch followed right alongside him.

She lifted a hand to her chest. As happy as she was to have her dad home, she suspected Patch was even happier. The dog had slept by the door every night since the accident, waiting for his human to come home. It had broken her heart all over again every night.

"Somebody sure is happy to have his favorite human home," Kate said.

Warren looked up at her with the ghost of a smile and reached down to pat his dog's head. "He's a good old boy."

"He is."

She watched as her dad struggled to lift a pot of water high enough to pour into the coffeemaker. From his wheelchair he sat an inch or so too low to be able to fill the coffeepot.

"I'll help you with that, Daddy," she said, and she stepped forward to take the pot of water from his hands.

Warren frowned, but relinquished the pot.

"Can't even make my own coffee anymore," he grumbled.

Kate poured the water into the brewer and then went to the cupboard for the coffee beans.

"We're gonna have to make some changes to the kitchen. But we're going to get it all figured out."

She ground the beans, added them to the mesh filter, and set the coffeepot to brew.

"There," she said. "Soon we'll have coffee and all will be right with the world. Isn't that what you always say? 'Ain't anything so bad a strong cup of coffee can't fix it.'"

"I might've proved myself wrong."

The defeat in her dad's voice broke her heart. Kate found herself at a loss for what to say. Her dad had always been the optimist in the family, but the accident had been devastating.

She took two mugs from the cupboard and placed them on the counter, then sat at the table while the coffee brewed. Gradually the rich aroma filled the kitchen, even the scent making her feel more awake.

"Alex will be here at eight to help you shower and work on your exercises," Kate said.

"Fantastic," her dad answered, but his bitter tone made it clear that it was anything but.

"He's no Cynthia, is he?" she asked, leaning forward conspiratorially, hoping to lighten the mood.

"What's that supposed to mean?"

Her dad seemed genuinely perplexed, and she had to smother a laugh.

"I saw the way you two looked at each other," she said.

Warren rolled his eyes. "Yeah, well, it doesn't matter now, does it? Maybe if we'd met before this stupid accident . . ."

"Right, because before the accident you would have had all sorts of reasons to be meeting pretty nurses up at the hospital."

Her dad's lips pulled upward for a moment, but the smile was gone almost as quickly as it had appeared. "There's no point thinkin' about that."

Kate exhaled. She wanted to say more. She wanted to convince him that just because his life was different didn't mean it was over. But the coffeepot interrupted, spitting the last of the coffee into the pot and indicating with a beep it was ready.

"I'll take my coffee with cream, please," she said. "Cups are on the counter."

Warren looked at her as if about to protest, but she held his gaze, daring him to challenge her. He knew better, and so he nodded once, then turned and wheeled over to the counter. With the counter set as high as it was, he had to pull the mug into his lap, then bring the pot down to his level to pour. He filled the first mug, set it on the counter, and filled the second. Then he wheeled over to the fridge to get the cream, which he added to each mug with the same slow procedure he'd used to pour the coffee.

Kate watched as he balanced a mug in his lap and began to wheel over toward her. The coffee splashed over the top, and her dad cursed under his breath. She had to refrain from going to help him. Instead, she opened a newspaper and pretended not to watch as he struggled.

It took a minute for the coffee to reach her, but she could see the pride on her dad's face as he handed her the drink.

"Thank you," she said, and took a sip, relishing the rich, warm liquid.

Kate waited for her dad to go get his coffee. Then she stood and headed out to the porch, walking slowly so that he could keep up, once again resisting the powerful urge to help him.

It was still dark outside. Only the barest sliver of light broke across the horizon. She sat on the cushioned porch swing, and her dad wheeled in beside her.

"A new day," he said.

Kate looked over at him. "Every day is."

She took a sip of her coffee as they gazed out at the sky together. Fiery pinks and oranges shot across the horizon, accented against the deep navy shade of the darkened sky and the purple patches of clouds. The air was pleasantly cool, with a soft breeze blowing across her skin.

"It's been too long since we've last sat out here like this," she said. For most of her life, it had been their morning routine.

"It has been awhile," Warren agreed.

Some of their deepest conversations had been held there, but this morning they sat in companionable silence.

As daylight stretched across the field, thoughts of the busy day ahead seeped through Kate's mind. Her dad had home care visits and physical therapy at various points over the course of the day. She had to rotate the cows in the fields and mend some fences that were getting pretty worn. Their hands, Owen and Dean, would, thankfully, show up around seven to help with the day's work. Then, midmorning, she was expecting a visit from Rowan Barnes from On the Range to pick up the restaurant's next order of beef—a full order this time for their opening.

Kate smiled at the thought of Rowan. Poor girl was so out of her element in Texas. Even from their brief interaction, Kate could tell Rowan generally carried herself with an air of confidence, bordering on cockiness. She'd seen it in Rowan's body language, the way she stood with her shoulders back, chin raised almost defiantly, and the fire in her eyes when she did business with Kate. It was clear she tried hard to maintain that air of confidence, despite the fact that when it came to Texas she had no idea what she was doing. It was actually pretty darn cute. Kate had enjoyed watching her look around the ranch, dark eyes wide with wonder. She suspected that Rowan hadn't spent much time up close and personal with any sort of livestock.

Kate finished her coffee and allowed herself one more minute to sit before starting the busy day. Both she and her dad had a lot of work ahead. It wouldn't necessarily be pleasant for either of them, but the end results would be worth it.

"I guess I'd better get started." She carried her coffee mug inside, changed into her work clothes, and pulled on her boots.

Her dad was still sitting on the porch when she went back outside.

"Do you need help with anything before I get to work?" she asked.

He just shook his head.

"Okay." She tried to think of something else to say, wanting to prolong the moment together. "Well, holler if you need anything. Owen and Dean will be here soon, and they can help as well."

"I'm good, Katie," her dad said.

There was a wistfulness in his voice, though. Kate was tempted to sit back down beside him, but there was too much work to get done, so she patted him on the back and headed over to the barn.

It's going to take some time to adjust, she reminded herself. Besides, he'd gotten out of bed and made coffee on his own. That was the progress she needed to focus on.

She wanted things to go back to normal as soon as possible. Of course, they were never going to go back to the way they'd been. They'd have to figure out some sort of new normal.

But they'd had their sunrise coffee.

Some things could be the same.

Kate did not have time for a jailbreak.

She sat atop her horse, Stryder, and worked to rotate the cattle. The cattle rotation was done every few days to prevent the grass in the fields from becoming grazed too thin. It simply involved moving the cows from one pasture to another, and was typically a quick and easy task to complete. She had only started with the longhorns, however, when she noticed the first of the escaped cattle.

"Darn it, not today," she said.

In defiance, a cow mooed from the roadway.

Thankfully she hadn't yet herded the longhorns out of their pasture, and she was able to make a quick exit and close the gate, containing them. Then she eased Stryder into a lope and took off toward the road. Owen was working on milking cows in the barn, and Dean was fixing a weak area of fence on the other side of the property.

Kate shook her head at herself. She should have done the fences a week ago. She'd helped on the ranch growing up, but she'd never been solely in charge before, and the enormity of the task settled heavy on her shoulders. There were a million moving parts, and she had to learn quickly how to juggle them all at once.

A handful of cattle meandered along the side of the road, snacking on grass as they went. It appeared only five or six had gotten out, and they wouldn't be able to go far, with cattle grates along the road only a few meters away from where they grazed. She was confident she could get them rounded up and herded back into their pasture—one without a broken fence—while her dad was still in his physical therapy. The last thing she wanted was for him to find escaped cattle his first week home. She needed him to know that she was in control of the ranch. He had enough to worry about without also worrying whether or not his daughter was going to run his home and livelihood into the ground.

Kate made quick time as she worked to steer the cows back to the ranch.

"Come on, girls. I don't have time for this today," she said to them as she rounded them up.

She heard the low rumble of a car on the road in the distance, and her heart rate quickened.

"Let's get you ladies back into the field where you can enjoy a nice sunny afternoon with some fresh green grass. How's that sound?" she asked, with increased urgency.

The cows plodded from the road toward the ranch and she breathed a sigh of relief. She just had to get them into their fenced-in field.

The car turned off of the highway and into the ranch drive. "Of course," Kate grumbled. "She comes *now*." This was not helping to present the ranch as operating as smoothly and professionally as ever. Her only saving grace was that it was Rowan Barnes, not Daniel Stanford, picking up the beef, and Rowan had never seen the ranch, or *any* ranch, operating any differently.

Because a bunch of cows running loose screams professional in any instance, Kate thought.

The car pulled in to park just as she was getting the last of the cows rounded up near their field. Rowan stepped out, pushing her sunglasses up onto the top of her short, dark hair, and taking in the sight before her. For just a moment, Kate forgot about the cows and took the time to watch as Rowan looked around. She wore a black tank top with ripped jeans and appeared to have stepped through the looking glass into some unknown world. She was more attractive than Kate remembered, with her outfit highlighting the contrast between her bold attitude and soft curves.

"Do me a favor and get that gate?" Kate called, bringing her attention back to the task at hand. She might as well make use of the extra set of hands.

Rowan froze, her eyes locked on the cows with a comical expression of horror. She hadn't even closed her car door yet, and from the look on her face Kate wondered if she was going to get back in and drive away. She looked as overwhelmed as Kate felt, and in that moment she wasn't the hotshot chef that Kate was supposed to impress.

"They won't bite, I swear," Kate said, softening her voice. "They'll just moo and get on with it."

Rowan didn't seem convinced. She appeared to have paled somewhat at the thought of getting anywhere near the cattle.

"You'd better be right," she said.

Kate watched her hesitate for a moment longer, before going

to the gate—making a wide arc around the cattle to get there—and pushing it open for Kate to herd the cows inside. She pressed herself flat against the gate and squeezed her eyes shut as the cows meandered past her. When one cow turned its head toward her out of curiosity, Rowan practically leapt out of the way, but she managed to stay with the gate and pushed it closed once the last of the cows was inside.

Kate let out a breath of relief and dismounted Stryder. She tied his lead to the wooden fence.

"Thank you," she said, turning to Rowan and wiping the sweat off her hands on her dirty jeans. "This lot decided to make a run for it this morning."

"They're all accounted for now?" Rowan asked, looking out at the cows. Kate did a quick count and then nodded. "They're all here."

She took a moment to watch Rowan study the cattle, her dark eyes wide with interest, and she tried to imagine feeling the same awe Rowan felt. As Rowan turned her gaze to Kate, her breath hitched slightly at the depth in Rowan's chocolate brown eyes. Or at the embarrassment at having been caught watching Rowan. Yeah, Kate reasoned, probably just the embarrassment.

"I'm glad I was able to help." Rowan smiled, warm undertones shining through in those brown eyes of hers. She had a dimple in her left cheek when she smiled.

Kate thought back on Rowan's look of fear as the cows had walked past, and she laughed. "You were really scared."

Rowan blushed and then straightened, pulling her confidence back into place. "They've already tried running away to avoid becoming steak dinner. The next step is clearly a revolt, and I have no doubt that in a fight between me and one of those massive things, I'd lose."

"They're gentle giants," Kate said. "That long grass out by the road is one big buffet to them. They're too full and happy to start any rebellion."

"You don't know that." Rowan set her hands on her hips. "Facing down an angry herd of cattle is a risk I'd rather not take."

Kate didn't know how Rowan managed to maintain a straight face, but she had her shoulders back and her chin raised ever-so-slightly. The utter confidence she attempted to project was too much for Kate, who was the first to break into laughter.

When was the last time she'd really laughed?

"How did the launch go?" Kate asked, not really wanting to shift back into work mode, but genuinely interested in the new restaurant and this new chef.

Rowan lit up. "Wonderful. We got a lot of great comments. The steak dinners were a hit. If everything runs this smoothly during our full launch, then we've got nothing to worry about."

"I didn't doubt that for a second," Kate said. "Daniel Stanford is an excellent chef, and you must be as well if he hired you as his sous chef."

Rowan's entire demeanor shifted. Gone was the forced confidence she'd tried to project earlier. Now, true pride and passion were evident in Rowan's smile.

"I'm not bad."

Even in the modest answer, Kate could hear Rowan's pride in her work.

"Are you feeling any more settled in Texas?" Kate asked. She should be leading Rowan in to get the meat for the order, but instead she was standing on the dusty gravel drive outside of the cow pasture, making small talk and not wanting that small talk to end.

Rowan looked at her for a breath before answering. "Honestly? Not really. I'm sure it's only a matter of time, but right now I miss home."

She hadn't been prepared for the honesty in Rowan's answer, and the moment of vulnerability hit her square in the chest. She'd known that Texas felt a little disorienting for Rowan, but she hadn't thought about the homesickness Rowan must be feeling, and what she must have sacrificed to follow her passion. She shifted her weight forward, leaning slightly closer to Rowan and wanting to offer her some kind of comfort.

"You must be really passionate about cooking to have moved here for the job," Kate said, hoping her admiration shone through.

Rowan met her eyes and held her gaze for a long moment, her features softening with the weight of Kate's words. "I am. This is all I've ever wanted to do. Ever since I was little, making play-dough pizzas for everyone. It's my dream job."

Kate could *feel* the passion in Rowan, who had left everything she knew for the chance at her dream. Kate could relate to that level of sacrifice, as well as the loneliness that came with it. Since her dad's accident, her life had consisted of her dad, the hospital, and the ranch. She had also stepped through the looking glass. Her world was familiar and yet entirely upside down.

"Have you been to the rodeo?" Kate asked, surprising even herself with the question.

Rowan laughed. "Um, that would be a no."

"Well now, there's a good way of getting introduced to Texas," Kate said. Suddenly the rodeo seemed like the fun night in Texas that they *both* needed. "Let's go."

Rowan looked caught off-guard, and Kate's stomach tightened in anticipation of Rowan's answer. She hoped she hadn't crossed a line. She found herself really wanting to show Rowan a little piece of her Texas.

"What day?" Rowan asked.

Kate smiled. "Well, normally the rodeo is only Friday and Saturday nights, but this week is the American finals, so we could go tomorrow night before your big launch if you'd like."

Rowan looked a little uncertain, but she nodded. "Why not?"

"Excellent," Kate said, already making plans in her mind. "I could pick you up and we could grab dinner beforehand? There's a famous Tex-Mex restaurant near the Stockyards. The food there is delicious. I think you'd really like it."

This time Rowan smiled widely. "You should've led with that. I'm not so sure about this whole rodeo thing, but I'll never say no to trying new foods."

Kate laughed. "Noted. I promise that even if you hate this 'rodeo thing' you'll have a delicious meal to compensate. Now, how about I pick you up tomorrow at five?"

"Sounds good," Rowan said.

This boldness was a new experience for Kate. She had certainly never invited clients to the rodeo before, but she hated the thought of Rowan being miserable in Texas without ever experiencing any of the quintessential Texas experiences that the state had to offer.

"Let's go get your order rung up, and you can write down your address and phone number while you're at it," Kate said.

She turned and led the way to the office while Rowan followed close behind. On the walk, Kate replayed the conversation in her mind.

I'm just being nice, she told herself. *Helping her adjust to living in a new place.* The offer certainly had nothing to do with Rowan's adorable dimpled smile or that biting sense of humor and bright laugh that she couldn't seem to get enough of.

It was a completely innocent invitation.

Kate could keep telling herself that.

Rowan had never had any interest in going to see a rodeo, and yet she could think of little else for the rest of the day.

She dropped the steaks off at On the Range, ready for Friday night's big launch, and then she went back to her empty mess of an apartment. She slumped down onto the couch and wondered lazily if she should unpack some boxes. Even just *one* box. She made no move to get up. Instead, she replayed the morning's events.

Rowan was unsure what to make of Kate. She was so very Texan. They had absolutely nothing in common. And yet Kate was warm and likable. Rowan felt like maybe they could even be friends. Of course, she wasn't about to tell Kate that she was gay any time soon, and so it would be a limited friendship, but still it would be nice to know a friendly face in Texas.

If nothing else, it would all make a good story to tell her friends back home. She couldn't wait to see the looks on their faces when she told them she had helped herd a group of escaped cows. She didn't know anyone in Portland who could say anything like that.

31

As if cued by the thoughts of home, her cell phone vibrated in her pocket. She pulled it out and smiled when she saw her dad's name on the screen.

"Hi, Dad," she said, sitting back and kicking her feet up onto her coffee table.

"Rowan, I've got your mom here, too. We were here missing you and wanted to give you a call and see how you're doing."

"It hasn't been that long since we last talked," Rowan said with amusement. Her parents had called her first thing in the morning the day after the soft launch to ask how it had gone. Paul and Emily Barnes had always been Rowan's biggest supporters.

"It's been ages," her mom said.

"I'm pretty sure it's been forty-eight hours."

"*Ages*," her mom stressed.

Rowan didn't want to admit that it had, in fact, felt like ages. She was a grown-ass woman who could live on her own. And yet, back home, she talked to her parents almost daily, and she saw them every few days. It was rare that they went a week without talking to or seeing each other, and if they did it was because they were all really busy. Now, Rowan was far away and alone.

"How's Texas going?" Emily asked, as though reading Rowan's thoughts. "Any better than when we last talked?"

Rowan shrugged, then realized that her parents couldn't see the gesture. "It's going. It'll take awhile to really settle in, I think. It's still hotter than hell, but it definitely helps to be keeping busy with work. I look forward to our full launch."

"We're so excited for you," Paul said. "We couldn't be prouder. I've been telling everyone to look for your name now that you're cooking in the big league."

"Dad, I'm a chef, not a celebrity," she said, rolling her eyes but grinning at her dad's sentiment.

"I don't see the difference," he stated.

She felt the blush creep up her neck and she smiled, glad just to hear her parents' voices. They had always been her cheerleaders.

"I'm going to the rodeo tonight," Rowan said.

"The rodeo?" her dad asked, as though he couldn't quite believe what he'd heard.

"I know." She shared the same tone of disbelief. "I'm still not quite sure what I've gotten myself into. I was invited to go, and I figured I might as well check it out. At least once. When in Rome, right?"

"Who are you going with?" Leave it to her mom to ask the hard questions.

"Her name's Kate."

"Her?" her mom asked. "A *special* her?"

"Mom, I've barely been here two weeks. Besides, trust me, this girl is as straight as they come. She's a bona fide Texas Southern belle cowgirl."

"And how did you meet this Texas cowgirl?"

"I picked up the steak for our restaurant from her family's ranch."

Her dad laughed. A loud belly laugh. The kind of big laugh that was always saved for moments when he was truly, deeply tickled.

"A *really* real cowgirl," he said.

"Born and raised," Rowan confirmed.

"That's brilliant."

She could practically see her dad clasping his hands together with a grin of delight on his face.

"I helped round up her cows today." She wished she could actually see the look on her dad's face, because she was pretty certain it was even better than what she was envisioning.

"You what?" he asked.

Rowan laughed at the surprise, and also horror, in her dad's voice.

"Oh, I'm sure it was quite a sight," Rowan said. "I wish you'd been there to see it. I pulled into the ranch and the cows were running everywhere. Kate was on her horse trying to round them up into their field. I opened the gate while she herded them all in."

Rowan smiled as she replayed the memory. Kate had been

33

especially sexy, riding her horse to round up the cows. She had the cowboy hat and boots and everything. Her flannel button-down shirt had been tucked into her jeans, and the entire outfit had highlighted every delicious curve.

"Anyway," she continued, "I'm not going to be given the title of 'ranch hand' any time soon, but those cows . . . they were *massive*. They could have charged if they wanted to."

"Honey, I think you're confusing them with bulls," her mom said.

"I'm pretty sure they're the same animal, just different genders," Rowan said. "I risked my life out there today. And as a 'thank you' Kate has offered to take me to the rodeo. Show me a bit of Texas."

Her mom laughed. "You did not risk your life. I can't stop picturing you trying to get the gate for a bunch of cattle, though. I so wish I'd been there."

"I hope you didn't touch them," her dad added. "You be careful around those cows."

"I don't intend on spending any more time around 'those cows.'"

"Good," he said, resolutely. He'd always been the cautious one in the family.

"Give us a call tomorrow and let us know how the rodeo was?" her mom added.

"I will. Absolutely. I'm sure I'll have all sorts of stories to tell."

"I'm glad to hear you're going out tonight," her dad said. "I worry about you way down there in Texas."

"I know, Dad, and I'm good. It's just going to be a bit of an adjustment."

"Home is here to welcome you back anytime," he added. "You know that, right? Go kick ass at this job, but if you don't like it, you don't have to stay."

"The job is great. Texas will take getting used to, but I'll be all right. I love you both."

"Call anytime," Emily said.

"Always."

Her parents each told her that they loved her, and Rowan turned off her phone, feeling less alone already. There was no cure for homesickness quite like hearing from her parents. They were her rocks. Her nerdy, lovable, wonderful rocks.

She would go to the rodeo. She would have fun and maybe take some photos to send home. It would be an adventure. A part of the Texas experience.

Kate was so very Texan.

What had she gotten herself into?

Chapter Four

"You're sure it's okay if I go out tonight, Daddy?" Kate asked, for what had to be the tenth time in the past hour. "I can cancel. I don't mind, really. Let's stay in with popcorn and a movie."

She didn't want to cancel. She had been looking forward to the rodeo from the instant she'd posed the invitation, but she couldn't help the guilt that coiled around her like a lasso, holding her to the ranch. She had more work on her to-do list than she could finish in a lifetime, and her dad needed her. His therapy appointment had not gone well. She'd gone inside after brushing down Stryder at the end of the day, and she'd found him sitting in his wheelchair, staring out the window, more defeated than she'd ever seen him in her life. He'd refused to talk about the afternoon other than to grumble about how much he hated PT as he wheeled out of the room. And now she was supposed to be leaving for a night out while he stayed home, miserable. It didn't sit right with her. Even if she was desperate for some *fun* in her life.

"I *want* you to go," he said. "The last thing I want is for you to cancel your plans to stay home with me. I don't want company. Home care will be by in a couple of hours. I have all the support I need." He softened. "I'll feel better knowing my baby girl is still able to go out and have a good time."

Kate frowned. That was the same answer he'd given the last nine times. She hadn't expected a different response this time, but still she didn't feel right leaving him. He would be taken care of. She *knew* that. But she wished there was a way of assuaging her guilt so she could actually relax and enjoy herself. Her dad was practically pushing her out the door, yet she couldn't let go of the feeling she was abandoning him and the ranch.

"You deserve a break," he continued. "You've been up at the hospital almost as much as I have. I'm thrilled you're going out tonight. I'll be here for you to look after when you get home."

She pulled out a dining-room chair and took a seat across from her dad so she could look him level in the eyes. "Only if you're certain."

"I'm beyond certain." His gaze didn't waver, and he gave a single resolute nod signaling it was decided.

Kate exhaled some of the guilt and nodded. She hated leaving him, but buried beneath the guilt of going out for the evening was an excitement she hadn't felt in a long time. There was something about Rowan she was drawn to. Maybe it was the spark in Rowan's dark eyes when she riffed on Texas. Maybe it was the vulnerability Kate had seen when Rowan admitted she was having a hard time adjusting. Maybe it was that, on top of those things, Rowan was super cute. That was a plus. Whatever it was, she looked forward to showing Rowan a small part of the Texas she loved.

Kate stood, kissed her dad's head, and hesitated, giving him one last questioning look.

"Go," he said.

She did as she was told—grabbed her keys off the iron cow-shaped wall hook, and headed out into the hot early evening.

She checked her hair and makeup in the truck's rearview mirror, and then pulled out of the drive, leaving her dad alone for the evening.

It took her about an hour to reach Rowan's apartment in the heart of Fort Worth. As she drove away from the ranch, her guilt began to dissipate, and nerves overtook her in its place. She replayed the invitation, wondering if the vague offer had been construed as a date or if she had simply come across as friendly. She wasn't sure which interpretation she hoped Rowan had formed. She took a few steadying breaths as she pulled up along the curb, parked, and headed up the stairs to knock on Rowan's door.

She told herself it was just a friendly offer to show Rowan Texas, but that didn't stop the butterflies from fluttering in her stomach as she waited for Rowan to answer. She couldn't remember the last time she had felt butterflies.

Gosh, it's like I'm thirteen again, she reprimanded herself, smoothing her hair behind her ears.

Rowan answered, and her dark eyes widened at the sight of Kate.

"Shit," Rowan said. "I'm sorry. This place is a mess. I didn't expect you to come up."

Kate watched with amusement as Rowan fumbled for her keys so she could close the door before Kate saw inside. It was too late, though. She had caught a glimpse of Rowan's living room, cluttered with boxes and piles of belongings.

"Hi," Kate said with a smile, resting a hand on Rowan's fore-arm to steady her. Rowan's skin was even softer than it looked. "Are you ready to go?"

Rowan met her eyes, then cast the briefest of glances over her, taking her in, and sending a wave of heat washing over her.

"Yeah. Let's do this," Rowan said with a nod.

Kate led the way downstairs to her truck, trying to remind herself to breathe. The butterflies swirled en masse within her, but despite the nerves she smiled. She was ready for an evening out, whatever it had in store.

"This place is one of the oldest restaurants in Fort Worth," Kate said as she pulled the truck into the parking lot.

It became evident that the restaurant Kate spoke of was, in fact, the run-down concrete building on the corner of the lot, and Rowan had no difficulty believing its age.

"They won't give you a menu," Kate said, still speaking excit-edly. "You can get enchiladas or fajitas in either chicken or beef. They keep it simple and delicious."

Rowan didn't think the dilapidated building was even open, and if it was, it was small and shady-looking. But she would trust Kate's recommendation.

"I know it doesn't look like much," Kate said, as though reading her mind, "but give it a shot. The food is *good*. I think even an expert such as yourself will agree."

"I'm trusting you," Rowan said, looking at the building with definite doubts.

She followed Kate in, surprised to find the restaurant seating was mostly outdoors in a large garden stretching out back. They did not even enter the building that she had first assessed. Kate gave her name to the hostess for the reservation, and the hostess seated them under the shade of a bright green tree. The entire garden was practically canopied in trees, there was so much foliage. Large fans kept the area somewhat cool, and for the first time since the move she found herself enjoying being outside.

"This place is seriously beautiful," Rowan said, looking around in awe. There were trees and flowery bushes and potted plants—greenery everywhere. In the middle of the garden was a large water feature, and a few smaller fountains were spaced throughout the rest of the venue. "Why didn't you tell me?"

"And miss the look on your face when you saw how very wrong your expectations were?" Kate leaned forward with a grin. "No thanks. Your expression right now is priceless."

"So, you have an evil streak. Duly noted."

"I don't know what you're talking about." Kate widened her eyes in an adorable, innocent gaze that brought a flush to Rowan's face. She was grateful when the waitress interrupted to take their order.

As Kate had explained in the car, there were just the two dishes, and the waitress explained the sides that would be brought out. Rowan settled on the beef fajitas while Kate went with the chicken, and they each ordered a margarita to go with their dinners. Rowan sat back and allowed herself a moment to take in the evening. The air was warm, but not scorching. A gentle breeze played lightly across her skin, a beautiful garden . . .

and a beautiful woman across from her. Kate wore a white tank top and light-blue jeans tucked into brown leather cowboy boots. Her hair was down for the first time that Rowan had seen, and it fell in soft waves over her back and shoulders, the rust-red accented with gold in the soft evening light. She had struggled to keep her eyes off Kate from the moment Kate had picked her up at her apartment, and the beautiful garden backdrop made the task that much more difficult. A small necklace in the shape of a cross hung over Kate's throat, a tangible reminder not to flirt with the conservative country girl from the South. Still, she allowed herself an indulgent moment of envisioning how soft the skin beneath that little silver cross would be.

That cross was probably the only thing keeping Rowan from getting herself into some major shit. It kept her grounded in reality when the evening had been confusing otherwise. Kate had picked her up from her apartment by coming up to the door, rather than just parking outside and waiting for her to come down. She'd held the truck door open. Rowan was unsure what to make of it all. Texas's Southern hospitality was virtually indistinguishable from what she normally would have assumed to be a date.

"So, tell me about Portland," Kate said, leaning forward. "What do you miss most?"

"My people." Rowan answered without missing a beat. She didn't have to think about her answer. "My parents. My friends. I've never left home before. I got my culinary degree at the Oregon Culinary School and lived at home while I studied. I'm not used to being so far away from everyone I love."

The waitress set the margaritas in front of them, and she took a long sip of the tangy lime drink. For the moment she was exactly where she wanted to be. This was the sort of Texas experience she'd been hoping for when she'd moved.

"That's a big move," Kate said, and admiration was evident in her gaze.

She nodded. "Yeah, I guess so."

"Tell me more," Kate said, and she leaned forward, capturing Rowan with her attention. "Why this job? Why Texas?"

"I applied on a whim," Rowan said. "My friend, Alycia, saw the call for applications for the position. It was a nationwide call for new talent. I didn't think I had a hope in hell of landing the job, but I figured it was worth throwing my hat into the ring. Somehow my application progressed to a Skype interview, which progressed to a job offer."

"And now here you are," Kate said.

"In Texas." She tried to make the begrudging statement come across as humorous, but she wasn't sure she'd managed to inject the right jovial tone into her voice.

"I have no doubt it's an adjustment," Kate said. "Texas admittedly has its own very distinct culture."

"And climate," Rowan added.

"You're a bit of a fish-out-of-water here."

"More like a fish in a frying pan. Does it ever cool off here?"

Kate laughed, her head falling back. "I promise you it does," she said. "Our winters get quite cold."

Rowan didn't believe that for a second. "Define cold."

"Around freezing," Kate answered. "It never stays below freezing long enough for snow to stick or anything like that, but it gets cold and wet enough for ice storms. There are usually a few days a year when the roads all shut down because of ice."

"So, hell *does* freeze over," Rowan murmured in amazement.

"Indeed, it does," Kate said, though she didn't laugh at Rowan's joke. Rowan was tempted to explain that she thought of Texas as hell more in terms of heat than the culture or the place itself, but she decided against it.

"I can't wait," Rowan said, instead. "It's hard to even go out to the grocery store. I feel like a vampire, with blackout shades on all of my windows. I thrive being outdoors in the sunshine, but with this heat it's impossible."

"I promise you, you'll acclimate," Kate said.

"Will I acclimate, or will I just become a frog in boiling water? Surely there has to be a point when the heat is simply too much for the human body."

"You're forgetting that I *work* outdoors," Kate said with a chuckle. "Trust me, it's manageable if you drink enough water and take precautions to keep yourself as cool and hydrated as possible. You probably won't die."

"Here I thought you were superhuman," Rowan said.

"Sorry to disappoint." Kate winked, and Rowan smiled in response.

The waitress interrupted to place their meals in front of them: a plate of meat, grilled vegetables, and rice for each of them. The sour cream, refried beans, and tortilla platter were served family style in the middle of the table. The rich smell of the grilled meats hit Rowan and her stomach growled.

"God, it smells amazing."

Kate smiled, visibly proud of herself.

Rowan opened the tortilla tray and was impressed to see that the tortillas were hand-rolled and fresh baked. These were not the mass-produced, store-bought kind. She picked one up and set it on her plate, marveling in the soft, warm dough. She added the meat, vegetables, and toppings, then took a bite, moaning out loud from the food that was possibly the best thing she'd ever eaten.

"So, does it live up to the chef's standards?"

She nodded heartily. "This is incredible."

Kate's eyes shone. "This place is a favorite of mine. Daddy used to bring me here on special occasions: birthdays, celebrations . . . As a kid, he'd bring me here to celebrate good report cards, and this was where we came when I was celebrating getting into college. This is Texas, so there are plenty of good Tex-Mex restaurants, but this one, there's just something special about it."

"There is," she agreed, touched that Kate had chosen to share such a special place with her.

Kate had a distant look on her face, and Rowan could see she was still in the memory.

"Tell me about him," Rowan said.

"My dad?"

Kate had shared openly about her dad a minute earlier, but Rowan saw some hesitancy now that she'd asked about him. She was curious as to what that was about.

"You and he are close?" she pressed gently.

"We are," Kate said, a smile forming on her lips, though it didn't reach her eyes. "He's my best friend. My mom left when I was young, and it's been the two of us. He took care of the ranch, and I would follow him around, trying to help with the animals. I was more trouble than help when I was little, I'm sure, but he always treated me as his number one ranch hand."

"And now you're a rancher with him," Rowan said.

"Yeah," Kate answered with a slow nod. "I guess I am."

Rowan wanted to understand the wistfulness in Kate's voice. She leaned forward on her elbows and held Kate's gaze with her own.

"What is it you're not saying?"

Kate shook her head. "Nothing."

Rowan rested a hand on Kate's forearm.

Eventually, Kate met her eyes and exhaled, worry creasing her face. "Just know that our business is as good as ever."

Rowan furrowed her brows, not understanding the leap, but nodded.

"Daddy was in an accident two months ago," Kate said. She spoke slowly, reciting the facts. "He was thrown from his horse."

The words had been spoken matter-of-factly, but the emotional impact hit Rowan like a punch, and she felt her breath catch in her chest. "How bad?" she asked.

"He severed his spine at the T3 nerve. He's paralyzed from the waist down."

"I'm *so* sorry." She squeezed Kate's forearm. She could only imagine the toll that accident had taken on Kate.

"Watching the emotional toll it's taken on him has been the worst," Kate said. "That part I can't fix."

Kate's shoulders slumped down, as though there was a heavy weight on them, and Rowan quickly connected the dots, realizing what the accident had meant for Kate and her life.

"You stepped in to take care of the ranch," Rowan said, more of a statement than a question. It was clear to her that Kate had stepped up. Her dad had been injured, and she'd jumped in with two feet, doing what needed to be done.

Kate nodded. For a moment she looked so vulnerable that Rowan wanted to go to her and wrap her arms around her, but then she watched Kate's defenses fall back in place.

"It doesn't affect the production of the ranch, I assure you. I grew up working right alongside Daddy. I know his order of operations like the back of my hand." Concern darkened Kate's green eyes.

"I don't care about that," Rowan said, surprised at the change in direction the conversation had taken. Business was the furthest thing from her mind.

The relief was visible as it washed over Kate, whose shoulders relaxed with her breath.

"Thank you," Kate whispered.

"Is he still in rehab?" Rowan didn't want to talk about business or beef. She wanted to know more about Kate.

"He got home last week."

"How's that been?"

"An adjustment to say the least," Kate said. "I think he was as excited as I was that I was going out tonight."

Kate sighed and Rowan could see the exhaustion in her eyes.

"I want to help," Kate continued, "but I've been in the way more than anything. Everything I do seems to frustrate him more."

"It's a big adjustment for him. And for you."

"Yeah," Kate said. "Everyone said it would be, but I still downplayed how hard it was going to be."

"I don't think there is any way to really prepare yourself."

Kate nodded. Then she glanced at her watch and changed the subject. "We should get going if we're going to make the rodeo."

Rowan didn't push the subject, grateful for the moment of vulnerability Kate had been willing to share. Instead, she watched as Kate flagged the waitress and insisted on paying for both of them. Once again, Rowan was confused. Southern hospitality or date? How did anyone ever know the difference in Texas?

"Ready?" Kate asked.

For the rodeo? Rowan thought to herself. She wasn't sure, but she was going to give it a go. She could cross that one off her bucket list, if nothing else.

"Let's do this."

Rowan walked alongside Kate, her eyes widening as she took in the shops along the narrow entrance to the historic Fort Worth Stockyards. Stores were selling all variety of kitschy Texas wear. Cowboy hats and boots, giant belt buckles in the shape of Texas, postcards, hot sauce, and everything jerky (beef, turkey, antelope, and even alligator). There were gaudy signs with slogans such as "We don't dial 911" alongside the image of a gun, which struck Rowan as both tacky and terrifying.

"What is this place?" Rowan asked.

Kate laughed. "Right here, this is tourist alley. But the Stockyards are a big part of Fort Worth's history, and the cattle industry especially. Livestock auctions used to take place here. It was *the* place for buying and selling cattle back in the day. Now, it's a tourist destination, a part of Texas culture, and a good place to go see the rodeo."

Rowan couldn't help smiling at Kate's enthusiasm. Her love for her home was evident. "You know, if you ever wanted to get out of ranching, you could be a tour guide, the way you're ready with all the facts and details about this place."

"I've missed my calling."

Rowan smiled and bumped Kate with her shoulder. She took in the sea of cowboy hats, and wondered how many of the people wearing them were even from Texas. Young children were dressed to the nines in full Western wear, riding mechanical horses, the type that took a quarter to operate, while parents snapped photos.

"I feel like I've stepped into another world," she admitted, as two children darted past them firing wooden pistols at each other.

"Embrace it," Kate said. "You know what they say. If you can't beat 'em, join 'em."

Rowan, wide-eyed, shook her head, not even sure where to start.

"You know what you need?" Kate asked. "A cowboy hat. C'mon!"

Rowan froze in horror at the idea, but Kate was already headed in the direction of the nearest shop. She started after Kate, trying to figure out how to get her to give up on that idea. Tex-Mex had been a great plan. Going to the rodeo was questionable, but she would give it a shot. A cowboy hat, though? That was where she absolutely, completely, without a doubt, drew the line.

Kate turned back to her and grabbed her hand. "You're a Texan now," she said. "You *need* one. It's a rite of passage."

Rowan had her arguments ready, but Kate's hand was soft in hers. Dammit, that softness distracted her until the next thing she knew Kate set a cowboy hat on her head and clasped her hands together with a delight that told her just how wrong for her the hat was. Large and unwieldy on her head, it even *felt* wrong. She didn't often wear *any* hat, let alone a cowboy hat. It was probably ruining her hair. She could only imagine how ridiculous she looked.

"It's perfect," Kate said, barely containing her laughter. "We're getting it."

Rowan wanted to take it off. She wanted to put it back on its rack and get out of the shop, and preferably even out of the Stockyards, but Kate's smile was addicting. If wearing the hat meant getting to see that smile, she'd wear the damn thing all night.

"This doesn't make me a Texan," she bit out.

Kate took the hat up to the front, insisting on buying it for Rowan. Then she pulled the price tag off and stepped toward Rowan to put it back on. This time, Rowan was very aware of Kate's nearness, and she breathed in Kate's soft floral scent. Kate's breasts brushed ever-so-slightly against her chest as Kate reached up to place the hat.

She swallowed hard at the light contact. "I guess I'm ready for the rodeo now," she said.

Kate led her through the rest of tourist alley and out to the main street. Cowboys stood in the evening sun, posing with longhorn cattle for tourist photos. A few brave souls took on a mechanical bull, while others attempted the cattle maze. She had to admit that some of the activities (*not* the mechanical bull riding) looked like fun. Kate bought their tickets for the rodeo and led her into the arena, which was blissfully cool. They found seats in the bleachers overlooking the dusty, dirt ring below.

"Can I get you anything to drink?" Rowan asked.

"A Dr Pepper would be great," Kate answered.

Rowan got up and went to the counter to buy a Dr Pepper and a Shiner beer, then returned to sit next to Kate, handing her the drink.

It wasn't long before the announcer came over the PA welcoming everyone. The lights dimmed and a solo rider came out. She carried the American flag and rode circles around the arena while "God Bless the USA" played. She started with the horse in a walk, then picked up speed as the music built until she was galloping in circles around the arena. The arena was more or less packed, and both the cheers and the music crescendoed. When the song ended, the rider stopped in the center of the arena, and everyone stood for the national anthem. The fanfare of the opening alone left Rowan feeling slightly mesmerized and a lot intimidated. What the hell was she in for?

Her knowledge of rodeos was nonexistent, other than knowing that it was a thing cowboys enjoyed, and it involved bull riding, which Rowan didn't think was a particularly animal-friendly or ethical pastime.

The rodeo kicked off with barrel racing, and she found herself enjoying watching the horse racers speed around the barrels. Kate explained that the object was to finish the course, which involved riding circles around barrels in a cloverleaf pattern, with the fastest time. It was fairly easy to understand as a spectator, and she found it oddly exhilarating to watch the speed and athleticism of the horses.

"I used to compete in this," Kate said.

Rowan watched the rider in the arena, and easily pictured Kate as the one leaning through the turns, her long hair whipping behind her, intense concentration on her face. The image made barrel racing a decidedly sexy sport.

Rowan cringed when the first bull burst out of the holding gate and cheered more for the bull than for the rider when the rider was tossed onto the ground a few seconds later.

Otherwise, she found that overall she was enjoying herself. The showmanship at the rodeo was way overdone, and some of the events seemed downright silly, but she got into the energy, cheering with the crowd. Kate explained the rules and scoring of each event as it came up. She admired the demonstration of skills with each event, and found she could appreciate the athletic ability each required. What she enjoyed most, however, was watching Kate, who leaned forward, rapt with attention. Her enthusiasm for each event was contagious.

At one point—what Rowan assumed to be the half-time portion of the rodeo—children were invited into the arena and started tossing all of their boots into a pile. The announcer gave the kids instructions, explaining the event, in which they all had to race to the center in a mad dash to be the first to find their boots.

"Did you do that as a kid?" Rowan asked.

Kate looked over at her with a wide grin that made Rowan's stomach flip and nodded. "Of course. I grew up with the rodeo. I started with boot racing, then graduated to mutton busting before finding my passion in barrel racing."

"What the hell is mutton busting?" Rowan asked. She was fairly certain she was going to find the answer ridiculous, and Kate did not disappoint.

"It's essentially a version of bull riding for little kids. They suit kids up in helmets and padding, and have them try to ride on the backs of sheep."

Rowan gaped at Kate, not sure if she was horrified or amused. "You'll see," Kate promised. "It's after the boot racing."

When the mutton busting event began, Rowan found herself overtaken with a fit of laughter. She worried for both the children and the sheep, and yet the sight before her was so utterly ridiculous she couldn't help the laughter that overtook her. If she had told herself about the event beforehand, she'd have thought it sounded awful, but watching it play out in front of her, she had to admit, was weirdly entertaining. She was having fun.

And then suddenly she wasn't having fun anymore. The moment the first calf was roped Rowan stopped enjoying the rodeo. She watched, unprepared for what was about to happen, as the rider rode out into the ring, lasso ready. A frightened calf bolted through the dirt toward the other side of the arena. The rider swung his rope in an overhead circle and lassoed the calf, which fell to its side with a terrified, high-pitched squeal. Rowan averted her eyes. She couldn't watch the baby cow in pain on the ground.

"The calves don't get hurt," Kate said, as though reading her mind.

"And you know that how?"

Kate's gaze was gentle, and she felt her response was perhaps too harsh, but her stomach was knotted as her mind replayed the calf hitting the ground. "You can't tell me that felt good."

"Probably not," Kate agreed, "but the calf is fine."

The announcer introduced the next rider. Rowan didn't watch, but she still heard the scared squeal as another calf hit the dirt ground.

"We can go," Kate said.

Rowan shook her head. She would wait out the calf roping event. The last thing she wanted to do was ruin what was a surprisingly wonderful evening. "No, it's fine."

Kate stood, though, and took Rowan's hand to pull her up as well. She led them toward the exit, and Rowan admitted to herself that she was glad Kate had made the decision for them.

Outside the arena the evening was much quieter. The sun had

nearly set. She could still hear the music and cheering coming from the arena, but the streets were quiet. The mass of people had thinned, probably for the rodeo, she presumed. Music came from many of the restaurants and bars, however, and she expected the Stockyards would be alive and busy well into the night.

"Are you okay?" Kate asked.

"I'm sorry," she answered. "I did want to watch the rodeo, but I wasn't prepared for the calf roping. Is that event really necessary?"

"Calf roping is an invaluable skill," Kate explained. "On my ranch, there have been times when I've had to be able to rope an escaped calf so it wouldn't run into danger. Cows are easy. Cows I can herd. The calves though, they're fast and feisty."

"That's different." Rowan tried to find the language to put her discomfort into words without insulting Kate. "That's to help the calf. That's part of your career. This . . . it feels wrong to watch it for entertainment."

"The rodeo is pretty much the only place to showcase these skills. It's a chance to win money for being talented in an area that would otherwise get overlooked. It showcases the skills I need to use every day in my career. It's not a meaningless activity."

Rowan chewed over that idea. She didn't want to devalue Kate's work, passion, and livelihood. She could see its importance. But at the same time, she could hear the calves squealing in her mind. "I understand its importance. I just don't think I can bring myself to get entertainment pleasure from it."

"I get that," Kate said.

Rowan hoped she did. She didn't want to come across as condescending. The last thing she wanted to do was insult Kate, who had been gracious and welcoming in introducing Rowan to Texas.

"I really did have a good time up until that last event," she said. "It was a lot more fun than I'd expected. To be honest I kinda expected to hate all of it."

Kate laughed. "I like that about you. How honest you are. It's refreshing."

Rowan felt a blush creep up to her cheeks and she looked away, hoping that the flush wouldn't be visible in the dark.

Then, she fell into step beside Kate, walking silently alongside her through the Stockyards, hoping her honesty hadn't driven a wedge between her and Kate. Kate said she liked her honesty, but a heaviness had settled into the air between them. She kicked herself, wishing she could undo the past thirty minutes, while still knowing that she'd have responded the exact same way to the calf roping, even with a do-over.

Not that it mattered. There was no do-over. All she could do was walk in silence and try to think of some way to bridge the distance that had formed between her and Kate, which suddenly felt as big as the difference between Portland and Texas.

Kate wanted to defend the rodeo. It was a part of her life. Her *culture*. She wanted Rowan to understand. And at the same time she felt incredibly touched at how deeply Rowan cared. She knew the calves were fine, and she wouldn't go to an event that harmed animals. But Rowan's concern was touching. She didn't want her to apologize for that.

"What would it take for me to get to see you on that?" Rowan asked, finally breaking the silence that had encompassed them.

She followed Rowan's gaze to a mechanical bull, surrounded by inflatable cushions, next to the road.

Kate hadn't ridden a mechanical bull in years, but Rowan's eyes shone again, no longer clouded with guilt, and she wanted to reclaim the lighthearted feel the evening had started with.

"I'll ride it if you will," she said evenly, holding Rowan's gaze.

Rowan's eyes widened and she shook her head. "I'm pretty sure I'd die. You're the cowgirl here. Come on. Show me how it's done."

Kate wavered, about to push Rowan to give it a go, when Rowan swung her gaze to a bar down the way.

"I'll tell you what," she said. "Show me how this is done, and I'll show you my incredible karaoke skills at the saloon over there."

A sign out front advertised karaoke, dancing, and shuffleboard.

"I'm really good," Rowan promised. "I'll even agree to sing you your favorite country song."

Kate held Rowan's gaze, as though weighing the decision, even though she knew she would take that deal. Finally, she nodded and held out her hand.

"Shake on it," she said. "There's no backing out if you get stage fright after I let myself get tossed from that thing."

Rowan grinned wide as though she'd won the lottery and took Kate's hand, giving it a single, firm shake. "Deal."

Kate couldn't help but laugh, even as nerves tightened within her stomach. She stepped up to the counter and paid for the single ride on the bull, wondering at those nerves. Sure, it had been a long time since she'd ridden one of these, but she rode horses daily, she helped train horses that were prone to bucking, and she had the balance and the core strength.

If Rowan weren't watching, she wondered if she would feel those same nerves. Were they for the bull or the cute city girl she was trying to impress?

She shook her head as she stepped up to the bull and pulled herself up by the handle, swinging her leg over.

Yeah, the nerves were entirely about impressing the cute city girl.

The operator started the bull slowly. It rocked and spun and dipped, but the movements were gentle, and Kate had no trouble hanging on. Then, once it was clear to the operator that she knew what she was doing, the mechanical bull began to move faster, the movements more jarring, tossing her in one direction and then the next.

Adrenaline coursed through her limbs as she fought to stay on.

The bull tossed forward, and she met Rowan's eyes, seeing the admiration in the gaze before the bull swung violently to the right. She almost lost her balance, but she managed to hang on.

She'd forgotten how much fun the challenge of the mechanical bull could be.

The bull moved faster still. She held onto the handle tighter with her left hand until a combination of a forward toss and sharp left turn tossed her onto the cushions below. She landed on her back, and then stood, straightening her clothes while she reoriented herself.

"Okay," Rowan said while she stepped out of the ring. "That was seriously badass."

Kate smiled but brushed off the compliment.

She met Rowan's eyes, the dark brown almost black in the evening light, but streaked with gold by the floodlights overhead.

"Seriously badass," Rowan said, her voice low.

Kate buzzed with the adrenaline that still coursed through her. She told herself that adrenaline caused the spark that traveled through her body. Rowan reached out to fix her hair, and her stomach tightened in response, her skin flushing, and she knew that the response was not adrenaline.

"I had better make this song a good one," Rowan said, breaking the eye contact and leading Kate toward the saloon at the end of the street.

Right, Kate thought, trying to pull herself back into reality. *Karaoke*.

Ricky's Saloon was a small dive of a Western bar with eclectic interior decor. Booths along the back wall were lined with black and white "cow print" fabric. The tables in the center of the room all had stools with metal backs that had a star in the center. A shuffleboard table was crammed in the corner, surrounded by wooden plaques with every Texas slogan imaginable, as though the owner had purchased every plaque possible from the Stockyards' shops. A mural of the Texas flag covered the entire wall behind the bar.

"What is this place?" Rowan whispered, looking around.

Kate bit her lips to keep from laughing at Rowan, who looked as confused and worried as if she'd stepped into the Twilight Zone. The bar was possibly too Texas for Texas. It was every stereotype amplified to the max, and way too over the top to be considered representative of Texas country and western bars. But Kate wasn't about to tell Rowan that.

53

"This," Kate said, "is the place where you make your country karaoke debut."

The place was by no means crowded, but a good number of people were mingling inside, for a weeknight. Enough that Kate would definitely *not* be getting up on stage and singing. Rowan, however, did not appear to have the same stage fright, and she walked confidently over to the binder of karaoke songs next to the stage. The bored-looking karaoke operator sat up straighter, brightening with the discovery that somebody was about to sing.

"All right," Rowan said, passing the book to Kate. "Choose your song."

Kate flipped through the songbook, looking for a country song she thought Rowan might know, before finally settling on "Ring of Fire" by Johnny Cash. Surely, even Rowan would know that one.

The karaoke operator queued up the song and Rowan jumped onto the stage, adjusting the cowboy hat on her head, and hooking her thumbs into her jean pockets. She danced a little through the opening guitar, smiling confidently at Kate.

And then she started to sing, and it became painfully clear that Rowan did *not* know the song. Either that, or she was completely tone deaf. Possibly both.

If Rowan was aware of how terrible she was, she didn't show it. She belted out each off-key note with confidence, fully committed to the song she had promised.

Some of the other bar patrons cringed at Rowan over their drinks. Kate had to press her lips together to smother her laugh.

But when Rowan smiled brightly at her, catching Kate's gaze with her intense, dark eyes, the smile that formed on Kate's face had nothing to do with amusement, and all of the off-key notes were forgotten.

Kate wouldn't have been caught dead on that stage. The mechanical bull was *far* less terrifying.

But Rowan commanded the stage. She commanded the room.

And she fully commanded Kate's attention.

When Rowan finished delivering on her promise of karaoke, she and Kate stepped back out into the quiet streets, and the two of them walked slowly back to Kate's truck, which was parked a block or so away, by the restaurant. The temperature was almost reasonable, and Rowan found herself in no rush to get back to her apartment. It was nice to have a friend in Texas. She'd missed having someone to hang out with. Phone conversations with Alycia weren't the same as being able to actually spend time with someone and talk face-to-face. She'd had fun at the Stockyards, even if the rodeo hadn't been her favorite experience.

When they reached the truck, Kate opened the door for Rowan, who climbed up into the passenger seat, still confused about this Southern hospitality thing.

"I enjoyed tonight." Kate echoed Rowan's thoughts, as she drove back toward Rowan's apartment. "I thought I would be distracted, worrying about my dad all night and feeling guilty for leaving him. I didn't. I had fun. I *needed* tonight. I haven't laughed as much in weeks as I have tonight."

Rowan turned toward Kate while speaking, taking in the details of her profile. Kate was focused on the road, but turned to her for a second, smiling warmly. "I enjoyed tonight, too. Calf roping aside. Thank you. For everything."

Kate pulled up in front of Rowan's apartment. She didn't want to get out and go back into her empty home that didn't feel like home.

"Don't get rid of the cowboy hat," Kate said. "You're a Texan now. Wear it with pride."

"Yeah, that's not happening," she said with a laugh. "I won't be wearing it around town. But I will keep it."

"Okay," Kate nodded. "Baby steps."

Rowan smiled and was about to reach for the door of the truck when Kate leaned in and kissed her. It was a quick kiss, but it was distinctly a kiss, not a peck. Kate's lips were soft and warm as they closed over hers, and Kate's hair smelled like strawberries.

Rowan's breath hitched and she leaned in, but in the time it took her brain to process what was happening and respond, Kate had pulled back.

"Good night, Rowan," Kate said with a gentle smile.

Rowan's head spun and her heart pounded hard in her chest. She raised an eyebrow and gave Kate a long look, unable to formulate words. Her thoughts flew in a million dizzying directions. She managed simply to smile back and let herself out of the truck, stopping at the stairs to her apartment to touch her lips and turn and wave back at Kate.

Rowan was pretty sure the kissing was *not* Southern hospitality.

Chapter Five

Kate untacked Stryder and finished brushing him down. Her horse was sweaty from a hard morning rounding up the cattle for rotation. She took her time as she brushed the dust and sweat out of his coat, then scraped the mud and rocks from his hooves. She enjoyed the quiet end-of-morning routine.

"Do you remember Rowan? She helped us round up the cattle the other day?" Kate asked her horse. "I may have kissed her last night."

She felt like a teenager, regaling her horse with the details, still smiling at the memory. She'd spent most of her day thus far thinking about the previous evening, enjoying the warm, happy thoughts. She hadn't planned on kissing Rowan, but in that moment it just felt *right*, and so she'd acted.

Kate laughed out loud at the memory. "You should've seen her face," she said to Stryder. She could still see Rowan's adorable happy and confused smile in her mind. Two things had become apparent throughout the evening. First, it had become clear that Rowan found her attractive. Kate had noticed the way Rowan watched her when she thought Kate wasn't paying attention. And second, Rowan very clearly read Kate as straight. Rowan had tried to keep things friendly and detached, despite the obvious attraction. Kate had enjoyed watching Rowan's confusion as she'd flirted throughout the evening, but when the flirting still had not cued Rowan in to the fact that the attraction was mutual, she'd decided a kiss would make things clear.

She smiled at the memory and turned her attention back to her horse. She reached into her bucket of treats and held a few of the grain nuggets out, palm flat, laughing as Stryder clumsily took them from her.

She finished brushing down Stryder, then led him back out to the pasture where she released him for an afternoon of sun-bathing and hay snacking.

"You headed out?" Owen called over to her. He was working on reinforcing the rest of the fences around the pastures to prevent another jailbreak.

"I am," she said. "Gotta get Daddy to his appointment. Cattle are rotated and the calves have been checked on. You and Dean are set to leave once those fences are done. We'll tag the new calves tomorrow."

"Sounds great," Owen said. "See you tomorrow, Kate."

She waved back at him and headed to the house. Warren had a physical therapy appointment back at the outpatient wing of his rehab facility. She would have been happy to never return, but the PT was a necessary part of her dad's recovery, and they would be going there for the long haul.

When she stepped into the house, she found her dad sitting in front of the unlit fireplace, staring into the concrete pit. She let out a long breath and watched him for a moment. As much as she didn't want to return to the rehab facility, she could only imagine her dad's resistance.

"Ready, Daddy?" she asked, stepping up behind him and resting a hand on his shoulder.

He gave a tired shrug.

"Yeah," she said. "I know." She gave him a pat on the shoulder for reassurance and then went to get the keys to the truck.

Warren wheeled out to the driveway, and she opened the truck door. She frowned as her dad grunted and struggled to lift himself into the truck. If they had a vehicle that was lower to the ground, the whole process would be so much easier. She needed a truck to haul the livestock trailer and pick up feed, but maybe she and her dad didn't *both* need a truck anymore. They could sell one in exchange for a car. She nodded resolutely to herself as she folded her dad's chair and tucked it into the backseat of the truck. Then she climbed into the driver's seat and pulled out onto the highway.

Two and a half months earlier, they had ridden in the truck together, heading to a cattle auction. She had sat in the passenger's seat with her veterinary textbooks in her lap so she could sneak in a few minutes of studying for her upcoming finals. Her dad had talked about the longhorns he wanted to procure for the upcoming season and the calves he hoped to sell. They'd both had such different plans from now. Now they were driving to the hospital in what was to be a weekly routine.

Warren stayed silent on the drive, and Kate didn't know what to say to him so she was silent as well. While her dad was in inpatient care, she had driven back and forth to the rehab facility a few times a day, trying to balance being with him while also trying to make sure the ranch didn't fall apart. Driving back to that all-too-familiar building, a knot of anxiety crept back in. With her dad home, things were hard but there was a level of reassurance that they would be okay. The rehab facility forced them to confront exactly what their future would look like. In rehab, it was impossible to ignore how much things had changed.

Kate pulled into the lot and parked the truck.

"Ready, Daddy?"

"I suppose."

She felt a little sick at the thought of going inside. She could imagine he was feeling that tenfold, though, so she swallowed down her own fears and tried to inject optimism into her voice. Her job was to keep him motivated and inspired.

"Just think how much stronger this will make you," she said as they headed inside. "Every day spent doing PT is one day closer to not needing this."

"It's not going to let me walk again," her dad said.

"Maybe not," she answered. "But walking is overrated. Just gets your boots dirty, and who needs that hassle? You're going to be unstoppable, Daddy. You're iron."

If he heard her, he didn't respond. He wheeled toward the entrance in silence.

Kate followed him to the outpatient ward check-in and the exercise room where he would work on building his upper-body strength over the next few months.

"Mr. Landreth, welcome back," the therapist said.

Kate took a chair and watched as Diane began to work with her dad. She started with a few fairly easy exercises before transitioning into the harder ones. Most of the work focused on developing the upper-body strength her dad would need to be able to function on his own, to be able to hoist himself in and out of chairs and to get around without the use of his legs. Warren Landreth was by no means a weak man, but he was also stocky, solid, and not used to having to lift such weight with his upper body alone.

Tears stung the back of her eyes as he struggled through exercise after exercise, and she looked away while taking a few deep breaths to steady her emotions. Her dad had always been her hero. She still saw him as she did when she was little, as someone who could do anything. It had been just the two of them for most of her life, and if playing the role of both parents while running the ranch had been hard, he'd never shown it. He'd been everything for Kate. He had an old baby photo of Kate on the fridge where she was standing in his cowboy boots which came up to her knees. She couldn't have been more than a year or so old. She'd been trying to stand in his boots ever since.

Now, her hero was trying to hold himself up on two parallel bars, his arms shaking and his face twisted with the effort.

"You can do it, Daddy," she said, stepping forward, wishing there was more she could offer than mere encouragement.

With a grunt Warren dropped himself, and the therapist assistants helped him back into his chair.

"We'll give you a few minutes and then try again," Diane said.

He shook his head and wiped the sweat from his brow. Kate knelt down in front of him with her hands on his knees.

"You're doing so great, Daddy. These exercises are so hard, and you're doing them all so much better than last week."

"You should go get some lunch," he said in response.

She shook her head. "I'm not hungry. I'm here to support you."

"You should go get some lunch," he said again, more sternly this time, leaving no room for argument.

She stood and looked at him, trying to find some tenderness behind his hard, pained gaze. "You sure?" she asked, hoping he'd change his mind.

He didn't. He nodded. Kate gave him a long look but saw no crack in his resolve, so she nodded. "I'll bring you a doughnut for after. Keep doing what you're doing."

She headed for the rehab hospital's small cafeteria. She'd had enough of their cafeteria food while her dad was in inpatient rehab. She'd be happy to never eat any of that food again, and she wasn't at all hungry. But she had nothing better to do, so she found herself in the checkout line with an egg salad sandwich in one hand and two doughnuts in the other.

She took the food to a table and pulled out her phone to aimlessly kill the time with social media and phone games.

She had to admit that an additional level of disappointment settled in when she opened her phone and there were still no calls or texts from Rowan. She tried not to overanalyze the radio silence. It had been less than twenty-four hours, after all. But her dad had kicked her out of his therapy session, and it was hard to not feel rejection from all angles.

She frowned and unwrapped her sandwich to take a bite. It tasted like cardboard, and probably had the nutritional content of cardboard as well.

Kate glanced at the time on her phone and gave herself five minutes to wallow, to let the pain of the past few months settle in and to let her thoughts dwell on feeling sorry for herself, thinking over the future she'd envisioned that was now never going to come to be. When the five minutes were up, she scrunched up the plastic wrap from her sandwich and tossed it in the trash. She picked up the doughnuts to take to her dad. She had to believe that there would be progress. He didn't believe, so she would believe enough for the two of them.

"I need two sirloin, medium and medium rare, two chicken, and one pork," the caller said, clipping the order to the line.

Rowan wiped her brow and then tossed the first of the steaks onto the grill. She smiled at the satisfying sizzle it made as it hit the heat, flames jumping up and licking the meat. That sound never got old.

The grill was a juggling act, and adrenaline coursed through her as she did her best to keep up, ensuring that each steak hit the grill and was pulled off with absolute precision timing. Forget about a steak for even thirty seconds, and it might come off the grill overcooked, and she would have to start it over, throwing off the timing of the meals for the entire table.

It was On the Range's official opening—the big launch—and the kitchen buzzed with an energy that had not come close to being paralleled at the soft launch. Orders flew in and out of the kitchen, and all of the chefs worked in tandem—like a machine—to get the dishes out as quickly as possible while attending to every minute detail. It was a pressure and an energy unlike anything she had ever experienced in her professional career.

"Rowan, what's the time on the rib eye?" Daniel asked, stepping over to her station.

"One more minute, chef," she answered in an almost military drill-like fashion.

Daniel nodded and moved down the line, checking the plates that were ready to be expedited. No plate left the kitchen without his approval, and she could hear him curse the *friturier* over a piece of chicken that was fried a darker amber than the crispy gold it was meant to be.

She didn't let herself glance at the offending plate or the fry chef. The juggling act left no room for even the slightest distraction. She blocked out the words and flipped two of the steaks in front of her.

Heat and smoke from the grill added to the pressure-cooker assault on her senses. Sweat and noise and chaos.

Rowan loved it.

She pulled the two cuts of sirloin from the grill and set them on plates, sliding them down the line for the *saucier* to add the cactus pear glaze to each.

Then she moved to the next order.

Set a ball down, add another in the air.

It was an almost-meditative dance. There was no room for homesickness, or stress, or daydreaming. There was only the grill.

"Rowan," Daniel said, returning with one of the plates she'd sent out, and she felt her stomach knot. "This steak is about a minute over. We need one more sirloin, medium-rare."

"Yes, chef," she said instantly putting another steak on the grill, her face burning from more than just the heat.

"It's all good," Daniel said, as though sensing the spiral her thoughts were taking. "Precision takes practice. Watch the clock with this one, and don't let one slipup get to you."

She nodded, and exhaled, letting go of the embarrassment to clear her head. She needed her focus.

They were slammed for the entirety of the evening. It was opening night in one of the most talked-about new restaurants in Fort Worth, and there was not a single lull between when the doors opened and when the final orders came in just after 11 p.m.

Her heart pounded as though she'd finished running a marathon. She pulled the final rib eye off the grill and watched with satisfaction as the sweet potato rajas and fried green tomatoes were plated next to it, and the waiter carried the dish out to the dining room.

There was nothing to do then but clean her station, pack her knives, and go home. The end of the evening was anticlimactic after the adrenaline-filled shift. She took her belongings to her car and started the ignition, still buzzing from her successful first real shift with On the Range. She hadn't cooked *perfectly,* but it was her first night *ever* in a high-pressure kitchen, and she was immensely proud of the job she'd done. She wanted to celebrate. The thought of going home to her empty, as yet unpacked apartment felt like tossing a wet towel on a fire, and she was not ready to kill the spark of energy just yet.

Instead, Rowan pulled out her phone, bringing up Kate's contact information. She had been meaning to touch base with her after their trip to the rodeo, but she had been uncertain what to say. She'd composed a handful of text messages earlier in the day and had discarded them all.

Getting kissed by the beautiful Texas cowgirl had been so far from what she expected from their evening out. Her head was still spinning. Kate was gorgeous, and engaging, and apparently not straight, which left Rowan feeling completely disarmed.

But, God, did she want to kiss Kate some more.

Emboldened from the evening's adrenaline, Rowan typed out a quick message and hit send before she could question herself.

Things I've learned about Texas: there is a place for the word "y'all" in absolutely every sentence; when people talk about the Cowboys, they're talking about football, not actual cowboys; and God might just forgive me for missing church if I cheer for the Cowboys.

Rowan glanced at the time displayed on her dash, and she cringed at the realization that it was nearly midnight. Nothing said playing-it-cool like midnight texting. She tossed her phone on her passenger seat and was about to put her car in reverse and drive home when the reply came through.

At the soft ding, she picked up her phone.

See? One of us! Now start wearing that cowboy hat of yours and you'll be indistinguishable from the rest of us Texans.

She smiled, about to type a reply when another message came through.

Okay. Almost indistinguishable. We need to work on that accent of yours.

64

Rowan laughed. *What accent? I do believe you're the one with the accent.*

It's called a drawl.

I stand corrected. She held her thumbs over her phone keyboard, trying to figure out the words to type that would open the door to spending more time with Kate.

The message from Kate came in first.

Have you ever ridden a horse?

Rowan looked at the message for a long time before answering, scared of what the follow-up question would be.

Not unless ponies at the zoo count.

They definitely do not, Kate wrote back. *Come over Sunday afternoon and I'll teach you to ride. Bring the hat. It's essential.*

Rowan groaned, but there was a smile on her face. She shook her head and took a deep breath before typing her response. When she'd thought of spending time with Kate, she'd envisioned dinner and beers. But sure, getting on top of a one-ton mammal . . . that seemed like fun.

What time? she asked.

She had absolutely no clue what the hell she was thinking. This was why late-night post-work text messaging with cute girls was never a good idea.

How about noon? Kate asked.

Noon sounds perfect.

Rowan was glad for the fact that her feeling of intimidation would not carry through over text messages. Now she just needed to prepare herself to appear just as cool and confident in person on Sunday.

What are you even doing awake so late? Rowan asked. *Don't you have to get up at the ass-crack of dawn?*

Couldn't sleep, Kate typed. *Alarm goes off in a couple hours.*

I'll let you go, Rowan said. *I'll see you Sunday.*

I can't wait.

Rowan couldn't either.

✳ ✳ ✳

Kate smiled as she set her phone on the table among all of the budget notes for the ranch. She went to take a sip of her coffee, but found the mug empty. That was her third cup. She could tell the caffeine had affected her as her hands were jittery and her heart beat a little faster than usual, but she did not feel any more awake than before she'd started that last cup.

She hadn't intended on staying up late trying to balance finances, but a hospital bill had been waiting in the mailbox when she and her dad got home from rehab, and when she'd tried to go to sleep, she had lain awake, stressing. She figured it was better to stay up and be productive, trying to solve the situation, rather than just lying in bed worrying.

The texts from Rowan were a welcome distraction from what had otherwise been a long and unpleasant night. Rowan was a breath of fresh air during a suffocating time in her life. She had such a quick sense of humor and a zest for new experiences. Seeing Texas through Rowan's eyes gave all of her mundane ranch life a certain magical quality. Their date to the rodeo (and Kate could now admit it was a date) had been so much more fun than she could have hoped. There was a tangible chemistry, but beyond her attraction to Rowan they had a natural, easy way of being together. It scared her a little to think Rowan might have the potential to grow into someone important. It was a terrible time for her to be dating anyone—for either one of them to be dating anyone—but that didn't stop the optimism from bubbling free in her chest, a warmth that Kate happily embraced.

She looked at the spreadsheet she'd created, feeling the warmth dissipate. Her mind could no longer process the numbers, so she closed her laptop. There was nothing more she could do for the night. The bills would all still be waiting in the morning. She would talk with her dad about selling his truck in exchange for a smaller vehicle. It would be more practical and would leave them with a little extra cash. Not enough, though. Never enough.

She rubbed her temples and folded her stacks of paper to put them away so that her dad wouldn't see them when he got up in the morning. She didn't want him stressing. There was nothing he could do to magically fix the budget, and she didn't want him worrying about anything other than his recovery. If he were to see her stressing about the finances he would become adamant about selling the ranch, and that wasn't a step she was willing to consider.

They had On the Range buying beef from them, and they could sell some cuts directly through local farmer's markets over the summer. They'd also be able to sell stock at auctions, and they had a number of calves this year that should run them a decent profit. They would pay the bills off a little at a time.

Kate could do it.

She only wished she could feel sure of that.

Chapter Six

Rowan pulled up the dusty drive to Landreth Ranch, her stomach tight in a combination of anticipation of seeing Kate and nerves about getting atop a horse. She had considered texting Kate to suggest a different activity, but she didn't want Kate to know how scared she was. She had gone as far as typing up the message, though.

She glanced over at the cowboy hat on the passenger seat next to her. It was out of place in her little hybrid hatchback, surrounded by the loud guitar and drums from the punk music coming through the stereo. That hat was *so* not her. It belonged in a truck with country music and a real rancher. She was a city girl from Portland. She would look about as natural in a cowboy hat as Santa Claus would look in a bikini. She put her car in park, shut off the ignition, and then rolled her eyes at the hat as she picked it up and stepped out of the car.

There appeared to be no limit to the things she would do for a pretty girl.

Rowan smiled at the thought of Kate. She was more than just a pretty girl. She was caring and warm, and if Rowan wearing the hat could win her one of those radiant smiles, then yeah, she'd wear the hat.

A large dog bounded up to her and she knelt to pet the animal, whose tail wagged vigorously.

She scratched behind the dog's ears. "Who's a good boy? Are you a good boy?"

The dog wagged his tail in response and licked her cheek.

"I see you've met Patch," Kate said.

Rowan looked up, squinting against the sun, to see Kate smiling down at her and the dog. Her stomach did a little flip.

She stood, wiping her hands on her jeans. Kate held Rowan with a tender gaze that made Rowan feel warm and vulnerable.

"So, hi," Rowan said, moving in a little closer.

"Hi," Kate said back.

Rowan was usually much better with words. Kate, however, stood there sexy as hell, and it was distracting. Sunlight reflected off the warm rust-red of her hair, which Rowan had the sudden urge to run her fingers through.

"Are you ready to learn to ride?" Kate asked, bringing her back to the task at hand.

"You know," Rowan hedged, "I was thinking maybe we could just take the horse for a walk."

"For a walk?"

"Yeah." She realized how utterly ridiculous she sounded, but was not able to stop the words as they came. "You know. Instead of riding, we'll walk beside the horses, and just lead them around the pastures."

"Like a dog," Kate finished. She raised an eyebrow and was very clearly trying not to laugh.

Rowan decided to keep going with it, more as a joke now than anything. "Dogs seem to like it. Why not horses as well? Relaxing for everyone. People and animals alike."

Kate could no longer contain the laugh. "It will be fine. I promise I won't kill you."

Death was only one of a number of terrifying scenarios running through her mind. She joked about taking the horses for a walk, and she played off her fear as comical, but there was truth behind that sarcasm. She knew what horses were capable of, as gentle as they might appear. It was not lost on her that Kate's dad was currently in a wheelchair because of a horse. That thought played over and over in her mind. But she knew better than to mention that fact. So she put the hat on her head and tried to relax into Kate's excitement for the afternoon.

She followed Kate toward the pasture where two horses were tied up to the wooden fence.

"This is Stryder." Kate patted the taller of the two, a dark brown, way-too-powerful-looking horse. Then she patted the other, a much shorter and stockier horse who was squat with a banana-shaped body, his stomach sagging down. "This is Mickey."

"I want to ride Mickey," Rowan said, without giving Kate a chance to assign her the muscle-y giant.

Kate frowned. "Are you sure? He tends to buck."

Rowan's eyes went wide and Kate laughed, pushing on her arm.

"He's a sweetheart," Kate said. "They both are. You can ride Mickey. The worst he's going to do is stop and chew on the grass every few steps."

"Not funny, Kate," Rowan said, but she realized she was smiling.

Kate held her fingers close together. "It was a little funny."

Rowan stepped closer to the horse, held out her hand, and then gently touched the horse's head. The horse paid her no mind, standing there in the sun, eyes half closed. She jumped back a bit when it shook its large head to brush away flies, but then she went back to petting the giant animal.

"Don't bite me, don't kick me, don't toss me to the ground, and we'll be fine. Got it?"

Mickey just shifted his weight, eyes lidded, looking like he was ready for a nap rather than a workout.

Kate rested her hand on Rowan's arm. "Really, you'll be fine. Mickey is a lazy old gelding. Before I left for college, I used to teach lessons with him. I've had little kids ride him. He'll saunter along about as awake as he is now."

Rowan looked at Kate, whose green eyes steadied her. She felt her elevated heart rate gradually return to normal. She had never once had the urge to ride a horse. Not even as a kid. She had always preferred her feet planted firmly on the ground.

"Let's get you mounted up, and I'll explain things from there," Kate said.

Kate untied Mickey and led him over to a small set of stairs, which she indicated for Rowan.

Her breath caught and her anxiety spiked. *Breathe*, she reminded herself. *People ride horses all the time.*

She moved toward the stairs.

"You're going to step up, put your left foot in the stirrup, and lift your right leg up and over."

She swallowed hard, trying to quell the panic that rose up from her chest and into her throat. "Do I have to?"

Kate held Mickey's reins in one hand but took one of Rowan's hands with her other. "You don't have to do anything. This is completely optional."

Rowan met Kate's grounding gaze until the wave of panic receded. "I'll give it a try."

Kate gave her hand a squeeze of support, and Rowan moved to the little steps. She did as she was instructed, put her left leg into the stirrup and swung her right leg over. She was sitting on a horse.

"I'm doing it," she said in amazement. She looked down at the ground, seeing it a good four feet below her. The fear remained, but she was surprised at how steady and balanced she felt in the saddle. She had expected to feel as though she could fall at any moment.

"You're doing it," Kate affirmed.

Rowan reached into her pocket for her cell phone. "Can you get a picture of this for me? I want to show everyone back home."

Kate took the phone and stepped back a few feet. Rowan smiled for the photo, envisioning what her parents and friends were going to say when she sent it to them.

"You look good up there," Kate said, as she handed the phone back to her.

71

She blushed. "I probably look terrified. Which I am."

Kate shook her head. "You look like a natural."

She watched as Kate untied Stryder, then stepped into the stirrup and lifted herself up and over. No steps necessary.

That, Rowan thought, *is what a natural looks like.*

Kate walked her horse over so Stryder stood in front of Rowan and Mickey, facing them.

"Okay," Kate said, "first of all, if you need to stop or slow down, pull back on Mickey's reins. Don't pull too hard. They're connected to the bit in his mouth. Just a gentle pull."

Rowan watched as Kate demonstrated with Stryder and then tried the movement herself.

"Excellent," Kate said. "Just like that."

Rowan gave it a few tries to make sure she had it down pat. She *definitely* wanted to know how to slow down and stop.

Kate demonstrated a few other simple steps such as how to get Mickey to move and turn. She had Rowan nudge Mickey into a walk by giving him a light squeeze with her heels.

Rowan didn't know how hard to squeeze and had visions of Mickey taking off in a gallop so she barely brushed her heels over Mickey's stomach.

Kate watched and laughed. "I don't think Mickey could even feel that. You're going to have to nudge him a little harder."

She tried again, and this time Mickey took a couple of steps forward and stopped.

"Horses are a little like people," Kate said. "People have different personalities and temperaments. So do horses. Some horses are boisterous and outgoing and want to run all over the place. Mickey is the horse equivalent of a soft-spoken introvert. I promise, you won't have to worry about him going too fast. The challenge for you will be to get him to keep moving."

Rowan scratched Mickey's neck. "I like you, Mickey." Slow, with many breaks, sounded perfect. She nudged Mickey forward, and the two of them walked slow circles around the fenced-in field. Kate had her change directions a few times, but they didn't do anything harder than that, for which she was exceedingly grateful. She'd seen the movies where one character gets on a horse that bolts, and they can do nothing but hold on, terrified. As Mickey slowed to a stop yet again, she started to realize the improbability of that happening to her.

A slight wind made the afternoon an almost-bearable temperature. Since moving to Texas, the sun had been unrelenting, and she was relieved to find that a few large clouds offered a break from that scorching sun. The afternoon was about as perfect as she could have imagined.

"How are you feeling?" Kate asked. "Still scared?"

She shrugged. "It's all right I suppose." But she smiled, letting Kate know that she was downplaying how good a time she was having.

Kate nodded with a matching smile. "Yeah. It's okay. Not too terrible."

Rowan looked down at Mickey, who sauntered lazily forward, head down, snacking on grass every few steps. She was still a little unsure about this horseback riding thing. She couldn't see herself wanting to ride just any horse. But she and Mickey? They could be pals.

Kate watched as Rowan relaxed into riding. At first, she'd thought Rowan was joking about her hesitation, but it quickly became clear Rowan was actually terrified of the animals. That fear surprised her. Growing up in Texas, she didn't know many people who were terrified of horses. She'd taught lessons for a number of years, but even when she'd encountered some uncertainty, she'd never really seen terror. Everyone she'd ever taught had, at the very least, *wanted* to learn to ride. As a rancher's kid, she couldn't recall her first time on a horse. Her baby album was filled with photos of her dad holding her on the backs of horses or riding with her in a baby carrier on his back. The horses had been her favorite part of growing up on the ranch. That and the baby cows. She'd always loved seeing the newborn calves.

She watched Rowan ride slow laps of the pasture. She didn't

think Rowan was even aware of the smile that had not left her face. She looked so proud, sitting atop Mickey as though she'd conquered Everest. Rowan wore a tank top that advertised a band Kate assumed had to be a punk or metal band, based on the neon creature plastered across the front. Her dark jeans were faded and worn out on the thigh. The cowboy hat on her head looked comically out of place, which only highlighted Rowan's easygoing, try-anything spirit, and made the whole surprisingly attractive. Kate smiled as she watched her, a lightness expanding in her chest.

In addition to watching Rowan learn to ride, though, Kate kept an eye on the sky. The clouds were moving in fast, and the wind had picked up significantly since they had started riding. She didn't want to make Rowan stop too soon because it was clear that Rowan was enjoying herself, but she also wanted them to be indoors before the rain hit.

"We should probably get the horses in," Kate said, as one of the gray clouds moved in overhead. "Storm's coming."

Rowan looked at the sky and then back at Kate. "What do you mean? It's not that cloudy."

Rowan was right. The sky was still largely open, with the sun shining brightly. But the horizon had darkened, and the clouds overhead were a dense dark gray, not puffy and white. Kate knew how to read the ever-changing Texas sky, and a darkening horizon was all it took to tell her they needed to get the horses in.

"The weather changes fast here," she explained.

Rowan followed her to the gate. "I haven't seen a single drop of rain since I got here a month ago."

"That sounds about right," Kate said. The weather in North Texas was fickle. The entire summer would be scorching sun, without the shadow of even a light cloud cover to offer any protection. The hot, dry summer would be bookended by two stormy seasons, with a cold, gray winter in between. Rowan had arrived at the end of the stormy season, and it seemed a late spring storm was about to hit.

Kate showed Rowan how to dismount and helped her off

Mickey. They led the two horses to the barn where the others waited in their stalls. She took the saddle and bridle off of Stryder, then helped Rowan untack Mickey.

"Thanks for the lesson," Rowan said. She stood beside Mickey, stroking his neck, clearly more interested in the animal than she had been an hour earlier.

"It wasn't as bad as you thought, was it?"

Rowan shook her head. "No. I suppose not. I didn't die, so I can't complain."

"I told you I would keep you alive."

"Well, I appreciate it. I think my parents would miss me if I died. I mean, I did up and leave them for Texas, but that betrayal aside, I suspect they want to keep me alive."

Kate laughed and grabbed the tack buckets so that they could brush the horses down.

"You're a character, Rowan Barnes." She handed Rowan one of the buckets. "You know that, right?"

Rowan shrugged. "I don't know what you're talking about." She looked at the bucket, taking inventory of the items inside.

"We'll start by brushing them down," Kate explained. "Then we'll clean their hooves to make sure no rocks are stuck in their feet, and then we can tuck them into their pens to rest."

Rowan grabbed Kate's arm, and when Kate looked over at her, she saw fresh fear in Rowan's eyes.

"Okay, I get the part about brushing," Rowan said. "Brushing I can do. But what's this about cleaning their hooves?"

"I'll walk you through it. Don't worry. It's not that hard."

Rowan looked as if she was about to say something, but Kate held up a hand to stop her. "I haven't killed you yet, remember. Trust me on this one."

Kate brushed down Stryder and helped Rowan finish up with Mickey. Then she pulled the hoof pick out of the bucket and showed Rowan how to get the horses to pick up their feet, and how to scrape out the mud and rocks, demonstrating with Stryder.

She held the hoof pick up to Rowan, who looked back and forth between her and the pick as though she were crazy.

Kate moved closer to Rowan.

"Stand with your shoulder next to Mickey's," she said.

She watched as Rowan tentatively did as she was instructed.

"Good." She stepped in behind Rowan, and then took Rowan's right hand, and moved it over to Mickey's front leg.

"You're going to brush your hand down his leg," she said, guiding Rowan's hand.

She could feel Rowan tense as her hand neared Mickey's hoof.

"Relax," she said against Rowan's ear.

She could feel Rowan's warmth, and breathed in Rowan's soft sandalwood scent. Rowan's arm was soft against hers, and she could feel the rise and fall of Rowan's chest with each breath.

Rowan swallowed and nodded.

"Good." Kate had to steady her own breathing as she helped guide Rowan's hand down Mickey's leg until they could squeeze the horse's fetlock, which urged Mickey to lazily shift his weight and lift his hoof.

Kate handed the hoof pick to Rowan, who tentatively used it to dig out the mud and rocks.

Kate stood back and let Rowan finish before helping her with the next hoof.

"You don't go easy on the newbies, do you?" Rowan said, once she finished.

Kate shrugged. "I could tell you were capable of cleaning his hooves. It's all a part of the lesson."

"Lucky me," Rowan said, but she was smiling.

Just as they tucked the horses into their pens, the rain began. It started hard and heavy, battering the barn roof.

"What the hell?" Rowan asked, looking out at the rain, which was coming down in buckets.

"I told you," Kate said. "The weather changes fast here."

Rowan stood at the entrance to the barn, looking at the sheet of water. "Not so much as a raindrop since the move. What is this? Is this the apocalypse? The next big flood?"

Kate laughed and stepped up next to Rowan. "Yeah, the storms here get pretty intense. We'll wait it out here, then head to the house."

Rowan, however, appeared to have other plans. She was already stepping out into the rain.

"What are you doing?" Kate called out, over the drumming of the water.

Rowan held out her arms and twirled. "I love the rain! I've *missed* the rain." She laughed and opened her mouth.

This was the happiest Kate had seen Rowan, and she smiled as she watched.

Rowan waved for Kate to join her.

Kate shook her head.

"Come on!" Rowan's clothes were soaking wet, clinging to her body after only a minute. Kate enjoyed being warm and dry. She was happy to stay tucked away within the cozy barn.

Rowan looked at Kate for a long moment, and then Rowan's cold, wet hands were taking hers and pulling her out into the water.

Kate screamed as rain splashed down onto her. She laughed, though, at the shock of cold water. She pulled the opposite direction, trying to pull Rowan back into the barn, but with only a half-effort, and let Rowan tug her farther into the rain.

"What are we doing?" Kate shouted over the water.

"We're having fun," Rowan shouted in reply. She let go of Kate's hands and twirled again. Then, she grabbed Kate's hand and spun her as well.

As Kate twirled, something happened. She felt lighter. It was a physical change, almost as much as it was an emotional change. The weight of the past couple months slipped off her shoulders, and she raised her arms to the sky and spun.

Rowan stopped her and steadied her by placing a hand on each shoulder. "Fun, right?"

Water dripped down Rowan's face. Her dark hair was plastered across her forehead, hanging over her eyes, but Kate could still make out the sparkle there.

Kate nodded. "It was—"

She was cut off by Rowan's lips on hers. Rowan took Kate's face in her hands and kissed her hard in the rainstorm, sending a spark through Kate, like lightning. Kate heard her own gasp of surprise, and then her eyes closed and she fell into the kiss.

She was vaguely aware that somewhere in the distance, a low roll of thunder traveled across the sky. Neither of them broke the kiss.

Her hands found Rowan's hips, and pulled her closer, pressing tight against her. Even through the cold water, Rowan's body was warm and soft.

Rowan's thumb traced over her jaw, and she opened her mouth to Rowan with a low moan.

Rowan claimed her with her mouth, and Kate dug her fingertips into Rowan's waist in a desperate attempt to hold on.

Rowan's teeth raked over her lower lip, sending a shock of heat through her.

Kate moved her hands to Rowan's back, wanting her closer, wanting more. She could hardly think. There was Rowan and her lips and tongue and hands and, oh God, it was everything.

The first few pellets of hail interrupted them.

Rowan pulled back, looking around at the little balls of ice as they hit the ground, clearly confused as to what was happening.

Kate was very used to hail, but even she needed a second for her brain to catch up before she could grab Rowan's hand and pull her back into the barn.

Rowan's eyes were wide as she looked out at the hail. "Holy shit. That hail's like, the size of a golf ball now."

Kate looked at the ice that had gathered on the ground. Golf ball was a bit of an exaggeration, but not much of one. It battered the barn noisily.

"My car," Rowan said, looking out helplessly.

Kate peered out at the little car sitting out on the exposed drive. "Shoot. I didn't even think about your car."

Rowan frowned, but then shook the thought from her mind. "It is what it is now. Hopefully it's not too dinged up."

Rowan turned and stepped into Kate and kissed her again. This time, slow and tender.

78

Kate breathed her in as Rowan's tongue gently brushed over her lower lip. She wasn't entirely sure what this thing between her and Rowan was, but it was intoxicating and invigorating. She'd never felt so lost in anyone before.

Rowan slid her hands into the back pockets of Kate's jeans, gently cupping her.

She rolled her hips gently forward, but broke the kiss, taking a moment to look into Rowan's cool, gray eyes, getting lost in their depths.

"That was . . ." Rowan began.

"Unexpected," Kate finished.

"Sexy as hell," Rowan amended.

"Mm, yes. That."

A slow smile spread across Rowan's face. "Kissing in a barn. Now *this* is the type of thing I hoped for when I moved to Texas."

Kate laughed and shook her head. "Oh, is that so?"

Rowan shrugged. "Well, maybe I hadn't pictured this *exact* scenario, but if I had, I might have moved here sooner."

That made Kate laugh harder.

Rowan pulled away and looked back outside. "Where'd the rain go?"

The rain had slowed to little more than a drizzle.

"In and out in the blink of an eye," Kate said.

"I don't even know how that's possible." Rowan looked out at the clearing skies with awe.

Kate shrugged. She didn't have a clue, but she had also never given it much thought. That was just how the weather was in Texas. She was never surprised by the quick changes.

"We should get you dried off," Kate said.

"I'll be fine."

"Nonsense," she argued. "I am not sending you home in that. Why don't you come inside? I'll lend you some of my clothes while we toss yours in the dryer so that you can be warm and dry for the drive home. It's a good long drive. You might as well be comfortable."

She didn't give Rowan a chance to answer. She took Rowan's hand and led her back to the house to dry off.

Rowan followed Kate, thinking of little else other than how soft and warm Kate's fingers were, intertwined with her own.

She didn't want to go inside and get dried off. She wanted to stay in the barn in that magical moment, getting lost in Kate. She didn't care that her clothes were wet and heavy with water. But Kate had taken her hand, and she could only follow.

Kate led them toward her ranch home. It was tucked away behind the main office, nestled next to a thick swatch of trees. Rowan had never seen more than a glimpse of the house before. It wasn't particularly large, but it had a special quality to it—a homeyness she was unaccustomed to. The combination of dark wood and light stone siding gave the place a warm, inviting appearance, and the large windows that faced the pastures were sure to fill the place with sunlight. Log pillars held the roof up, overhanging the large, wrap-around porch, which held a couple of porch chairs with large cushions.

"This place is gorgeous," she said.

"Thanks," Kate said. "My dad built it when my parents first got married."

"He *built* this?"

"Not entirely on his own. He had help. But yes. The ranch was my dad's dream. This house was my mom's. He wanted to make it real for her."

"Wow," Rowan breathed, taking in the detail in the porch railing.

"I think my dad thought that if he could give my mom the house she wanted, she would be okay with living on a Texas ranch."

Rowan paused, realizing she had never heard Kate talk about her mom before.

Kate gave a small shrug and shook her head. "She wasn't meant for ranch life."

Kate pushed open the front door. Rowan knew the conversation was over and followed her inside.

"Wait here," Kate said, and she left Rowan standing by the front door, returning a moment later with two giant towels. She wrapped one of the towels around Rowan, pulling her close as she did.

Rowan liked the closeness. She lifted a corner of the towel to Kate's face and brushed Kate's wet hair back, then traced the towel along the curves of Kate's face, drying her. Then she toweled dry her own face, and tousled her hair so that it was no longer dripping wet.

When she finished, she saw Kate watching her with a look of combined adoration and amusement.

"What?" Rowan asked.

"You're just cute. That's all."

She felt a blush rise to her cheeks, and she had to look away from Kate's gaze.

"Come on." Kate took Rowan's hand again, leading her through the house toward the bedroom.

Rowan stood in the entry while Kate went to the closet to find clothes for her to change into.

"I'll find you a T-shirt and some sweatpants," Kate said. "Hang on."

She nodded and wrapped her towel tighter around herself as she looked around the room.

The room struck her as very "Kate." It was warm and feminine, with country décor and what appeared to be hand-crafted wood furniture, quilted blankets, and a framed painting of horses running across a field hanging on the wall.

She moved into the room to look at the framed photo that rested on Kate's nightstand. The photo was a man with a little girl in cowboy boots on his shoulders. She knew it instantly to be Kate and her dad, and she smiled at the little girl with copper hair in twin braids, who was grinning as she squinted into the sun, toward the camera. She felt her heart tug toward Kate, while she also felt a knot of homesickness settle into her stomach.

This place—it was clear it was everything to Kate.

The way Portland was everything to her.

Kate stepped next to her holding a folded pair of sweats and a white T-shirt.

"You were adorable." Rowan looked over at Kate.

"I still am," Kate said with a wink. Then she held the clothes out to Rowan. "These should fit."

"Thanks." She accepted the clothes.

"There's a bathroom just out in the hall," Kate said. "I'll change quickly as well. And then we could put your clothes in the dryer and have some tea while we wait?"

Rowan looked at Kate, surprised at the sudden shyness she saw, and nodded with a smile. She wasn't in any rush to leave. As far as she was concerned, the more time she could spend with Kate, the better.

"That sounds wonderful," Rowan said.

Kate gave a shy smile, and Rowan headed for the bathroom to change.

This wasn't her home, but she was grateful for the time she got to spend in Kate's world. She made Texas a little more comfortable.

Kate went to the kitchen to put the kettle on for some tea and saw her dad sitting in a big recliner in the adjoining living room, reading the newspaper.

"You doin' okay, Daddy?" she asked after she switched on the kettle.

Her dad gave a small nod, but didn't look up from his newspaper. Kate turned and saw Rowan move into the room.

"Daddy," Kate said, "this is Rowan. She's the grill chef who picks up the beef for On the Range. I taught her to ride Mickey today. Or I tried to until the rain interrupted us."

Her dad looked up and gave Rowan a polite but distant smile and nod. "Nice to meet ya, Rowan. Name's Warren Landreth."

Rowan stepped over to him and held out a hand. "It's a pleasure," she said as he shook her hand.

"We're going to make some tea while Rowan's clothes dry," Kate said. "Would you like any?"

He shook his head. "No, thank you, Katie. I'm just gonna read the newspaper until the home care folks show up for my afternoon torture session."

"You're getting stronger already," she said. "I can tell."

She saw the eye-roll and was about to say more when Rowan spoke instead.

"Anything interesting happening in the world?" Rowan motioned toward the newspaper with her head.

"Is there ever?" Warren asked. "Same old depressing stuff. Politics. Crime. Terror. The usual. I might as well be reading a tabloid magazine."

"Hey now," Rowan said. "You should take the news more seriously. If you haven't started building your underground bunker yet, you should get on that. I hear the end of the world is coming any day."

Warren gave a single laugh. His smile had widened, and it reached his eyes. "I like you."

Rowan took a seat on the couch, and Kate stood for a moment watching the two of them.

"What do you take in your tea?" Kate asked.

Rowan met her gaze, and even from across the room she felt herself melt into Rowan's warmth.

"Just sugar, please," Rowan said. "And just a little. Not Texas sweet tea level."

Kate laughed. "Got it. All the sugar."

She winked and went to the kitchen to make the tea. As she was putting tea bags into two mugs, she couldn't help but overhear the conversation between Rowan and her dad.

"So, what is this torture that you have to go do this afternoon?" she heard Rowan ask.

She tensed and was surprised when her dad answered.

"It's all this therapy garbage they've got me doing. I'm sure Katie's told you about my accident? Anyway, I swear they're not doing it to see me improve. They get off on watching me in pain. Sadists, the bunch of them."

"Daddy—" Kate said.

At the same time, Rowan said, "Bastards."

Kate looked over at Rowan but was caught off guard when she heard her dad laugh.

"Yeah," he said. "The only reason I'm going to participate in their torture is so that I can get fast enough to chase them down and give them a beating for everything they're putting me through."

"They have no idea what they're creating," Rowan said.

"They sure don't," Warren agreed. "They had better watch themselves."

Kate didn't know what was happening, but she warmed at the sight of Rowan and her dad laughing together in the living room. It had been too long since she'd seen him laugh freely like that.

"They're only doing it to help you," Kate said, once the laughter had died down.

She saw her dad shoot Rowan a look and overheard him say, "Hear that? Why did I raise such an optimist? She's insufferable."

"Daddy!" Kate argued, but she was laughing as well.

From the stove, the kettle whistled, and she pulled it from the burner to pour into the mugs.

"Actually," her dad called from the living room, "if it's not too much trouble, I think I will have some tea with y'all after all."

She looked at him and smiled over at Rowan, hoping she could see her gratitude. She pulled a third mug down from the cupboard.

"We'd love to have you join us," Rowan said.

Kate poured the water into the mugs and then went to the counter to get the sugar.

"So, Rowan, your accent, you're not from Texas, are ya?"

"That I'm not," Rowan answered. "Born and raised in Oregon."

"And how are you liking Texas so far?"

Kate stirred the sugar into the tea, still smiling as she listened to the two of them get along.

"It's not home," Rowan said.

And Kate's smile fell.

"But it's growing on me."

She turned and saw Rowan smiling over at her, but this time when she smiled back, Kate knew her smile didn't reach her eyes.

She joined her dad and Rowan and tried to tell herself to have a good time. She had, after all, known Rowan did not consider Texas home. But hearing the words articulated created a grain of fear that settled into her mind, no matter how much she tried not to get ahead of herself.

The sun was just starting to set when Rowan got home for the evening. She was still smiling as she let herself into her apartment, setting her keys and cowboy hat on the little shelf by the door and turning on the lights.

As soon as she stepped in, her mood dampened. She felt as if she were living in a hotel room. Well, if a hotel room were cluttered with boxes. The apartment was just four walls that Rowan happened to be sleeping in.

God, she missed her apartment in Portland. She missed the large bay window overlooking the wooded park with its quiet man-made lake, where she would sit and watch the joggers and morning taekwondo groups while sipping the coffee she picked up from Joe's Coffee Shop just downstairs. This apartment looked out onto the brick wall of the building across from her. She wasn't sure where the nearest coffee shop was, but she was fairly certain they didn't brew Joe's special midnight dark roast that she'd gotten so hooked on. She missed her living room with her friends sprawled out, having wine and cheese night, and watching B-rated horror flicks. This apartment had silence. And boxes.

She went over to the boxes that had taken up residency on her dining-room table and opened the box nearest her. It was full of books. One at a time, she pulled out the familiar stories. She set them on the bookshelf that stood vacant next to her television, until the shelf had a collection of familiar stories, characters, and places. She sat down on her couch and looked at her bookshelf. It was *something* familiar at least.

She couldn't stand the thought of unpacking all of the boxes. That felt too much like settling in, and she wasn't ready to settle into Texas. Books, though. She could handle unpacking books.

A small something to make the place feel a little less cold.

Of course, after spending the day at Kate's ranch, her apartment may as well have been a prison. Kate's place oozed sentimentality, family, *home*. The knot of homesickness had settled in when she'd first stepped inside and had not yet let up.

Rowan tried to shift her thoughts and think of something else.

She had survived riding a horse. That was something. She had known she was scared, but she hadn't realized how terrified she was until she got off the horse and her heart rate came back down to normal. In the end, she was prouder than she would ever admit out loud. She was glad Kate had pushed her.

Kate.

The thought of her brought a rush of warmth to Rowan. She had certainly not intended on kissing Kate in the rain, but by God if it wasn't the best kiss she'd ever experienced.

She didn't know what she and Kate were doing together exactly, other than the kissing, but she enjoyed whatever was between them. After her rough start at work, it was nice to have something to enjoy about Texas.

Rowan opened her phone and looked at the picture that Kate had taken of her on the horse. She looked ridiculous with her Texas cowboy hat, gripping the reins tightly, fear evident in her eyes. She laughed and opened her messages to send the picture to Alycia, but she stopped before hitting send. She still hadn't really had a chance to talk to Alycia, and she felt clingy and desperate and all the things she didn't like feeling with her partner in crime, best friend, ride or die. She texted the picture to her parents instead.

Wow. You look great! her dad texted back.

I look ridiculous, she thought.

Alycia would have seen that. She would have laughed.

She closed her phone, feeling more alone in Texas than ever.

Chapter Seven

The water was cool on Rowan's skin as she swam the length of the small pool, a delicious contrast to the hot sun, which beat down fiery and unforgiving. The fact that nearly every apartment complex came with a pool was one of Texas's only saving graces. She was fairly certain she'd die without it. She flipped onto her back and floated in the small patch of shade provided by the nearby oak tree, closing her eyes and allowing her thoughts to drift along with her.

She thought of Kate and the kiss they'd shared in the rain, and at the thought she felt the corners of her mouth tug upward.

It had been a good kiss.

A *damn* good kiss.

She could still feel Kate's lips on hers—soft and warm and eager. And Kate's hands, tugging at her waist, pulling her closer.

Even floating in the cold water, she felt the warmth spread through her at the thought.

She flipped over again and dove beneath the water as though submersing herself could cool her thoughts.

When she resurfaced, she swam over to the edge of the pool, grabbed her towel and sat down on one of the pool chairs, letting the sun dry her skin.

She picked up her phone, which she had left beside her towel and her apartment keys.

She hadn't told her friends about Kate, and she wanted to call or message them. It felt strange and hollow not to have them to talk to. She told them about all of her dates, usually immediately after the date ended. Now she had been on two dates and she hadn't shared a thing.

But Alycia was busy. Too busy to talk apparently. And it felt wrong to share with Kris and Hannah before her. Alycia was always the first one to know, and Rowan was certain Alycia would be upset to hear about Kate from the others and not directly from Rowan.

Rowan opened her photos and looked at the one of her riding Mickey, the smile falling easily back into place. She had to admit that although she had been terrified, learning to ride had been a lot of fun. They hadn't done anything crazy. They'd just sauntered through the pasture, slow and relaxing, in the afternoon sun, beside a pretty girl. It was actually kinda perfect.

She decided to share the photo, and she opened her Instagram account to post the photo for her friends and family to see, along with the caption, "All right, rodeo. I'm ready."

She was still smiling as she hit post, and then went to the homepage to scroll through the pictures that her friends had shared. She had been so busy with the move and the new job and Kate she'd hardly been on social media since she'd arrived in Texas. As she scrolled through her friends' pictures, she felt a level of comfort settle in. For a moment, she didn't feel a world away.

She saw the photos of her friends' cats, the colorful macarons from the new bakeshop that had opened in the city, Hannah's new tattoo, and photos of nature and green spaces (which Texas desperately lacked).

Then she saw the photos of her friends at their favorite bar, and her good mood deflated, her heart sinking. Kris, Hannah, and Alycia were all smiling for photos together. Rowan wasn't there. She was supposed to be in those photos with them.

If it had been just the three of them, Rowan would still have felt like she was missing out, but there was a fourth woman in the photos—one she didn't recognize—and as irrational as it may have been, she couldn't help but look at the pictures and feel as though she had been replaced. The woman stood next to Alycia in one of the photos, with her arm around Alycia's shoulder, both of them making silly faces for the camera. Rowan didn't recognize the woman, and yet she had an obvious connection with Alycia.

A lump formed in the back of Rowan's throat, and she set her phone down, not wanting to see any more. Except the images still burned the backs of her eyelids.

She got up and jumped back into the pool, feeling the shock of cold as it hit her sun-heated skin. But the tightness in her chest didn't loosen, and she no longer felt light and relaxed, floating beneath the oak tree.

She was in Texas, where the sun was actively trying to murder her, where Jesus billboards lined the interstate, where she might possibly be the only unarmed civilian . . .

Where she felt trapped.

Kate was exhausted. She sat in the cafeteria of the rehabilitation hospital, sipping on coffee and staring out at nothing while she waited to feel energized. Work on the ranch was always busy, physical work, but that morning they'd had a calf birth that she'd had to oversee on top of the everyday work that needed to be done. All of which she had to cram into a shorter time frame than she would have liked, so that she could finish early and drive her dad to his rehab appointment.

Which he was adamant she take no part in.

So she sat in the cafeteria until she finished her cup of coffee.

Once the cup was empty, and Kate was left to just stare into space, she glanced at her watch. Only about fifteen minutes were left in her dad's appointment, so she figured she could make her way back to the physical therapy room and see how he was doing. She tossed her cardboard cup and then headed down the hall, hating the apprehension she felt.

She was tired of feeling like a monster for trying to help.

"I don't give a damn what this is supposed to do for me."

Kate heard her dad's voice, louder than usual, just before she stepped into the room.

"Is it going to make my legs work?" Warren continued. "No? Then you can leave me alone."

She hung back as she entered the room. Her dad had his back to her, but she could see his arms were folded across his chest.

As a physiotherapist, Diane must have heard it all because to her credit she did not appear bothered by the scolding. She stood there looking as patient and warm as ever.

"Mr. Landreth—" Diane began.

"No. I don't need this garbage. It's not doing anything for me. I'm not *gonna* get better. I want to be left alone."

"Daddy." Kate stepped in and moved over toward her dad. "You know this is not about walking again. It's about building the strength for you to move around in other ways. Diane is here to help you. Take a few deep breaths and try again in a few minutes."

Warren spun his chair to face her, and she saw the combination of anger and hurt in his hard gaze. "Damn it, Katie, I don't *want* to take a few deep breaths. I don't want to try again in a few minutes. I want to go home."

She had no idea whether she should back down or push harder. She had been raised to respect authority, but at the same time her dad *needed* rehabilitation and she wouldn't be helping him if she didn't push him at the times when he wasn't able to push himself.

"Daddy," she said softly, kneeling in front of him. "I know you don't want to do this. I know it's hard and painful and tiring. But we're almost done for the day. If we can get through fifteen more minutes of this, then we can go home to a cold beer and dinner. I'll make your favorite chicken pot pie."

"It's not we."

The words were spoken firmly with a hard edge Kate had never heard from her dad before.

"What?"

"You keep saying 'we.' *We're* almost done. If *we* can get through

91

fifteen more minutes. It's not *we;* it's *me.* I'm the only one in this chair. I say I'm done."

She took a step back, feeling the words hit her like a blow. The past couple of months had been hell for her dad, but they hadn't exactly been easy for her.

"I'm trying to help you," she said. "I know you're the only one in a wheelchair, but you're not alone in this. We're in this together."

"We're not," he snapped. "You have no idea what this is like. We're not a team. This is not your burden. It's mine, and only mine."

"It's been a hard day." Diane stepped forward, her voice thick with empathy. "We can call it here. You did a lot today, Mr. Landreth. I know sometimes progress doesn't feel like progress, but you did good today."

Warren scoffed.

Diane met Kate's eyes as she continued. "This is a bad day. That's all. Bad days happen."

Kate nodded and tried to believe her. The words didn't make her dad's anger any less hurtful. She was trying to be strong for the both of them, but that only seemed to make things worse.

"We'll see you in a few days," she said to Diane and headed for her truck, her dad following behind her.

The drive home was made in silence. She felt the tension in her jaw as she bit down to keep from verbalizing her anger. All of the extra work she'd done . . . her exhausting morning trying to run the ranch essentially on her own.

"I oversaw the birth of a calf today," she said, as they pulled up into the drive, unable to contain the words any longer. "I cleaned the horse stalls and rotated cattle. I booked an appointment for the farrier to change the shoes on the horses. I'm *trying* to keep everything together for us, but I need you to meet me halfway. I can't do this all on my own. I need your help."

"I didn't ask you to do this at all," he said. "I don't need your help. I didn't want you to come here and keep the ranch running. I told you we should sell the livestock. Hell, even the ranch itself. We'd pay off all of my medical bills and I could move somewhere accessible, where I wouldn't have to spend all day looking out at the life I used to have. It's gone for me, Katie. If you want to keep it running, then that's your choice, but don't pretend you're doin' it for me."

Kate shook her head. *He's just hurt.* She was certain he didn't want to lose the ranch any more than she did. This place was their home. It was his dream. He'd never be able to do all the things he used to, but the wheelchair wasn't a death sentence. Dean and Owen were helping to make the ranch more accessible, and he'd be able to start helping with the day-to-day operations. She could see it all so clearly. Why couldn't he?

She parked the truck and got her dad's wheelchair out of the back.

"Come on," she said. "I'll make dinner."

"Don't," he said. "I'm not hungry."

She swallowed the hurt and watched as her dad slid down into the wheelchair and wheeled himself toward the house.

"Fine," she said after him, too softly for him to hear.

She didn't go inside. She sat on the porch, trying to fight the tears that burned behind her eyelids.

Eventually, she found herself pulling out her phone and hitting the call button.

"Hey stranger."

At the sound of Rowan's warm, friendly voice, she felt the tension melt away. "Hi you," she said. "I know it's a little last minute, but I was wondering if you wanted to grab some dinner with me? I know a great taco place."

Kate could make her chicken pot pie another day. She didn't feel like cooking, and she didn't really want to stay in alone. She wanted to get out, be away from the ranch, and forget about all of it for one night.

She waited for Rowan to answer, hope building within her, and when Rowan finally spoke, Kate heard the smile in her voice.

"Tacos sound perfect."

Chapter Eight

Rowan could tell she was going to like the place as soon as they parked next to the taqueria. Indie rock music played over the speakers, carrying out into the alley—a refreshing change from the country music that she had been hearing everywhere. The rich scent of grilled meats clung to the air, making her stomach water before she even stepped inside.

"I used to come here when I was in school," Kate said. "It was my go-to, post-class dinner spot. The food is fast, cheap, and delicious."

A winning combination if Rowan had ever heard one.

They stepped inside, and she looked over the yellow menu board above the cashier. The place was hardly a traditional taqueria, offering a combination of Mexican- and Texan-inspired tacos: everything from *tacos al pastor* to fried chicken and beef brisket tacos, all at $2 apiece.

"This place is legit," Rowan said. "Chicken and *nopales*. I definitely haven't seen tacos featuring cacti in Portland." She'd seen cactus cooked on cooking shows before, but she'd never had the chance to try it for herself.

"You might never eat tacos from a kit again after this."

Rowan nearly choked, and immediately began defending herself. "I haven't had a taco from a kit since childhood. There's no way I would eat anything so full of sodium. Why eat packaged crap like that when it is so easy to make tacos from scratch?"

Kate answered with a bright, teasing smile that said her comment had hit its mark. Rowan felt her cheeks redden.

"You were teasing me."

"I was teasing you." The playfulness that creased the corners of Kate's eyes tied Rowan's stomach in knots.

She had to break the gaze before she leaned in to kiss Kate right in the middle of the food line.

"So what should I get?" she asked, looking back at the menu and forcing herself to focus on the task at hand.

"Really, anything," Kate said. "You can't go wrong with any of the dishes."

"Helpful," she said, rolling her eyes in Kate's direction.

Kate laughed. "I am, aren't I?"

Rowan settled on the fried chicken taco, the chicken and *nopales* taco, the ancho chile-marinated pork taco, and the grilled Baja shrimp taco: a diverse selection to get acquainted with the place.

Graffiti-style wall art advertised that the place made the best margaritas in Fort Worth—"made with *real* tequila."

"I think I need to be the judge of this," Rowan decided, and she ordered a prickly pear margarita to accompany her dinner.

Kate laughed and ordered her food and margarita as well. They took a seat on the patio while they waited.

The restaurant had a young, industrial feel to it. The patio was shaded with sheets of corrugated metal, and large overhead cage fans kept the area pleasantly cool. Garage doors served as windows, separating the patio and the main restaurant, and the concrete walls of the patio were adorned with bright monster murals.

Rowan took a slow sip of her prickly pear margarita, closing her eyes and nodding. The sweetness of the prickly pear balanced perfectly against the tang of the lime and the salt rim. It was cold and refreshing, and without a doubt the best margarita she'd tried.

Kate sat across from her and took a sip of her margarita as well; however, she stared out at the restaurant with a pensive gaze. Her brows were pulled ever so slightly together, leaving a faint crease across her forehead, and her eyes lacked their usual sparkle. She hadn't sounded like her usual bright and happy self on the phone earlier either, and had seemed distracted on the drive over.

"So," Rowan began, trying to find a way to gently broach the subject, "what's going on?"

Kate looked back over at her with a small shrug and a smile. "Not too much."

Rowan, wasn't convinced. She reached across the table and placed her hand on Kate's to convey her genuine interest in whatever was bothering her. "Try again."

Kate let out a breath and met her eyes. Rowan could see her warring over what to say. Rowan got the impression Kate wasn't used to opening up to others. She was strong and stoic, and usually the one that *other* people turned to. Rowan didn't want to push her, but she gave Kate's hand a squeeze and held her gaze.

"It was a long day," Kate said at last. "Therapy was rough. Daddy, I know it's hard for him, but he's kinda awful to be around right now. I know he doesn't mean the things he says, it's his anger talking, but he's been mean to the people trying to help him. Nurses, home care . . ."

"You," Rowan finished.

Kate let out a breath, as though happy to finally have that fact articulated, and she nodded. "He was snappy with me tonight when I tried to motivate him to get through his therapy session. He's been short with people, myself included, since the accident, but tonight was the harshest he's been. I'm trying to be optimistic and encourage him to keep going, but my optimism only frustrates him. What am I supposed to do? Just give up with him? He makes it sound like things have been great for me, and I don't understand what he's going through, but it hasn't exactly been the easiest time for me, either. I spent nearly two months driving back and forth almost constantly between the ranch and the rehabilitation hospital. They're a good hour's drive apart. We don't have to make the drive as often now, but I still have to drive him a few times a week for his therapy. I dropped out of school, I dropped *everything* to help him, to help *us* keep the ranch."

Rowan set down her drink and reached across the table to take Kate's hands in hers.

"Veterinary school was my dream," Kate said. "It was impossibly hard to get in, and I had to drop out. I was able to withdraw from my classes without academic penalty, but I can't imagine being able to go back. Not if I have to run the ranch at the same time. It may have been my dream, but I don't want it at the cost of the ranch."

Kate sighed, the tension falling from her face, replaced with sadness. Then she shook her head, visibly pulling her armor back into place. "I'm sorry, I don't mean to complain. Today, well, today was a hard day. I just wish he'd appreciate the fact that he's not the only one this is hard on."

Rowan squeezed Kate's hands. "You don't have to apologize for anything. I'm sorry that today was rough."

Kate met her gaze, and her armor fell away again. "Today has been the worst, sure, but it's all been rough. I feel like I'm alone in this."

"For what it's worth," Rowan said, "I'm here. Anytime you need to talk."

"Thank you." Gratitude filled Kate's eyes. Then she surprised Rowan by adding, "I'm trying to keep it all together. But it's a lot."

Rowan nodded, though she could only imagine how hard Kate's situation was, trying to take care of her dad *and* the ranch all at the same time.

"Rowan," the voice boomed over the loudspeaker. "Your tacos are ready."

She got up and went inside to the counter, where she picked up the metal tray with tacos for both her and Kate. They looked and smelled amazing. Rowan eyed Kate's order, not entirely sure she wanted to share the tacos.

"These tacos will make things a little better," she said, setting the tray on the middle of the table. "I can almost guarantee it."

"Thank you," Kate said. "I really needed this."

"I think I should be thanking *you*. This was your idea. And a brilliant one at that."

This time, Kate's smile brightened, and Rowan was relieved to see the warmth return to the summer green of her eyes.

Rowan looked down at her food, debating for a minute about where to start before picking up her ancho-marinated pork taco. A lime wedge sat next to each taco. Rowan squeezed the lime over the top and then took a bite and moaned. The ancho chile offered a kick of heat, but it was balanced perfectly with the sweetness of the pineapple salsa and the tang of the lime.

"This is heaven."

"Right?" Kate asked around a mouthful of brisket taco.

"I will defer to you for all of my dining choices from now on. It seems you're a bit of an expert."

Kate laughed. "Hardly. I just hate cooking and ate out a lot when I was living in the city for school."

"Wait a minute." Rowan held up a hand. "You *hate* cooking?"

Kate looked up at Rowan from under her eyelashes. "Guilty."

Rowan shook her head. "We're going to need to fix that."

"Oh, we are, are we?" Kate raised an eyebrow in a decidedly sexy look.

Rowan nodded. "You made me get on a horse, so yeah, now you get to try cooking with me."

Kate scrunched up her nose. "Fine."

"I promise, I'll make it worth your while," Rowan said.

Kate held her gaze. "Is that so?"

She nodded. "Definitely. I'll make sure it's a very enjoyable cooking experience."

Color rose to Kate's cheeks, and she took a long drink of her margarita.

Rowan picked up her fried chicken taco and was as impressed with it as she had been with her pork taco. Fried chicken and coleslaw in a taco. She'd never considered the combination before, but as she bit in she wondered why not. It made perfect sense.

"This is the kind of place my friends back home would love," Rowan said. "Alycia and Kris and Hannah. Going out and trying new foods is our Friday night thing. This would be the type of place that would become a regular in the rotation. In fact, there's a taco truck we go to pretty regularly. It doesn't have quite as many options as here, and they're definitely not choices as diverse, but they do an amazing steak and poblano taco."

"Tell me about your friends," Kate said.

"They're the best," Rowan answered without hesitation. "Alycia, Kris, and I have all been friends since high school. I kinda had a rough time in school until I met them. I wasn't exactly popular. I struggled with my weight and, well, teens are mean. Plus, I was the only out lesbian in my school at the time. It was pretty much hell. But Alycia, Kris, and I all ended up in a film class together and we've been inseparable ever since. When Kris started dating Hannah, she became a part of the group, like she had been there the whole time. Alycia and I were roommates through college, so we're especially close. She's my person."

Rowan thought about Alycia, and how they had hardly talked since her move. "She *was* my person, anyway."

"What does that mean?"

She frowned, not wanting to kill the mood. "The move has been hard. I guess I didn't think it would change much between us, but she's been busy, and we've hardly had a chance to talk. I didn't realize that being in a different state would matter so much."

Kate leaned in closer, her gaze gentle and caring.

"I guess I was naive about the move. I thought things would stay mostly the same, except I'd be working at my dream job in Texas." she sighed. "It sounds silly now when I say that out loud."

"Leaving home was never really part of the plan, was it?" Kate asked. There was no judgment in her voice, just a gentle acknowledgment.

99

"God, no. I love Portland. I'm really close with my parents, and I have a great group of friends. I have good roots there. But the job? It was too good to pass up. It's not the kind of opportunity you say no to."

Kate was quiet for a long moment, but her eyes shone with admiration when she looked at Rowan. When she spoke, her voice was low and quiet. "It was brave of you to move here like that."

Rowan shrugged. It didn't feel brave. It felt scary and lonely.

Kate took a long sip of her margarita, and her gaze was no longer holding Rowan's as she looked out at the restaurant with a distant, indiscernible expression.

"Is everything okay?" Rowan asked.

Kate nodded. Rowan didn't believe her.

"Talk to me?" she begged.

Kate exhaled slowly, clearly weighing whether or not she should voice whatever was on her mind. "What exactly are we doing?"

"Eating tacos?" Rowan answered in question, not sure what exactly Kate was asking.

"I mean in a more general sense, smart aleck," Kate said. "I like you. And I think you like me."

"I do," Rowan acknowledged.

"I'm actually *really* enjoying getting to know you. I think there might be something kinda special sparking between the two of us."

Rowan agreed, but she didn't say so, waiting for the "but" that she knew was coming.

"I don't want to get ahead of ourselves, but I think there's potential here. And yet you're not exactly grounded here, are you?" Kate asked. "I saw your apartment when I picked you up for dinner. Your things are still in boxes. And when you talk about Portland . . . it's all present tense. It's not just where you're from. You're still there at heart."

"I haven't even been here two months," Rowan said.

"I know," Kate replied. "And like I said, I'm not trying to put the cart before the horse, so to speak, but I don't know where all of that leaves me if we get involved. I have so much going on in my life. Everything with Daddy . . . I need to be careful right now, that's all."

"This isn't a vacation," Rowan said. "My *job* is here. I'm not about to pack up and move home. I'm trying to settle in. I really am."

Kate nodded, but she looked sad. Rowan could understand where Kate was coming from, but she wasn't sure what she was supposed to say. She couldn't say that Texas all of a sudden felt like home. It *wasn't* home. She wasn't sure it ever would be. On good days Texas was a new adventure. The rest of the time it was more like a bad dream that she couldn't wake up from.

"I'm sorry," she said.

"It's fine," Kate answered. "Let's enjoy our dinner. I didn't mean to make things so heavy. I think I just need us to slow down a little while you figure some things out."

"Okay." Rowan took a bite of her Baja shrimp taco. The dressing was rich and flavorful and the shrimp well seasoned, but she couldn't enjoy it. Kate was the best thing about Texas, but Rowan's heart was in Portland. She couldn't wave a wand and make her homesickness disappear, even if it meant that she couldn't commit to Kate.

She tried to relax back into the conversation. They could enjoy the evening as friends if nothing else. She needed a friend in Texas, even if that wasn't everything she wanted.

Kate sat on the porch with an ice-cold sweet tea, listening to the cicadas singing in the trees, and watching the lightning bugs flicker through the bushes. It was quiet on the ranch away from the Dallas/Fort Worth metroplex's constant roar of traffic, but she couldn't relax, because her mind played through a memory reel with a deafening intensity.

She had been six when her mom left. She had kissed Kate goodnight one night, and in the morning she was gone. Kate woke that day to find her dad sitting on the porch. She had been too young to recognize that anything was wrong, and she'd gone out there tugging at his shirt and begging him for breakfast until he'd broken down and started sobbing. It was the first of only a couple of times that she could ever recall seeing her dad cry.

Kate used to wonder what she would say to her mom if she ever saw her again. Now, she hoped that day never came.

She thought back on her evening with Rowan, her stomach still twisted in guilty knots. She'd asked Rowan to dinner because she'd wanted an evening of easy conversation and laughter. Spending time with Rowan was meant to cheer her up. She should have enjoyed the tacos and flirting and maybe even some kissing afterward. She was really sad there had been no kissing. Rather than relax into the evening, she had heard Rowan talk about her friends and Portland, and all she could see was their inevitable end. Rowan didn't want to be in Texas.

And yet she'd known that from the start, and she was still the one to ask Rowan out, to kiss Rowan, to make all the first moves.

Kate took a drink of her tea. The entire evening had gone wrong. She'd opened up to Rowan, and suddenly things had felt more intimate. She'd shared something of herself, and that opened her up to loss. She couldn't take any more loss.

She looked out at the pastures, seeing the barest outline of the cattle silhouetted in the pale moonlight. Stars peppered the night sky in a multitude that couldn't be seen through the light pollution in the city. She could see constellations, the North Star, and even the faint line of the Milky Way.

When her dad had caught her kissing her first girlfriend at fifteen—before she had even understood her own sexuality, let alone thought about telling him—she had run out to the pasture, lain down, and looked up at the stars until the panic subsided and she was able to go inside and talk to him. She'd lain in that same field, looking up at the stars, while she applied to colleges. In her naivete she'd believed she was making a decision that would affect the rest of her life. She'd lain under those same stars when she got to the ranch the night of her dad's accident. She hadn't moved back yet, but she needed to let Patch outside, and once she got there, she allowed herself to fall apart. Everything had changed in a day, but those stars, that field, always the same.

Now she sat on the porch with her tea, seeing those same stars, wondering what her life might look like in a year. She hoped the ranch would still be running. She hoped to God she could be sitting out on the same porch in a year's time.

Her thoughts flashed back to Rowan.

There was no point in even hoping that Rowan would feature in that image. She didn't have time for distractions, and she didn't have time for heartbreak when it didn't work out. *Everything* was riding on her shoulders.

A shooting star flashed across the sky. She quickly closed her eyes and wished for the ranch to be okay.

She felt silly, like a child, placing her faith in something as juvenile as a shooting star, but she *needed* the wish to come true. She needed to make it come true.

Chapter Nine

When Rowan was nine, her parents had taken her to Disneyland. She vividly remembered standing in front of Cinderella's castle, looking up at the palace, in complete awe and reverence while she fought the crowd for the opportunity to hug Cinderella herself. She had been old enough to *know* it was all a charade, but she had been completely absorbed in it all the same. She was in a whole different world: one that she had not realized existed.

Being in Texas felt pretty much exactly the same, except the princesses were cowboys, their tiaras were rifles, and she didn't look forward to meeting any of them.

But she definitely felt she was in a whole different world. She had moved to Texas, bound and determined to be independent, and now she was lost in the giant world that existed outside of her own small corner of the universe.

That trip to Disneyland had been the only time she had left Oregon prior to her move. Her parents worked hard to get by and didn't have a lot of money to put toward vacations. Any extra money she had been able to save went toward her school tuition. She'd always wanted to travel and see what else existed in the world, but she'd always assumed she'd go on vacation—always returning home to Portland.

She sat on her couch with her laptop open, looking up the cost of a flight home. If she flew out of Texas on a Sunday morning, she could spend a couple of days with friends and family before flying back in on Tuesday in time for her work shift. It would break the bank, but God, it was tempting. Even just a day with her people . . .

Her mouse hovered over the "purchase" button that she *knew* she couldn't click, but she felt an almost irresistible urge to do so anyway.

Her mind flashed to Kate, and she once again saw the worry in her eyes when she'd commented on Rowan's still-packed boxes. At the time Kate's concern felt unfair, but maybe it was justified. She moved the mouse away from the "purchase" button. It was possible that in her homesickness she wasn't giving Texas a fair chance. She lived here, but she had one foot out the door.

She exited the travel site and brought up her search engine. She typed in, "Best things to do in Fort Worth, Texas."

Kate had called her a tourist, but she had been wrong about that. Rowan hadn't even taken the time to see Texas as a tourist. She had driven her U-Haul to her new apartment and waited for it to feel like home. She hadn't seen the city, besides what Kate had shown her and her drive to work, which still required GPS mapping so she didn't turn down a wrong street and get horribly lost. Maybe she needed to see what the tourists would see in Fort Worth before she could hope to see the place as a local.

She looked up the reviews of various places, activities, and restaurants in the area. She had the night off work, and she decided that this time she wasn't going to stay in and wallow in thoughts about the things she *wasn't* doing with her friends in Portland.

The sheer number of activities that the internet suggested was overwhelming, and she had no idea where to start. Evidently the city was quite large, and Rowan barely even knew her own little corner.

It was time for that to change.

The fountains in Sundance Square were alight with jets of water shooting into the air, illuminated in various colors. Rowan found it strangely meditative to watch the plumes shoot from the ground in short streams, medium streams, tall streams. Sundance Square was crowded with people, even though it was a Monday night. People sat at tables around the fountain area with coffee and pastries from the nearby shops. Children dashed through the jets of water, and she watched as the security worker occasionally pulled one aside to point out the sign that clearly delineated the appropriate hours for fountain play, as though even the pre-schoolers and toddlers should have been able to read the sign and know better. Parents tried to reinforce the rule, but the water was right there and oh so tempting in the heat. A man walked his puppy, who like the children had to play in the water. The puppy jumped around happily, trying to nip at the jets of water. On the far side of the square, a country band played, and she found herself tapping her foot in time with the music, despite her aversion to any music with a twang.

She liked Sundance Square. There was a lighthearted vibe to the area. Nobody was in a rush. There were stores and restaurants, country bars and coffee shops. It was an enjoyable place to spend an evening out.

She sipped a lemonade while people-watching. She'd been nervous about going to the square on her own, but she was hardly the only one there alone. One man worked on a laptop while a woman a few tables over had a sketchbook open, trying to capture the fountains.

Rowan finished her lemonade and just sat for a while. As enjoyable as it was she did wish she had people to share the evening with. But the evening was about familiarizing herself with Texas. The loneliness of being stuck there was a whole different issue. She wasn't going to solve all of her homesickness, or her problems with Texas, in one night.

She thought of her neighbor, Dave: pro-God, pro-gun, pro-life. She was most likely never going to solve all of her problems with Texas.

One thing at a time, she told herself.

As the sun began to set, children and families headed home for the night, but the square did not go completely quiet. She sat by the fountains until she found herself growing hungry, and decided to check out the BBQ joint on the corner. If she was making a list of things she had to do as a tourist, then surely Texas BBQ needed to be at the top.

She smelled smoked meat as she made her way down the sidewalk to the small restaurant with the neon BBQ sign. Country music blasted through the front door, which was propped open, and a chalkboard sign next to it advertised "burnt ends" as the daily special.

She felt a spark of excitement as she stepped inside. There was a lot about Texas Rowan had been less than enthusiastic about. But the state was known for its BBQ. As a grill chef, she had to appreciate that if there was one thing this state did right, it was cooking meat. In that regard, she wanted to soak up everything about the Texas experience.

She got in line and read over the menu while she waited to order her food. She watched as a large brisket was pulled from the smoker and set down on the counter to be sliced. She eyed the plates of everyone in front of her, each different type of meat looking as good as the rest. She wanted to try them all, but that would be impossible.

Reason 412 why she needed her friends to be in Texas with her: She needed people to help her order and eat all of the food she wanted to try.

As she approached the counter, she saw a cooler full of ice and beer, as well as a couple of drink dispensers offering lemonade, sweet tea, and fountain drinks. She grabbed a beer and stepped up to the counter, not entirely settled on what she was going to try until she actually heard herself order the beef brisket platter.

She watched as the brisket was sliced and heaped high on her tray. Her eyes widened at the sheer volume of meat that was handed to her. More meat than anyone should ever be served anywhere.

She supposed it was true, what they said about everything being bigger in Texas.

The brisket was tender and nicely infused with smoke, and she tried it with every one of the half-dozen sauces on the table. She ate slowly, taking her time as she tried to identify all of the flavors in the spice rub. She didn't own a smoker so it wasn't like she would be able to re-create the dish anyway, but still she wanted to learn everything about what went into making such delicious brisket. She wondered what Kate would have thought of this place. Was it a good representation of Texas BBQ, or did Rowan need to keep searching? She made a mental note to ask Kate for BBQ recommendations. Maybe they could make a point of trying the *best* Texas BBQ together.

She chased her food with her cold Shiner bock beer, trying only halfheartedly to chase away the thoughts of Kate. The two of them could really be something, but she understood Kate's hesitation. Kate's Texas roots ran deep while Rowan had barely touched down. Still, she hoped Kate would see she was branching out, that she was trying, that she was *settling in*.

Even if she hardly felt settled.

She barely made it through a quarter of her brisket platter before she could no longer make herself eat another bite. She looked at the massive amount of meat remaining with guilt, not wanting it to go to waste, but surely nobody could have eaten that much food.

She finished off her beer, admitted her brisket defeat, and then headed back out to walk with no set direction, just to get a sense for the area.

Sundance Square had fewer tourist trinkets than the Stockyards, but she found a variety of Texas-shaped belt buckles in store windows. She wished her friends were there. They'd have made it a scavenger hunt to see who could have found the largest and gaudiest of the belt buckles. They'd have people-watched with her, making up conversations in silly voices and putting on bad Southern drawls. Then they'd have talked about their days. They'd have listened to Rowan talk about hers.

Instead, it was only her.

She sat in front of the fountains again and pulled out her

phone, tired of her only conversation being in her own mind. She missed her friends. She missed Alycia. She felt needy and clingy, but she pushed the feelings aside and hit the call button. She could either sit in the square lonely, or she could extend the olive branch and make the call.

Alycia answered on the third ring. "Rowan!"

Relief hit her like a tidal wave, and she closed her eyes, smiling at the warm sound of her best friend's voice.

"Hey Aly-cat."

Alycia laughed. "Bestie, I've missed you!"

And just like that everything was right in the world again.

"Tell me all about the job. Is it everything you dreamed of? Is Texas still *Texas*? Has your neighbor figured out that you're a lesbian and started a prayer circle to save you from the satanic lure of the ladies?"

Rowan laughed. "And then some, yes, and probably. Every time I go in to work, I still feel like it's a dream. Like, am I *really* working in Daniel Stanford's kitchen? It's *hard*. It's the hardest job I've ever had. And I'm not perfect at it, but I'm managing, and I've already grown so much as a chef. No more cutting potatoes into little fucking footballs until my fingers ache."

She thought about the shifts she'd worked so far. None of them had been flawless, the way she'd have liked. Each night there was a steak or two that got sent back, a little overcooked or a little undercooked. But she tried hard not to let that shake her confidence. The amount of moving parts that were on the go in any one night made perfection nearly impossible. She didn't think she was doing too badly. Between Kate and the move and work, she had a million things on her mind, and yet she was able to focus enough to get most of the steaks done flawlessly.

"I'm so proud of you," Alycia said, and Rowan could hear that the statement was genuine.

"And the food here . . ." she continued, shifting the focus off her work. "My God, it's a foodie paradise. I can't wait to show you, Kris, and Hannah around. I went out for BBQ tonight and tried the smoked brisket. It was *so* good, and now I'm in a food coma. I understand now why Texas is the gold standard of BBQ in America."

Alycia laughed. "I'm glad you're having a good time."

Rowan sobered, wanting to be honest with her best friend. "There's parts of this move that I love, truly. But it's been rough. I still haven't unpacked any of my stuff. I'm so glad that I'm here. I want to try all of the food, and I want to learn all of the grilling techniques. But I don't want to *live* here. It's hard to see this place as home. I know this move is good for me, and it's my dream job, but I miss my family and friends. I miss *you*."

"I miss you, too," Alycia said. "It's not the same without you here. I was watching some bad horror movies last weekend, and it wasn't half as fun without you there to laugh at them with me. Julie couldn't stop rolling her eyes at the bad graphics, and I was like, *'but that's what makes this movie so great!'* She didn't get it."

"Julie?" Rowan asked.

"Oh my God," Alycia said. "It really *has* been forever since we've talked. Have I not told you about Julie?"

"Um, no," Rowan said, and her mind flashed back to the Instagram post she'd seen ... the fourth woman standing in her place, with her friends.

"Wow," Alycia said. "Julie's my new girlfriend. We've been together, well, almost two months now, I guess."

The words were a punch to Rowan's stomach. "Two months?"

"Yeah," Alycia said. "We met shortly after you moved. She's so great. It hasn't been that long, but I really think she might be *the one*. You'd love her. She's a teacher, smart, caring, sexy as hell, and she treats me *so* well."

"I'm happy for you," Rowan said. She knew the words sounded flat, but they were the best she could manage, given the giant knot in her stomach. Alycia had been in a relationship for *two months*, and this was the first Rowan was hearing about it.

"How about you?" Alycia asked. "Have you met anyone in Texas? Is there even a queer scene there or do you have to go underground?"

Kate's gentle smile came to mind, and the knot in Rowan's stomach eased a little. "I've maybe met someone. We're still figuring out what exactly it is."

"Tell me more," Alycia said. "I want to know all of the details."

She didn't particularly want to talk. She wanted to go home, crawl into bed, and not think about the fact that her best friend had been in a relationship for two months without telling her. But Alycia's eagerness came through, and thinking about Kate made her feel a little better.

"Do you remember that cattle ranch I was sent to for work? To pick up the steaks? She works there. She's been showing me around Texas, she took me to the rodeo of all things, and we've kissed a couple times. There's not much to tell beyond that."

"She's a cattle rancher?" Alycia asked with a laugh. Behind the amusement, Rowan could hear a note of judgment in her friend's voice.

A wave of defensiveness washed over her. "It's her family's ranch. You should see the place. The property is gorgeous, complete with Texas longhorns and horses. She actually taught me to ride."

This made Alycia laugh harder. "You on a horse? It all sounds like something out of a Western movie. So very Texan. Does she talk with the silly accent, and say 'y'all'?"

The defensiveness swelled bigger. "Everyone here says 'y'all.'"

"That's so cute," Alycia said. "I can picture it in my mind. I'm glad you're happy, Rowan. If I get a chance to come visit, you'll have to introduce me to her."

If she got a chance to visit. Not *when*. Before Rowan moved, Alycia had talked almost nonstop about coming down to visit her, but now that visit was moved from the planning category to the maybe category, which pretty much meant it was in the never category.

"I will," was all Rowan said.

"I'm glad we finally got the chance to catch up," Alycia said. "It's been too damn long, bestie. But I've got to run, because Julie is coming over. Talk again soon?"

"Yeah, of course," she said, thinking all the while that the radio silence had not been from her end.

She said good-bye to Alycia and hit "end" on her phone. Even just last year Alycia would have called Rowan after every date for a full recap, good or bad. Now her best friend was in a relationship, and she hadn't even thought to tell Rowan.

She watched the fountains shoot water in rhythmic plumes until her breathing steadied and anger began to replace the sadness within her. She had moved to Texas for her *dream* job. It wasn't some whim. And despite the distance she was doing her best to keep in contact with Alycia. That contact had to go two ways. She would never have thought that their friendship was so fragile it couldn't handle distance, but if it was, then she didn't know why she should bother trying at all. This move was the hardest thing she'd ever done. She needed her friends. And yet Alycia didn't seem to care that she was sitting in her apartment, lonely and homesick.

Rowan missed Portland like hell, but suddenly it seemed like the things she was holding onto were not entirely worth it.

She looked around Sundance Square and pictured Kate there with her. It was easy to envision sitting across from Kate with a coffee and a pastry, holding hands, talking, laughing.

This place was unfamiliar and not entirely likable. But it wasn't entirely *unlikable*, either. Kate was here, and that reason alone was worth giving Texas a chance. She could enjoy being a tourist for a while. Maybe she could even find herself liking her life in Texas.

Chapter Ten

Kate shoveled fresh straw into the horse stalls in the barn. Her limbs were heavy with exhaustion from the physical labor she'd done all morning, and yet she didn't slow as she systematically cleaned each stall. She enjoyed the work. It was an almost hypnotic task, and she allowed herself to get lost in the simple, repetitive movements. It was exactly what she needed. Mindless, yet busy enough it kept her thoughts from wandering. From worrying about paying off her dad's medical bills to her dad's anger at her when she tried to help him with his therapy, she was mentally and emotionally drained. Add to that the guilt over her last conversation with Rowan, and she felt like an all-around failure.

"You want a hand with that?" Dean asked from the doorway of the barn, pulling her from her thoughts.

"I'm good, Dean. Thanks."

Dean made no move to leave. "It's just that you usually have customers come by on Friday morning, don't you?"

Was it really Friday?

Kate looked at her watch which confirmed that it was in fact Friday and that it was already nearly midmorning. Which meant Rowan would be coming by to pick up the steaks for the restaurant. She came by to pick up beef on Mondays and Fridays.

"Shoot," she murmured under her breath.

She wasn't ready to see Rowan. She hadn't heard from her since their taco dinner, and she was fairly certain their conversation had painted her as a crazy U-Haul lesbian, insisting that Rowan commit to her and Texas. Any spark that had existed between the two of them had surely been extinguished, and while she wanted to protect herself she had not intended on humiliating herself in the process, which was precisely what she had done.

It was barely their third date, and she had practically begged Rowan to promise that she would never leave.

"Do you think that you could handle the customer orders today?" Kate asked.

Dean looked at her for a long moment. "Is everything okay?" he asked.

She nodded. "I'm just really tired. I haven't been sleeping well, and I don't know that I'm much of a people person today."

Dean looked nervous, and she could see he was wavering over whether or not he could fill the orders.

"You wouldn't have to do much," she promised. "It's just the one order today. Rowan from On the Range will come by. Her order is prepackaged in coolers, labeled with her invoice number. All you have to do is take the check and fill out a receipt. They're in the top left drawer of the desk. You can leave the check in there as well. It's really easy. You can call me if you have any problems, but I promise you'll be fine."

Dean nodded, but he didn't leave the barn. He stepped toward where she was working, and leaned against the side of the stall.

"Why don't you take a couple of days off?" he suggested. "You're working yourself to death. Owen and I can handle the ranch. Take the weekend. I'll come in Saturday and Sunday this week."

Kate saw the concern on his face. He wanted so badly to help her out. The truth was she didn't know what she'd do with a couple of days off. She felt like she was out in the middle of the ocean. If she was working, she was treading water. If she stopped, she'd drown. Everything would be too overwhelming. The only thing she could do was to keep up with the routine. Keep the ranch going. Keep her dad going. Keep going.

"I'm good," she promised.

Dean pursed his lips and nodded. He clearly wanted to say more, but then he straightened and put on his usual smile. Kate was glad to see that he wasn't going to push the matter.

"I've got the customers today." He clasped her shoulder as he stood and exited the barn.

"Thanks," she called, before turning back to the straw, using the pitchfork to spread it in an even layer along the floor of the stall.

She progressed from one stall to the next, steadily cleaning out and replacing the dirty straw, ensuring each stall had a soft cushion for the horses.

She didn't hear the barn door open and jumped when she felt a hand on her shoulder.

She turned to find Rowan standing in front of her, stifling a laugh.

"What are you doing here?" Kate asked, as she tried to will her heart rate to come back down to normal.

Rowan shrugged so casually it was almost infuriating. "It's Friday. I pick up the steaks for our weekend service on Friday."

"Yes, I'm well aware," Kate said. "Dean said he would take care of payments for me while I finished up the milking."

Rowan nodded, still visibly trying to keep herself from smiling. "Yeah. I'm all paid and good to go. I thought I would stop by and see you before I left."

Rowan shifted ever so slightly forward. Kate felt as though the barn shrank around her with that simple move. The air between them hummed. Her body ached to move closer, to close the distance. Her mind shouted at her to move back, to protect herself. Kate stood in place.

"You scared me half to death," she said, trying to look angry, but she was fighting a smile now as well.

"I'm . . . sorry." Rowan barely managed to get the words out.

Kate swatted her shoulder. "You are not."

115

Rowan batted her eyelashes at Kate, looking as innocent as possible, and this time Kate couldn't stop the laughter.

"Don't try to cute your way out of this," she said.

"Is that what I'm doing?" Rowan asked, again with that subtle shift forward.

Kate nodded and swallowed. "Yes. I'm pretty sure that's what you're doing. It's not fair. You're too adorable."

"I'm dashing and charming," Rowan said, pulling her shoulders back and standing a little taller.

"Whatever you say." Kate rolled her eyes, but internally agreed with Rowan's claim.

"That's right." Rowan's smile got wider, and Kate was further pulled into the warmth. She had to stop herself from getting too caught up in Rowan.

"So," Kate started, "you got your steaks."

Rowan nodded.

"And yet here you are."

Rowan nodded again. "Very astute observation."

This time she took a small step forward, and Kate put a hand out to stop her. She couldn't take the closeness. It was too much. Too intense.

"Rowan," she began.

"I know," Rowan said. "I went out last night to explore Fort Worth."

Kate arched an eyebrow, not sure how the conversation gone off to that sudden tangent.

"And I unpacked a couple of boxes." Rowan took her hand. "I know I don't have roots here. I get why that's scary. But you're right. I should make more of an effort to actually *be* here. This is where I live now. I don't plan on going anywhere."

Kate swallowed, simultaneously wanting to believe Rowan and wanting to keep her guard up. Hope swelled within her and she tried desperately to tamp it down.

"I wanted to see you," Rowan said. "That's why I came to the barn. I've missed you. And I wanted to ask if you had plans for the Fourth of July?"

Rowan's eyes were clear pools, and she sank into them. This time she was the one who shifted closer.

"I hadn't given it any thought," she said.

"Come with me to the Fort Worth Fourth? I read about it online, and it looks like a really big event."

Kate nodded. "I've been a few times. You'll like it. You can try all of the Texas deep-fried creations, along with tubing on the Trinity River and of course a Texas-caliber fireworks show."

"What does that even mean, Texas-caliber?"

"You'll see when we go," Kate said.

"So you're in?"

Kate nodded. "For the Fourth I'm in. But you're going to have to stop being so adorable. It's making it really hard to play things safe."

"Keep being adorable," Rowan said. "Got it."

Rowan winked and turned to leave the barn, and Kate sank down onto a stool.

Yeah, there was nothing safe about any of this.

Rowan thought of Kate as she worked, her mind flashing to Kate's warm smile, and her gentle posture as she'd stood across from Rowan in the barn. It had been so tempting to close the distance between the two of them. She had been sure Kate wouldn't have stopped her. That electric hum between the two of them, they'd *both* felt it, she knew. But she wanted more than just a kiss in the barn, no matter how great a kiss it would have been. She wanted to show Kate that she was sticking around.

"Rowan," Daniel called, interrupting her thoughts. She could hear the impatience in his voice. "Tell me, what's wrong with this steak?"

She looked down at the steak in question, and her stomach dropped. One side of the steak had dark brown grill marks, while the other side looked like it had barely touched the grill. "The sear is uneven," she said quietly.

"Pay attention to your work," he said. "Even sear. All of the cuts. No excuses."

"Yes, chef."

He let out a frustrated breath of air and went back to expediting orders, leaving her burning with embarrassment. It was clear that he was losing his patience with her. The first few shifts, he'd been gentle in his corrections, helping her grow into her role. Now, he sounded frustrated, and even a little angry.

She was angry with herself. She never should have plated that steak. Daniel Stanford expected perfection, and that steak was about as far from perfection as you could get. The uneven sear meant that it would also have an uneven cook, with part of it being rare, while the other side edged closer to well-done. She'd been in the kitchen long enough now to know better, and yet not only had she not noticed and corrected the issue while cooking the steak, but she hadn't noticed when she'd pulled it off the grill and plated it.

She'd been distracted and had made a stupid novice mistake.

A mistake that had no place in any professional kitchen, and certainly not Daniel Stanford's kitchen.

The heat on her face had nothing to do with the grill she stood behind. She blew out a long breath and looked up at the next order before tossing a T-bone steak and a pork tenderloin onto the grill.

Tell me what's wrong with this steak.

The anger had been evident in his voice. Anger and disappointment.

She tried to push the memory of that anger from her mind, but she heard his voice over and over, an awful echo.

She had worked in kitchens her entire adult life. She knew that it wasn't a career for the weak. Through culinary school, she'd watched her peers get ripped apart over little details: forgotten garnishes, vegetables chopped unevenly, sauces too thick or too thin . . . Mistakes weren't taken lightly, and so she didn't make mistakes. She prided herself in her perfection. Attention to detail. Getting things exactly right.

She wasn't the one who got yelled at for something as careless as an uneven sear.

She pulled the T-bone and the pork tenderloin off the grill and slid them down the line, and then tossed two sirloins and a filet mignon onto the grill.

It was one uneven sear, she told herself. She had to let it go and move on.

Except that it wasn't one uneven sear.

"Rowan, this tenderloin is overcooked and dry. Start it again."

Daniel's voice had an even harder edge this time.

"Yes, chef," she managed to say around the shame that sat thick and painful in the back of her throat. She set another pork tenderloin on the grill, watching it studiously, determined not to overcook it.

Except that her over-attention to the pork tenderloin resulted in her sending out an undercooked sirloin.

And as she tried not to *under*cook it again when she redid the order, she wound up *over*cooking the damn thing.

She knew how to cook meat. She hadn't landed such a prestigious position by accident. But based on the evening's performance, nobody would ever have guessed that. Rowan lived and breathed food. Cooking was the one thing she was truly passionate about in her life. It was more than a *career* path for her; it was a *life* path.

And yet the further she got into the weeds, the harder it was to get back out.

Order after order came back to her: mistake after mistake.

Daniel's anger grew.

She barely made it through the evening, and when the night was over, she felt the weight of the shame settle heavy onto her chest.

"What the hell was that tonight?" he asked, cornering her as she wiped down her station.

She could only manage to shrug and shake her head. There were no words. The embarrassment strangled her, making it impossible to think, to speak, to breathe.

"I know you're better than that," Daniel said, his words low and cold. "I've *seen* you cook better than that. Which is the only reason I'm not firing you right now. You had more food come back than go out tonight. I don't know what the hell is going on with you, but you need to get it together. We're done for the week. You've got a couple of days to regroup. Come back and get it right. Don't fuck it up again."

"Yes, chef," she managed.

Daniel exhaled in frustration, then left her to clean her station.

She scrubbed down the grill, but she couldn't scrub away the harsh sting of failure.

She wouldn't get another chance. She had to be perfect next time.

There was no room for error.

Kate sat in the tub, surrounded by bubbles with a glass of wine beside her, and tried to relax. She had drawn the bath about ten minutes earlier, but the stress of the day had yet to wash off of her. She took another drink of wine, and waited for some semblance of relaxation to sink in.

The ranch had lost one of their bigger buyers. It wasn't anything she had done, and she couldn't have done anything differently, but that didn't mean she didn't feel the weight of failure land square on her shoulders. They'd made a good bit of money at a nearby community market over the weekend, and so at least they had that, but it wasn't enough to carry the loss of this client, not with the added expenses they had this year.

Kate wished she was more business-minded. She had grown up on the ranch and knew how the day-to-day operations were run. She could easily transition into those without any break in operations, but she had never been responsible for the business part, and her dad was checked out, uninterested in helping.

She frowned, feeling her stress spike again at the thought of her dad.

Tomorrow was the Fourth of July, and Kate was leaving him home by himself. Not that he *wanted* to do anything for the Fourth of July. She'd asked him, and he said he wanted to spend the night in, yet she felt guilty leaving him alone on the holiday. And at the same time, she didn't feel that guilty, given how snappy he had been with her recently. She couldn't do anything right.

Sell the ranch, he kept pushing.

Except she knew he didn't want that.

She didn't want that.

Selling the ranch was simply not an option.

She shook her head as though she could shake out the thoughts. She was tired of all the stress, of constantly feeling like she was on the brink of losing everything.

Her phone buzzed from beside the tub, and she reached for it, welcoming the distraction. She felt her mood shift the instant she read Rowan's name on the screen.

So we're doing the tubing tomorrow, right? Rowan asked.

Kate smiled at her phone like a teenager. *We'd better be. It's the best part of the festival.*

So I should bring a bathing suit then?

She swallowed. She maybe hadn't thought this through, because her stomach tightened at just the thought of Rowan in a bathing suit.

Yeah. And a towel, she answered, as though her mind was not screaming warning bells.

She squeezed her eyes shut. She needed her life to stop feeling like a high-wire act. One misstep . . .

I'm looking forward to seeing you tomorrow, Rowan wrote.

Kate read the message and relaxed into the warm bathwater.

She was looking forward to that as well, dangerous or not.

Chapter Eleven

Rowan hadn't been so nervous for a date in as long as she could remember. Maybe when she was in high school, but she doubted even then. She had dated plenty, but she couldn't remember another time when she'd really cared about the outcome. She'd always kept things fun—low risk, low stakes. With Kate, though . . . Kate was special. She wanted it to work with Kate. And that terrified her.

Rowan carefully styled her hair and changed her outfit no less than five times before finally settling on a pair of cut-off jeans and a black-band tank top.

Then she waited for Kate, who had offered to drive, to swing by and pick her up.

At the gentle knock on her door, she stood, quickly straightening her clothes and hair before going to open the door. She grabbed her keys and her bag with her towel and slipped out quickly, not wanting Kate to see that she had done some sorting, but the bulk of her belongings remained scattered in half-unpacked boxes.

She pulled the door closed quickly and smiled up at Kate, who stood there looking impossibly pretty, dressed in a soft, sleeveless yellow sundress that fell just above her knees, exposing her long legs. She still wore her cowboy boots, which came up to her mid-calf, and Rowan decided the boots were maybe the sexiest thing she had ever seen.

"Wow." Rowan's gaze traced over every curve. "You look amazing."

Kate's cheeks turned a soft rose shade.

"Thank you," she said. "So do you."

Rowan smiled at the sincerity in Kate's voice. They headed down the stairs, and Kate opened the passenger door of her truck for Rowan who climbed in, excited for the day ahead.

"Are you prepared to eat a *lot* of fried food?" Kate asked.

"Oh, I'm ready." She had heard rumors of Texas's deep-fried creations, and she was eager to try out the most inventive and purely indulgent deep-fried goody she could find.

Kate laughed. "You say that now."

Kate pulled into the crowded parking lot and was lucky enough to find a lone parking spot near the back. Rowan looked out at the crowd of people all making their way to the main pavilion and saw the white tops of the food vendor tents.

"Wow," she said.

"Fourth of July is kind of a big deal here," Kate answered.

"I see that."

She followed Kate into the crowd. The day was sticky with a heat that clung to her skin. The sun sat high and fat in the sky, shining down on the festival. There were children with elaborate face paint in strollers and seated on parents' shoulders, holding tight to balloons and stuffed animals. The smell of fried food, sugar, and grilled meats carried through the area, and she heard the bass thump of the live band playing in the distance. It was almost overwhelming, the cacophony that assaulted her senses.

"So, where do we go for this river tubing?" she asked, still trying to get her bearing.

Kate laughed and took her hand, leading her through the crowd toward the river, where she saw a couple of booths with bright green rubber inner tubes stacked to the side.

"We sign a waiver, rent the tube, and then get on the river," Kate explained. "A little ways down, we'll get off and a shuttle will pick up the tubes and bring us back here."

Rowan nodded, taking it all in.

"Surely you must have tubing in Oregon," Kate said.

"Our rivers move," Rowan answered.

Kate's laughter was warm and bright, and it melted Rowan, even more than the hot sun.

After she and Kate signed their waivers and paid their fee, they carried their inner tubes down to the river.

Kate pulled the sundress off over her head and kicked off her boots so that she was standing in her bikini, ready for the river. Rowan was completely unprepared for the visual, and she swallowed hard while taking in Kate's soft curves, the smooth expanse of her tight stomach, the swell of her breasts, only barely covered by the soft green fabric . . .

"God," Rowan said under her breath, trying to pull her thoughts out of the gutter.

Kate arched an eyebrow at her with a knowing smile on her face, which made Rowan's face burn red.

"So not fair," Rowan said. "I can't be expected to think when you're standing there in . . . *that*."

Kate stepped closer and teased the bottom of Rowan's tank top, her fingers just barely brushing across her stomach, making it clench tightly.

"You might not want to tube in this," Kate said.

Rowan nodded, but seeing Kate standing in front of her, toned and soft and *perfect*, she felt suddenly self-conscious.

"Turn around," she said.

Kate met her gaze, her eyes soft with concern and confusion.

Rowan gave a small, self-deprecating smile and a shrug.

Kate arched an eyebrow but said nothing, turning around to let Rowan change.

She pulled off her shirt and shorts, then wrapped her arms around herself to cover her too-round stomach. She had bikini shorts on, covering her thighs, but she wished she'd thought to bring an extra tank top to cover her stomach. She wasn't typically self-conscious about her body anymore, but Kate stood there looking impossibly perfect, and Rowan couldn't help but wonder if she could measure up.

"Ready?" Rowan asked, starting toward the water before Kate could say anything.

"Hey," Kate said.

Rowan stopped and reluctantly turned.

Kate's gaze was gentle as it traced across her body, sending goosebumps across her skin.

"You are so incredibly beautiful." Kate stepped over to her and gently unwrapped her arms. Kate's thumb brushed over Rowan's stomach, and she closed her eyes against the soft touch.

Rowan didn't feel beautiful, but Kate sounded sincere, and some of her self-consciousness eased.

"I'm sorry," she said, automatically. "I'm just a little self-conscious about my body."

"You don't need to be," Kate promised. "You have a great body."

Rowan smiled at Kate's words.

"In fact," Kate continued, leaning in and speaking into her ear, "I have all sorts of things that I'd like to do to your body."

Rowan's breath caught. She didn't get to ask a follow-up question because Kate moved away, picked up her inner tube, and headed for the water, leaving her standing there trying to collect herself.

"You're evil, Kate Landreth," she said, racing to catch up and get her tube in the water.

Kate just grinned, sat down in her tube, and kicked herself away from the river's edge.

Rowan shook her head, but laughed and got into her own tube.

The water was wonderfully cool against the heat of the day. Rowan sat with her feet and hands dangling in the water, and floated down the river alongside Kate.

And just like that, she *got* it. River tubing made sense, and she realized she'd been missing out. The sun was hot as it beat down on them, but no longer unbearably so, with their feet dangling in the cool river. Kate held tight to Rowan's tube so that they didn't drift apart. They got to relax as they drifted slowly downstream, listening to the music and laughter from the festival.

"Maybe I misjudged Texas," Rowan said as they floated lazily.

Kate looked over, green eyes shining as her mouth curved up into a smile. "Oh yeah?"

"Yeah. I expected flat, hot, and boring. Turns out it's only two of those things."

Kate laughed and splashed her. She yelped as the water hit her stomach.

"I'm glad we're not boring you to death here," Kate said.

Rowan took in Kate's impossibly long legs and her slightly tanned skin dusted with a few freckles.

"I'm definitely not bored," she said, her voice low.

Kate held her gaze, and the heat between them burned hotter than the Texas sun.

"Tubing the Comal, south of Austin, is even better," Kate said after a long moment. "I think you'd like it."

"Take me there one day?"

Kate nodded.

"I should make a Texas bucket list," Rowan said. "A grand list of all of the places to see and things to do. Then we can do them together."

"It's going to be a long list," Kate answered. "It's a big state. There's a lot you need to see. It might take a while."

Rowan nodded as if she was thinking it over. "I might be okay with that."

Rowan and Kate walked hand in hand through the crowds of people as the sun began to set, taking in the music and looking at the various Texas trinkets sold by the craft vendors—candles, knitted clothes, little garden creatures, kitchen plaques.

Rowan traced her fingers over a wooden cutting board in the shape of Texas. "What is it with Texans and loving the shape of their state so much?"

Kate just shrugged. "We're proud of our state."

Rowan bit her tongue from making a sarcastic remark about that overinflated Texas pride she saw everywhere. "I guess I can understand that, but I don't have Oregon-shaped items lying around my place, and I love Oregon."

"You're missing out." Kate nudged Rowan with her elbow. "A missed opportunity to represent."

Rowan rolled her eyes, but she pulled out her wallet. "I'll buy it."

Kate laughed. "Really? You want a Texas-shaped cutting board?"

"As a chef I can never have too many cutting boards." And she hoped that maybe some of that Texas pride would begin to wear off on her.

"You'd better be careful," Kate said. "You're going to be a full-blown Texan before you know it."

"I don't know that I'd go that far." Rowan held up a hand to stop Kate. She finished paying, collected the bag with her new cutting board, and took Kate's hand again. "I'll take the cowboy hat and the cutting board, but I'm not going to deck out my apartment with a million of those metal stars, and I'll be damned if I ever hang a wall plaque with a picture of a gun on it."

Kate cringed, and Rowan immediately knew why.

"Oh my God, don't tell me you have one of those!" Rowan cried in shock and surprise.

"To be fair," Kate began, "that wasn't my choice; it was Daddy's. But guns are a big deal on the ranch. You've got to know how to shoot to protect the cattle, calves especially, from animals like coyotes. I grew up around guns. They've always been a part of my life."

She fell silent, thinking about Kate—sweet, gentle Kate—holding a gun. The image didn't compute, and it didn't sit well with her.

"I'd never own a weapon that is intended for anything other than hunting," Kate said. "And I don't love that everyone and his dog can buy a gun. But as ranchers there are times we need them."

Rowan felt the differences between herself and Kate as if they were a physical distance between them. She cared about Kate, she was attracted to Kate, and yet she didn't understand Kate's world *at all*. Oregon felt like another world. She hadn't expected everything and everyone to be so different.

Kate closed the distance by slipping her hand into Rowan's. "I like that we're so different," she said, as though reading Rowan's mind.

"Yeah?"

Kate nodded. "You see the world in a way that is so new to me. Everything I grew up with—all the mundane, boring day-to-day stuff—it's all new when I get to see it with you. Showing you Texas feels special."

Rowan couldn't find words around the sudden emotion that caught in her throat; instead, she leaned in and kissed Kate's cheek.

"What was that for?" Kate asked.

She just shrugged and kept walking.

When they came to the fried food vendor, she stopped in her tracks, staring at the long menu with a mix of awe and horror. Kate hadn't been lying when she said that Texas offered deep-fried *everything*. The sign boasted deep-fried pickles, deep-fried cheesecake, deep-fried ice cream, deep-fried Oreos, deep-fried Oreos stuffed inside of a chocolate chip cookie . . . If you could dream it, it was on the list. Even if you *couldn't* dream it, it was on the list.

"How does one deep fry Kool-Aid?" Rowan asked, staring at the menu board and shaking her head slowly back and forth.

"Easy," Kate said, as though deep-frying Kool-Aid was the most natural thing in the world. "They freeze the Kool-Aid into cubes, batter it, fry it, and toss it in some sugar."

"But . . ." Rowan started, losing the words before they could come out of her mouth. "As a chef, I can't tell if I'm appalled or intrigued."

"Well, you'll have to try it then."

"Oh absolutely. Trying deep-fried everything is at the top of this Texas bucket list of mine."

Kate laughed. "That's the spirit!"

Rowan looked around at the crowd, scoping out the tables and the lineup. "Why don't you grab us a table, and I'll go order a couple of deep-fried creations?"

"On it," Kate said, and she headed off into the crowd to find an open space at the picnic tables.

Rowan stood and looked back up at the menu board. Some of the creations sounded tasty, and some of them sounded border-line monstrous. She settled on the deep-fried Oreos, deep-fried Oreos stuffed inside of chocolate chip cookies, fried pickles, and fried Kool-Aid (because why the hell not?). There was probably enough grease in that order alone to fuel a campfire for a good twelve hours and certainly enough to clog at least one of her arteries, but in the name of science she couldn't pare that list down. She *had* to try them all.

She got up to the front and ordered two of each of the items so that Kate could join her in the experimentation, and then she stood back to wait, watching the staff frantically deep-fry food to keep up with everyone's orders.

"Rowan," the man at the stand called after a few minutes.

She stepped up and was handed a tray of cookies and a tray of fried pickles. She carried the food over to the picnic table where Kate was waiting, and then went back for the last little tray of fried Kool-Aid. Except, as it turned out, that wasn't the last tray. The man handed her two trays of fried Kool-Aid, and then called her back to pick up another tray of fried pickles and another tray of cookies.

She could hear Kate laughing while she herself could only stare in horror as she numbly carried all of the fried food over to the picnic table.

The man called her again and passed her two more trays of cookies. So many cookies. A never-ending amount of deep-fried sweets rolled in powdered sugar.

"Is this the last of it?" she asked, holding her breath while she waited for his response.

The man nodded, and she let out her breath in relief.

"I don't know what I did wrong," she said, carrying the armful of cookies to the table, which was already covered in fried food.

Kate was doubled over laughing while she tried to do the calculations in her head to figure out where she had gone so wrong.

"I swear I only ordered two of everything," she said, sitting down across from Kate and looking at the mountain of food in front of them.

"One cookie doesn't mean one cookie," Kate said through her laughter. "It means one *serving* of cookies."

"Oh God." Rowan looked at the massive amount of fried food in front of her. "The sign should be much clearer."

Kate wiped tears out of her eyes and sucked in air, trying to control herself but apparently failing, because she only wound up laughing harder.

Rowan looked around at the people in line and at the tables next to them. "Does anyone want any fried cookies, pickles, or Kool-Aid?" she asked. "I ordered too much. Help!"

The man at the table next to her chuckled, but offered to take a tray of the cookies. A family in line took the second tray of fried Kool-Aid balls. But Kate and Rowan were still left with far too much food.

"I can't even order the food right," Rowan said, aghast at all of the cookies still in front of them.

Kate's laughter had subsided, but her green eyes still shone with amusement. She reached out and took Rowan's hands in hers. "It's all good. Besides, you've made some new friends." Kate swung her head toward the family that was happily eating the fried Kool-Aid. The youngest child's face was covered with powdered sugar from the bottom of his chin, all the way up to his nose, and he looked completely delighted as he reached for another.

She nodded and met Kate's gaze, feeling some of her embarrassment subside. The way Kate looked at her . . . she flushed with a different kind of heat. "What should I try first?"

Kate pushed over the two different types of cookies. "I'm partial to the deep-fried Oreos. You can never go wrong with Oreos."

Rowan picked up the Oreo stuffed inside a chocolate chip cookie, because it all sounded too indulgent to be real. Sure enough, it was a deep-fried mass of melted chocolate-chip cookie dough, stuffed with a melted chocolate Oreo and melted Oreo cream, all rolled up into a one-million-calorie ball of deliciousness.

"Who the hell thinks of these things?" she asked.

"Every year there are contests for who can come up with the next fried creation," Kate said. "Texans are always trying to outdo each other on the fried food front. If it *can* be deep-fried, it probably *has* been deep-fried."

Rowan tried a fried Kool-Aid bite next, followed by the fried pickles. The truth was, all of the fried creations were good, but for the most part she found them all a little too rich. The fried pickles were her favorite because the acidity of the pickles offset some of the heaviness of the fried dough.

There was still way too much food left by the time she and Kate had finished. Eventually she was so full she couldn't have managed another bite, and she had to concede defeat.

Rowan continued trying to pawn off the extra untouched fried platters on unsuspecting fairgoers.

"I haven't eaten this much food since I was a teenager, pigging out at the fair with my friends," Kate said.

"I haven't eaten this much food ever."

Kate laughed. "Admit it. It was pretty darn good."

She shook her head. "I will admit that it was interesting."

Kate kicked her playfully under the table.

"Okay, fine, it was good."

Kate grinned, clearly happy to have won.

Rowan felt bad having to throw out all the excess fried food, but there was nothing more she could do.

She and Kate headed back into the crowd, taking in the vendors and game booths.

She would describe the entire night so far as interesting, but also "pretty darn good" as Kate might say. The festival was fun, vibrant, *alive*. There was something that felt special about it.

It was a night she didn't want to forget.

The instant she saw the game booth, she grabbed Kate's hand and pulled her forward. "You said you're good at shooting!"

The game's booth was set up with rifles and little moving metal targets.

"Win me the stuffed elephant?" Rowan asked, looking up at Kate with her hands clasped in front of her, her eyes wide and her smile hopeful.

Kate rolled her eyes with a laugh in response, but stepped up toward the booth.

"On one condition though," Kate said. She held up one finger and her eyes had a playful shine.

"Anything," Rowan promised, though her stomach knotted at what she might be promising.

"You have to give it a try, too," Kate said. "I'll walk you through it, but you're going to play as well."

Rowan wished she hadn't agreed to anything. "I'm going to make a fool of myself in front of the Texans."

Kate began to put her wallet away.

"Okay, fine!" she agreed. "I'll do it."

Kate smiled and handed a five-dollar bill to the guy working the stand, who handed Kate the little pellet rifle and wished her luck in a monotone voice.

"You hold it like this," Kate demonstrated how to hold the gun.

Rowan nodded. It seemed easy enough. Butt of the gun on her shoulder. Finger on the trigger. Pull trigger. Hit target.

"You're going to want to take a deep breath to steady yourself and pull the trigger on the exhale," Kate said. "Like this."

She watched Kate fire the pellet rifle and knock down the first target.

"Wow." Rowan was genuinely impressed at the ease with which Kate hit the target. She still hadn't tried it herself, but she sensed it wasn't as easy as Kate made it look.

Kate readied herself again and knocked down the next target. The targets moved faster. Kate knocked down another. Faster still. Another hit. Kate fired all eight of her pellets and hit all eight of the targets.

"Nicely done," the worker said, no longer sounding so bored.

"Which one of the prizes do you want? You knocked down all of the targets so you can pick from any of them."

"I'll take the elephant," Kate said, taking the smiling stuffed elephant and pulling it close.

Rowan reached for the elephant, but Kate shook her head. "Not so fast. You're up."

Rowan looked over at the targets, which were being returned to their upright position. "I can't now. You made it look so easy. I'm going to make a fool of myself in comparison."

Kate hugged the elephant. "I think I'll name him Walter."

Rowan's mouth dropped open. "Um, no. She's clearly a she, and her name is clearly Beatrice."

Kate swung her head toward the booth and then looked at Rowan expectantly.

She begrudgingly stepped forward and handed the man five dollars. Then she picked up the pellet rifle and tried to hold it the way Kate had.

Kate walked her through all the steps, but her first shot hit the backboard, a good foot too high to have even had a hope of hitting the targets.

"See? I suck at this."

Kate gently corrected her stance, and ran her hands over Rowan's bare arms to fix how she was holding the rifle.

Rowan's next shot was closer, but still nowhere near hitting a target. It went like that for the first seven of her shots. On the last, with Kate's guidance, she managed to hit the largest of the targets.

Kate cheered.

"No prize," the man said, bored again.

But Kate was already handing Rowan the elephant and pulling her into a big celebratory hug.

"You did it!" Kate said.

Rowan didn't even try to wipe the smile from her face. She *did* do it.

"I don't know why that was so oddly satisfying," she said.

Kate grinned and bumped her with her shoulder.

"I'm still never going to hang a gun placard on my wall," Rowan said. "And I'll always rally for gun control, no matter how satisfying that little target game was."

"I'll rally right along with you," Kate said. "I'm with you about the need for restrictions. Needing guns on the ranch and thinking they have a place for personal use and everyday carry are totally different. It's not black or white."

Rowan nodded, even though she wasn't sure what to think. She felt disoriented in this new world.

She hugged Beatrice close, already thinking of how she was going to tell everyone back home that she'd hit the moving target.

"My friends aren't going to believe me," she said.

"I may have got a video."

Rowan looked at Kate, her smile growing wider. "I'm sure you were trying to get something to embarrass me with later, but I hit the target, so thank you."

Kate laughed. "Well darn, my plans were foiled."

Rowan slipped her arm into Kate's and rested her head on her shoulder for a moment before they continued walking. Kate was foiling a number of her plans. Her world felt tilted on its axis. Nothing was what she knew it to be.

And yet she felt oddly balanced.

Kate could have walked hand in hand with Rowan all night. Rowan's hand was soft and warm around hers, and she had spent the evening laughing and smiling, more than she had in months. However, she found herself growing exhausted from the noise of the music and trying to navigate through the thick crowd. She loved the energy of the Fourth of July and the festival, but she was a country girl at heart, and the bustle eventually became too much for her.

"Come on." She weaved through the crowd, toward the parking lot. "I know somewhere a little quieter where we can watch the fireworks."

She led the way back to the truck, where the music was muted and distant, and they were away from the mass of people. The air was stiller and quieter. She could breathe again.

Rowan hugged her stuffed elephant to her chest, clearly in love with Beatrice. Kate hadn't shot targets in one of those game booths in years. Not since high school, she figured. There was little challenge in it for her, and she found the game to be tired and repetitive. But winning that elephant for Rowan had been one of the highlights of her night.

Kate climbed up on the hood of her truck and motioned for Rowan to join her, sitting back against the windshield, her feet stretched out in front of her.

Rowan looked at her like she was crazy. "What are we doing?"

She patted the hood of the truck next to her. "We're sitting to watch the fireworks."

Rowan raised an eyebrow but said nothing as she climbed up onto the hood and took a seat next to her.

Rowan was warm, pressed against the length of Kate's side, and her breathing was a calming lull. They intertwined their fingers and when Rowan traced her thumb over the back of Kate's hand, it was so easy for her to imagine those hands elsewhere. It would have been so easy to lose herself in Rowan.

She knew that Rowan was trying to like Texas for her, and she wanted to believe Rowan actually *could* like Texas. Despite all of the reasons to worry, she couldn't seem to pull herself away. Rowan was hardheaded and stubborn and skeptical of the South, but she was also open and adventurous and funny. Kate had been serious when she told Rowan she enjoyed seeing Texas through Rowan's eyes. And Rowan made her laugh—deep belly laughter that made her forget about all of the stress she was under. She should run from Rowan before Rowan ran from Texas, but despite her fears hope welled inside of her.

"Tell me something about you," Kate said, looking over at Rowan, taking in the strong set of Rowan's jaw, tracing the line up to the small tattoo of a chef's knife and spatula that rested behind her ear.

"Like what?"

She shrugged. "Anything. Everything. Did you always know you wanted to be a chef?"

"Not *always*. When I was a kid, I'm sure I wanted to be something ridiculous like a superhero or a movie star."

Kate smiled, but she didn't laugh along with Rowan. "I'm serious. When did you get into food?"

Rowan looked at her for a long moment before answering. "I started cooking in high school. I didn't exactly win the metabolism lottery. Growing up, most of my friends could eat whatever they wanted and not gain an ounce while I struggled with my weight. In middle school I was picked on pretty badly because of it. I got to the point where I did some unhealthy things to try to lose the weight. Then in high school I had to take a home economics class, and I really enjoyed the cooking component. I was good at it, and it was fun. I started studying cooking and nutrition in my spare time and got into trying to cook healthy food that tasted good. I lost some of the weight, which was initially what got me hooked on cooking, but I didn't really stick with it for that reason. I'm passionate about ethical food, but beyond that I'm not particular. I love creating tasty, healthy meals, and I love pure indulgence and deep-fried creations."

She grinned over at Kate as though the last sentence could lighten the conversation, but Kate didn't want to keep things surface level with Rowan. She wanted to *know* her.

"That must have been hard," Kate said, "the bullying."

Rowan shrugged. "Yeah. But it made me really appreciative of the people who were in my corner. I think that's part of why I've had such a hard time being away from my friends. They're my people. It took me a long time to find them, and it's weird not having them as part of my day-to-day life."

Kate brushed a hand through Rowan's hair, twirling a lock of it around her index finger. "I like how loyal you are." She liked to think that maybe one day, she'd be Rowan's person, and that Rowan would be that loyal to *her*.

Rowan met her gaze, giving her a gentle smile that caused Kate's stomach to tighten.

"Tell me about you," Rowan said. "I can't imagine it was easy for you, coming out as gay in the Bible Belt."

Kate thought for a moment about how to answer. "You know, it really wasn't that bad."

Rowan looked at her, clearly skeptical.

"Everyone thinks Texas is this conservative nightmare for queer people, but that hasn't been my experience. I've met people, and I've dated people, who have certainly found Texas to be a very homophobic place. I think it depends on where in Texas people live. The DFW area hasn't been bad. I have a friend, Jeff, who grew up in East Texas, and he could tell you some horror stories. My dad took a little while to adjust, but he never stopped loving and supporting me. I never worried about getting kicked out of my home, and I have never really feared for my safety."

"I definitely expected Texas to be a conservative nightmare," Rowan admitted. "I'm happy to have been wrong."

"Wait," Kate said, sitting up and looking at Rowan with a grin. "Say that again."

"What?" Rowan asked, a smirk tugging at her lips,

Kate looked at her, eagerly awaiting the words once more.

Rowan met her gaze, and Kate watched the teasing defiance softened into compliance. "That I was wrong?"

She nodded and pressed her lips together to hide her smile.

Rowan elbowed her. "Don't get used to me saying that."

"Oh, it's too late," she said.

Rowan rolled her eyes and Kate leaned in, kissing her lightly on the cheek.

"What did you think of your first Texan Fourth of July?" Kate asked.

"It was everything I hoped it would be, and nothing I could have even imagined, all at once."

She laughed. "Yeah, it's crazy big, isn't it?"

"That's one way of putting it."

"Daddy used to bring me here every year," Kate said. "I'd get all hopped up on the sugary foods, and Daddy would carry me around on his shoulders. Half the time I'd fall asleep before the fireworks."

She could feel Rowan looking at her, but she looked up at the stars, not turning to meet that gaze.

"You know," Kate continued, "I always thought he'd carry his grandkids around like that."

It seemed like such a silly thing to be sad about in the grand scheme of things. There were so many other bigger plans and visions that had been derailed by her dad's accident. But she felt the sadness anyway.

"How's he doing?" Rowan asked.

"Still stubborn as ever."

Rowan laughed. "Yeah. He seemed like a very—how do I say it?—set in his ways sort of guy?"

"Yeah, well, you're one to talk." Kate elbowed Rowan with a smile.

"Hey, I know what I want, and I make it happen. There's nothing wrong with that."

"No, there isn't. It happens to be one of the things I like most about you."

"Really?" Rowan asked.

Kate nodded. "You're driven. I like that."

Rowan looked at her, dark eyes softening at her words. Kate could get lost in the warm depths of those eyes.

"You moved to Texas," Kate said. "You wanted the job, and you risked everything to move all the way out here for it."

Rowan shrugged dismissively.

"It was brave," Kate said.

Even in the moonlight she could see the color rise to Rowan's cheeks.

"You know what you want and you give it your all." Kate lay back, resting her head against the windshield, looking up at the sky. She just hoped Rowan wanted to stay more than she wanted to be back in Portland.

"I want you." Rowan cut through the silence.

She looked over at Rowan who was propped up on an elbow, gazing down at her.

"You're right about me," Rowan said softly. "I want *you*, and that means I'm in this."

Rowan didn't give her a chance to respond. Instead, she leaned down and captured Kate's lips with her own. Kate's breath caught in her chest at the softness of Rowan's lips. She was distantly aware that she let out a soft moan as she reached up, taking Rowan's face in her hands.

Rowan's tongue brushed across her lower lip, and she opened her mouth to Rowan's tender exploration.

Rowan shifted over her. Her breasts pressed against Kate as she settled her weight over her.

Kate allowed herself to get lost in Rowan's tender touch and warm, gentle kiss. She gave herself over to the sensation, letting go of all of her stress and worries, living completely in the moment.

A loud *boom* pulled her attention back to the present. Rowan rolled onto her back, and they both looked up to see fireworks exploding across the sky above the festival grounds.

"Perfect timing," Rowan said.

Kate had to agree. She rested her shoulder against Rowan and watched the explosions light up the sky in a variety of shapes and colors, all the while breathing in Rowan's soft, safe scent, and feeling Rowan's skin against her own.

It was the most perfect moment she had ever experienced.

She looked over at Rowan who was rapt with attention to the fireworks display.

It was at that moment Kate knew she could very well be falling for Rowan. She hoped that she could trust Rowan to be there to catch her.

Chapter Twelve

Rowan woke up and stretched sleepily, smiling as she recalled the night before: tubing the Trinity river, eating way too much fried food (her stomach still hurt a bit from all of the cookies), and watching the fireworks with Kate. She'd wanted to invite Kate up when she dropped her off. She had seen the hope in Kate's eyes, the desire that matched her own. But she knew that Kate needed to see she was committed, and her apartment was still a mess of boxes, so she'd kissed Kate goodnight and somehow used all of her willpower to pull herself from Kate's truck.

Still, the memory of Kate's mouth, and hands, and incredibly soft body . . .

She groaned and ran her hands through her hair.

Sunlight streamed in through her bedroom window, and she lay in bed, looking at her mess of an apartment. Boxes were half-open, with belongings strewn all over from when she'd had to dig around to find items that she'd needed in her day-to-day life. Nothing was sorted. Her bookshelves were built, but only a few books were on them. Her pictures were in frames, stacked in piles, collecting dust. The thought of unpacking was both stressful due to the amount of work to be done and anxiety-provoking due to the permanence it suggested.

Rowan climbed out of bed and dressed in a light tank top and pair of shorts—work clothes. She surveyed the living room, deciding to start with the kitchen as that was the room with the most belongings already unpacked. She cranked the volume on one of her favorite Portland punk bands and began sorting her pots and pans.

As she worked, she found herself less overwhelmed by the task and more energized. Empty boxes were stacked outside her front door, as kitchenware, books, DVDs, and her vinyl record collection made their way onto shelves. The place started to feel a little more like it belonged to her, and she found the familiarity surprisingly comforting. She had been so sad at the thought of making a home in Texas that she hadn't realized how much she needed a little corner of the state to feel like her own.

By the time the last box was emptied, she was sweaty and tired. It had taken her the better part of the morning, and there was still a lot of sorting to be done. She hadn't started hanging her wall art or photographs yet. But she felt a massive sense of pride and relief.

She needed to take the cardboard boxes downstairs to the recycle bin. She gathered an armful of boxes, stacking a few of the smaller ones into one large box. They weren't heavy, but they were large and awkward. She'd rather get them to the bin in as few trips as possible, though.

She was rounding the corner at the bottom of the stairs when she nearly collided with Dave, who was turning to head up the stairs.

"I'm sorry." Rowan shifted the boxes in her arms so she could see better.

"What's with all the boxes?" Dave asked.

Rowan hated his tendency to try to start a conversation every time they saw one another. Why couldn't it be enough to give a simple nod of acknowledgement, or even just a "hello," and be on their way?

"I'm finally getting around to some unpacking," she said, and used her gaze to indicate the boxes in her arms and the recycle bin, hoping he'd take the hint and let her get back to what she was doing, rather than keep her standing there holding a ton of giant boxes.

He got the wrong hint.

"Here, let me help you with those," he said, and before Rowan could object he took a few boxes from her arms.

Rowan frowned at his imposition but didn't protest. There was no point. She might as well just let him dump the boxes. He wouldn't leave her alone otherwise.

"I've been meaning to touch base with you," Dave said, "see how you're settlin' in."

"I'm good."

"It was a big move for you. Are you starting to make some friends around here?" Dave asked.

Rowan looked over at him, and his smile was warm and genuine. She let out a breath. He was a nice enough guy, if a bit pushy. She decided to answer him more honestly.

"It's been a hard transition, but I think I'm becoming a little more settled. I may even come to like it here a little bit, heat and all. Though I'll deny that if you ever tell anyone."

Dave's laugh was loud and oddly contagious.

"Listen," he said, once his laughter subsided, "it's my birthday coming up, and I'm having a bit of a get-together with a bunch of the neighbors. We're going to meet up down by the pool area and grill up some hot dogs and hamburgers. Have a few beers. It'll all be really relaxed. You should join us. It'll be a good chance to get to know some of the folks around here."

"When is it?" she asked, hoping that it was an evening she worked so that she didn't have to lie about being busy.

"It's Sunday evening," Dave answered, crushing her hope. "A few of my church friends are going to come by, too. It'll all be really casual."

Rowan wracked her brain to make up an excuse.

"Feel free to bring your partner. I'm sure she'd be welcome."

Rowan stopped walking, unable to find any words to respond. She wasn't sure what surprised her more, the fact that her neighbor somehow knew she was gay, or the fact that this gun-loving, God-loving, pro-life uber-Texan didn't appear bothered in the slightest.

"I saw y'all when she picked you up yesterday," Dave said as if reading her thoughts. "I'm not blind. I know a date when I see one. She's really pretty."

She was fairly certain her jaw was on the ground. She nodded and tried to think of what to say, all the while trying to assess her neighbor's reaction.

"I get it," Dave said as he heaved the boxes in his arms into the recycle bin. "You're in the Bible Belt. But we're not all homophobic and close-minded down here, ya know. Sure, some are, but I'm sure you'd find that anywhere. Come join us Sunday. Bring your girl. Y'all are welcome here."

"Okay," she nodded, still dumbfounded.

Dave took the rest of the boxes from her and tossed them into the bin.

"Great," he said, as they turned and headed back to the apartment. "I'm looking forward to seeing you there. Hey, do you plan to watch the game tonight?"

And just like that the conversation flipped over to football. Rowan had nothing to contribute, but Dave happily talked about his predictions for the game, the players he had high hopes for, and the ones who'd let him down recently.

She nodded while he talked, but guilt tugged at her for the snap assumptions she'd made about him.

Kate sat atop Stryder, riding slow circles around the large pasture out back. The sun beat down on her, and she relaxed into the gentle rhythm of his stride. There was a lot to love about growing up on the cattle ranch. She loved the cows, she loved living in the country away from the city noise and lights, and as a kid she had loved all of the space to run, the trees to climb, and the mud to play in. But more than anything, she had loved the horses.

She eased Stryder from a walk into a trot.

Her dad had always had a natural gift with animals. He had been gentle and fair as a rancher, just as he'd been as a parent. She had grown up admiring the soft-spoken way in which he approached the livestock. It was clear he had formed a bond with each of them.

Which was why it was especially unfair that riding was what landed him in the wheelchair.

It hadn't been rider error. It was an unfortunate accident, and there was no way to predict or prevent such a thing. The horse, Pip, had gotten spooked. Her dad didn't know what had spooked him. It could have been a mouse, or a snake, or a stick that resembled a snake. He had landed on the ground before he'd had a chance to even sense that Pip had startled, and now nothing was the same.

Kate eased Stryder into a lope.

She tried to turn off her thoughts as she exercised Stryder, riding fast circles around the pasture. She was tired of thinking. There was too much to think about constantly. The ranch, finances, her dad, Rowan . . .

It was all too much.

So she rode, letting the stress slip away as she focused on ensuring that Stryder retained the correct lead, eventually maneuvering in figure eights as she would in a barrel race.

Stryder huffed and shook his head, his thick mane whipping in the wind as she rode.

The tension eased.

Eventually she slowed back to a trot, then a walk, and let Stryder cool down, sauntering slowly around the arena.

"You're a good old horse, you know that?" she asked the horse, who simply kept walking in response.

She thought about the veterinary classes she'd had to withdraw from, following her dad's accident. She had worked so incredibly hard to get into veterinary school, and the courses had been everything she'd hoped they would be, and more. She had been in the first year of her classes, and the courses were still broad, covering the basics before she could get into the really interesting material, and yet she had been completely enamored with her studies. She was *meant* for the program. She had been especially looking forward to studying horse anatomy, with the hope of one day being able to travel to various nearby ranches to treat the cattle and horses that needed care.

There was no point thinking about that.

Sure, she wanted to be able to care for sick animals, but not at the cost of losing the ranch and the animals that she loved.

She took Styder into the barn and untacked him before heading back to the house.

She was surprised to find her dad sitting on the porch and watching her as she walked back to the house.

"You looked like you were having fun out there," he said.

Kate hesitated, her hand on the porch rail. She knew her dad would have loved to be in that field riding.

He patted the chair next to him. "It's okay, Katie, I like watching you ride. I've *always* loved watching you with the animals."

She took a seat next to her dad. "It should be you out there."

He shrugged. "It is what it is."

She said nothing, staring out at the pastures, her dad quiet beside her.

"How was the Fort Worth Fourth last night?" he asked after a bit.

She smiled at the memory of the night before. "Good. I ate way too much fried food, floated the river, and watched the fireworks. I had a nice night."

"I'm glad to hear it," he said. "How's Rowan?"

Kate blushed against her will at the mere mention of Rowan. "She's good. I think she enjoyed the festival."

She felt her dad's eyes on her, and she turned to meet his gaze, raising an eyebrow at the intense look her dad was giving her.

"What?" she asked.

"I like Rowan," he said.

She nodded. "So do I."

"Then why do I hear hesitation in your voice when you talk about her?"

She looked back out to the pasture. "I don't know what you're talking about."

"I always could read you like a book," he said. "You've never been great at keeping things from me, and you're a terrible liar."

"It's complicated," she said.

"How so?"

The stress rose within her. "Daddy, she's not from here. She doesn't *want* to be from here. I see her trying to adjust to life in Texas, but trying to love Texas and actually loving Texas are two very different things."

"Katie," her dad said in that parenting tone that told her he was about to point out the flaws in her logic.

She shook her head and held out a hand to stop him. "No. Please don't. Don't tell me I'm wrong, or that I'm overthinking things, or whatever it is that you're about to say. It might all be true, but that doesn't change the fact that I'm *scared*."

"What are you scared of?"

"That she's going to leave," Kate said.

"Anyone could leave. She's no more likely than anyone else."

"Come on," she said, the frustration growing within her. "You as much as anybody should understand what it's like to love somebody who can't feel *home* here."

Warren Landreth was silent for a long time.

Kate fought the emotion within her as she thought back to her dad, wiping his own tears to explain to her that her mom had left. Only now, thinking about how she would feel if Rowan left, she felt his own pain as well as hers, and the intensity of the memory overwhelmed her.

"She's not your mom, you know," he said at last.

Embarrassment washed over Kate at her transparency, but voicing the fear didn't diminish its power. "It's exactly the same. You always said that Mom didn't want to stay on the ranch. That she wanted to travel, see the world, live somewhere exciting. How is this different?"

"Your mom wasn't happy here, and for the longest time I was able to tell myself it was because she wanted more than living on a Texas ranch, and maybe that was a part of it, but things had been rocky between us. It's possible she'd have left anyway, but

I'd be doing her and you an injustice if I didn't own my role in her leaving. I worked too hard. I didn't put in the effort. Ultimately, *I* didn't make her happy."

"She chose to leave us. Not just you. She left me. That's on her, not you."

She saw her dad shrug. "Maybe. But I don't want you thinking it's as black and white as your mom not liking Texas. I may not have been a great husband, but you're an amazing daughter, and her leaving you is something I'll never be able to comprehend."

"Thanks, Daddy."

"Give Rowan a fair chance," her dad said. "She may leave, it's true. But don't assume she will, just because it's what your mother chose. They're not the same, Katie."

She nodded.

As if on cue, her phone rang and Rowan's name lit up across the display. Despite the fears, she still smiled.

"It's her?" Warren asked.

Kate nodded.

"Take the call," he said, wheeling inside to give her some privacy.

Warning bells rang in her head, but the desire to talk to Rowan won.

"Hi." Kate sank back into the porch chair.

"So, my neighbor has invited us to his birthday grilling party at our complex," Rowan said, leaping straight into the conversation. "As in, you as my date. Attending as a couple. I know you want to take things slow, and I don't want to make any presumptions, but if you'd like to join me, then I'd really like that."

Kate smiled as she listened, and when Rowan finished she asked, "Are you done rambling?"

"Yes."

"I'd love to go with you," Kate said, despite the worry knotting in her stomach. "You know, as a couple."

"Now you're just mocking me and my nervousness," Rowan said.

Kate smiled and rested her feet on the porch rails. "I would never."

"I thought we could pop in for a little while, have a drink or two, get to know some of my neighbors, and then I could give you that cooking lesson I still owe you."

"I was hoping you'd forgotten about that," Kate said.

"Oh, I definitely did not forget. In fact, I've been planning what complicated recipe to start you on. I'm thinking something flambéed." Rowan lowered her voice. "You're not scared of fire are you?"

Kate swallowed hard, choosing to respond to the surface content of the words, not the underlying spark. "Is this about the horseback riding thing? Because a, you could have said no, and b, you enjoyed it."

"And you'll enjoy cooking with me. Trust me."

Kate rolled her eyes at Rowan, who was stealing her own reassurances to use against her.

"It's a good thing you're cute," Kate said.

"So I'll see you Sunday?" Rowan asked.

"I'll be there."

"Great," Rowan said. "Does 3 p.m. work?"

"It does. What should I bring?"

"Just your gorgeous self," Rowan said.

Kate felt herself warm at the compliment, and wasn't sure how Rowan did it—how she could make her melt so easily. She said good-bye, and put the phone down beside her, waiting for the butterflies in her stomach to disperse.

Because of course there were butterflies.

Why did there have to be butterflies?

It didn't really matter what her dad said or didn't say to her. She would continue to be terrified of Rowan, and she would continue to be unable to pull herself away to safety.

You're not scared of fire, are you?

No, Kate had never been particularly scared of fire, but at the moment she was terrified of getting burned.

Chapter Thirteen

Rowan was still unsure about the party, but since she'd invited Kate she figured she had go.

Dammit. Why couldn't I have invited her for dinner? I didn't have to invite her to the party, just because Dave invited us.

But the answer came to her easily. She wanted to show Kate she was settling in, and gathering with the neighbors was one way of doing exactly that. And also if she was being honest, she had been touched to have been invited. She'd always been an extrovert, thriving in social situations and in getting to know and connect with others, and was finding it exhausting being so alone all the time.

Still, she didn't expect to have anything in common with anyone there. Dave had to be at least fifteen to twenty years older than her, and he was Texan through and through. It wasn't like they would suddenly be best buddies. They wouldn't be going to check out local music or calling each other to talk about their dates. He wasn't going to be Alycia, Kris, or Hannah.

She sighed as she continued to war with herself. Back and forth went the arguments for and against going to this party. All the while she knew she would go regardless. She hoped there would at least be good food and beer. She and Kate would put in an appearance, but they didn't have to stay long.

The gentle knock on her door pulled her from her internal debate.

Kate was as beautiful as ever, her jeans hugging the curve of her hips and highlighting her long legs. A soft blue tank top showed off her lightly tanned arms. Her hair was down, but pushed back with the sunglasses that sat atop her head. The sight of her made Rowan forget all of her hesitation.

She'd be with Kate. That's all that mattered.

"You've got to stop doing that," Rowan said.

Kate arched an eyebrow.

"You always show up at my door looking like *that*, and I'm left all speechless. So, hi."

Kate laughed and leaned in to kiss her lightly, leaving her further speechless. "Hi."

"Now that was just cruel."

"You're right. There should be absolutely no kissing. Got it."

Rowan pulled Kate in and kissed her, then stepped back and nonchalantly grabbed the case of beer she'd purchased to take to the birthday BBQ.

"Can I get you to carry these?" She handed the beer to Kate, who took it with a smile.

She then grabbed the platter of beef skewers she'd prepared for the grill, and her keys to lock up her apartment.

"I didn't know we were supposed to bring food," Kate said. "I could have prepared something."

"We aren't expected to bring anything. I'm a chef, though. A grill chef at that. I couldn't *not* bring something."

"This is going to be the first time I get to try your cooking." Kate moved a step closer to Rowan.

Rowan had to focus on what she was doing as she locked her apartment, distracted by Kate's soft scent of strawberries.

"I will cook you a proper meal soon," Rowan promised, once her apartment was locked up. She lowered her voice. "Trust me. I'll make it worth the wait."

A flush rose to Kate's cheeks.

"Come on," Rowan said with satisfaction, knowing her words had distracted Kate. "We don't want to be late, do we?"

Kate fell into step beside her, and she didn't feel as nervous about the party.

The smoke from the charcoal wafted toward them before they turned the corner to the pool area, and the smell of the grill and the meat was a familiar comfort. Dave stood in front of the grill, flipping burgers. The pool was gated, with a grill area that had tables and chairs already set out. A handful of people sat around, talking and laughing. They all looked to be Dave's age or older, and Rowan was about ninety-nine percent certain they would have nothing in common. She had never been one to hold her tongue, and she didn't like faking interest. She enjoyed getting to know new people but tended to avoid social situations where she'd have to put on a front or be inauthentic in any way. Just because Dave wasn't actively homophobic didn't mean the rest of her neighbors would be so tolerant. She braced herself for a lecture about God.

As if sensing her apprehension, Kate slipped her hand into Rowan's and squeezed lightly.

Rowan's nervousness slipped away as she met Kate's warm green eyes.

As she pulled open the gate to the pool and grill area, Dave turned and waved with a big warm smile. "Rowan! You made it."

She held up the tray of skewers. "Happy birthday, neighbor. I hope the grill isn't too full. We come bearing skewers and beer."

Dave held up his hands in delight. "Wonderful! You can set the drinks in the cooler, but I'll take one of them if you don't mind. And we've got plenty of room on the grill for some skewers."

She went to the grill, took a pair of tongs, and placed a handful of skewers on. Then she turned to find Kate unpacking the beers into the cooler, handing one to Dave, and then grabbing one for both Rowan and herself.

Rowan took the beer from Kate and held it up in Dave's direction. "Happy birthday," she said, clinking her bottle against his.

"Thank you. Now introduce me to this girl of yours," he said, already smiling at Kate and extending his hand to her.

151

"This is Kate," Rowan said. "Kate, this is my neighbor, Dave."

"It's nice to meet you, Dave," Kate said. She didn't look even a bit nervous as she shook Dave's hand, as friendly and sociable as ever.

Rowan envied Kate's warm, easy way of interacting with people. People were drawn to her. The kindness *seeped* from her. And it wasn't forced or faked. Kate was just a genuinely *good* human.

And here she was with Rowan—a fact that Rowan was, frankly, amazed by.

"Come on. I'll introduce y'all to everyone," Dave said.

Rowan and Kate followed him over to where the others were sitting.

"That's Lou," Dave said, pointing to a man about the same age as him, with a thick gray moustache and a Cowboys ball cap. "He lives across from us."

Rowan held up a hand in a wave, but Dave continued his introductions before she could tell Lou it was nice to meet him.

"Betty and Randall here live in the apartment below you. And that's Cindy from a few units down."

Rowan mentally filed all of the names and introduced herself and Kate to the group.

"So you're new to Texas?" Cindy asked.

Rowan nodded. "I moved here from Portland for work."

"What do you do?" Lou asked.

She wished she could shift the spotlight off herself, but the questions seemed friendly enough. "I'm the grill chef at On the Range, a new restaurant that opened a couple of months ago."

"Wow," Betty said with genuine admiration in her eyes. "I've heard a lot of talk about that place. You must be a pretty excellent chef."

Rowan shrugged. After her one disastrous night, she had been more on top of her game, but she was still overthinking things and had made a couple careless errors. She was on thin ice with Daniel, and she hated herself for it. She took pride in her culinary skill, but lately she was far from excellent.

"She's being modest," Kate cut in, nudging her.

She looked over at Kate with one eyebrow arched. "Is that so? You haven't even tried my cooking yet."

"Yeah, well, I know things."

Rowan laughed.

"So wait," Lou interjected. "You're a grill chef?"

She nodded.

"And you're letting Dave over there cook the burgers?"

Dave had moved over to the grill and was using his metal spatula to poke at the burgers, presumably to check their doneness.

"Hey, Dave, you're fired," Lou called out as the group laughed. "Hand over the grill to Rowan here."

She shook her head, trying to avoid taking responsibility, but the group was clearly not having it.

"Last time Dave grilled for us, half of the burgers were burnt beyond recognition. The other half were bleeding."

Dave motioned Rowan over, and she took the metal spatula from him.

As she watched the burgers and turned her skewers on occasion, she listened to Kate easily conversing with the others. She didn't seem to struggle coming up with conversation topics and quickly got lost in an argument over college football with Lou.

"On the Range is a pretty big deal," Betty said, stepping over to the grill.

"I was lucky to get the job," Rowan said.

"Randall and I own a restaurant nearby, the Down Home Diner. I would love to chat with you about food sometime. I'm always wanting to learn new techniques, and there's bound to be so much I could learn from you." Betty sounded genuinely in awe of Rowan, which was a new experience for her. She'd always felt certain she had the skills to be at the top of her game, but to have another chef in admiration of her, and want to learn from her . . . She felt pride well within her.

"Tell me about your restaurant," she said.

Betty's wide, warm smile made it clear she shared Rowan's passion. "We do casual Southern comfort food mostly. Nothing fancy, but if you haven't tried proper biscuits and gravy yet, you should stop in."

"I haven't tried the biscuits and gravy yet," Rowan said. "What other dishes do you do? I haven't tried most Southern comfort dishes, to be honest. I'm still on a mission to try all of the Texas cuisine I can."

"Well then, y'all have to stop by," Betty said.

She listened while Betty told her about the food she and Randall cooked, explaining the importance of the perfect sausage for the sausage gravy, and the right way to make creamed corn.

If there was one conversation that never got dull for Rowan, it was talk of cooking. Maybe she did have something in common with her neighbors.

She pulled the skewers from the grill and gave the burgers another minute. The conversation paused while the group came over to get food, taking skewers and selecting buns and toppings for their burgers.

"What did you put in the seasoning for these skewers?" Dave asked, moaning as he took a bite out of one, hardly letting it hit his plate before it got to his mouth.

"If I told you that, I'd have to kill you," Rowan said. She got a burger for herself and Kate, turning to find Kate looking at her proudly. Rowan gave Kate a quick kiss.

Lou cast a sideways glance and frowned at the two of them, but said nothing. The rest of the neighbors were warm and accepting, so she chose to ignore the quick judgment she saw flash across his face. It was a nice afternoon, and she didn't need to let the opinion of one Texan affect that. Especially not when she'd expected worse reactions from the entire group.

Rowan took a seat, and Kate pulled up the chair beside her.

She had thought that she would be itching to leave the party, but she found herself having a good time.

And she found herself *wanting* to stay and get to know her neighbors.

✳ ✳ ✳

It was dark by the time Kate followed Rowan up to her apartment. In fact, they had stayed until the very end of the party and walked back with Dave, helping him carry up all of his grill tools and leftover food. Rowan was talking animatedly with Dave about the latest episode of *Survivor*, a show they both apparently watched religiously. Kate tried to keep her delight from showing as she listened to Rowan and Dave make plans to get together to watch the program when it next aired.

From the outside Rowan and Dave could not have appeared more different. She could understand why Rowan had been hesitant to get to know Dave, who was an older generation down-home Texan. There had been times throughout the evening when she saw that Rowan still had to bite her tongue. Someone had made an offhand comment about "liberal snowflakes," and she'd watched as Rowan physically ached to say something but bit back the words. They didn't all see eye to eye on everything. But there was more that they had in common than separated them.

Upstairs Rowan helped Dave set down the grill tools and food on his counter.

"Happy birthday, Dave," Rowan said. "And thanks for inviting us."

"It was great getting to know y'all," Dave said, and he pulled Rowan into a big hug.

Kate smiled as she watched the exchange. "It was nice meeting you, too," she said.

Dave waved, and Rowan unlocked the door to her own apartment.

As Rowan shut the door behind them, Kate stepped into her, placing her hands on Rowan's hips to pull Rowan flush against her so she could kiss her, slowly and deeply. She felt Rowan's surprised intake of breath as she gave into the kiss, pulling Kate tighter against her and opening her mouth to Kate.

Just as quickly as Kate had initiated the kiss, however, she stepped back, a satisfied smile on her face.

"What was that for?" Rowan asked, taking Kate's hands, and

155

sending little sparks up Kate's arms as she traced her thumbs over the backs of Kate's hands.

Kate shrugged. "It was nice seeing you get to know your neighbors. I know this move has been hard on you, and that's been scary for me. But seeing you today . . . It made me a little less worried. I know you miss your friends, but you're going to find yourself a community here."

Rowan nodded, but a trace of sadness passed across her features and did not go unnoticed by Kate.

"I know it doesn't make being away from your friends and family any easier," Kate said.

"I'll be okay. You're right. I'll find a community here. And, besides, I have you. That alone makes Texas pretty great." Rowan's confident smile slipped back into place, but Kate knew it was masking her homesickness.

Kate looked around the apartment.

"You unpacked," she said. The place was noticeably more like a home than the last time she had seen Rowan's apartment. It felt like Rowan now—comfortable and warm while also colorful and bold.

"I live here now," Rowan said. "It's time that I settle in."

Kate noticed some framed photos hanging on the wall, and she stepped over to them for a closer look. Rowan stepped up behind her, resting a hand on the small of her back.

"This one is my dad and me." Rowan pointed to the top photo, in which Rowan was smiling next to an older man who was tall and thin, with wire-rimmed glasses, in front of a *Star Wars* movie poster. "And this one is my mom and me." She pointed to the photo of her and a woman with long, blond hair, each with a backpack on, smiling in front of a waterfall.

"They're both so blond." Kate marveled at how different from Rowan they looked.

Rowan laughed. "I'm adopted."

Kate turned to Rowan, who was smiling in amusement when she met her eyes.

"I didn't know that," Kate said.

Rowan shrugged. "I was adopted at birth. It doesn't tend to come up because it's not really a big deal. It's a small part of my story. My parents always wanted kids, but they felt there were already children out there who needed homes, and rather than try for a child biologically they chose to adopt me."

"Do you know your birth family?" Kate asked.

Rowan shook her head. "I've never really wanted to. This is my family." She tapped the photo frames. "I definitely got my sense of humor from my dad. He's the king of puns and corny Dad jokes. He and I grew up watching bad sci-fi and horror movies together. He took me to my first punk concert when I was eight. I'm told I make the same facial expression as him when I'm skeptical or amused. I got my love of nature from my mom. When I was little, she would take me for walks and point out all of the different types of birds and flowers. She's gentle and patient, and she takes the time to notice all of those details I don't always notice. I wish I could see the world the way she does, but I tend to blunder my way through things. She's also the adventurous and fearless one in the family. My dad is a lot more reserved. I think I'm somewhere in the middle of the two of them."

Kate laughed at Rowan's self-description. "They sound wonderful."

"They are," Rowan said. "I miss them. I've never really been away from them like this. Summer camp for a week each summer as a child, but that's about it. We talk on the phone, of course, but I haven't seen them in a couple of months. It's weird."

Kate thought about her relationship with her own dad. They had never gone months without seeing each other, and she couldn't imagine living so far away from him. Suddenly, the fact that Rowan was there even trying to make it work in Texas seemed impressive. She hadn't *really* considered everything Rowan was giving up to make it work in Texas.

Rowan was *trying*, and Kate had been too caught up in her own fears to see that.

Kate interlaced her fingers with Rowan's and looked around

the rest of Rowan's place. There was a poster from a punk rock band that Kate had never heard of on the wall, the DVD stand was packed with '80s horror movie classics, and her bookshelf was an eclectic mix of horror, feminist literature, and cookbooks.

"This place is very you," Kate said.

"It definitely feels good not to be living out of boxes anymore," Rowan said.

Kate laughed. "I bet."

Rowan took Kate by the hand and led her into the kitchen. "Are you ready for your cooking lesson?"

"You know," Kate said, trying to think of a way to get out of showing Rowan just how helpless she was in the kitchen, "I think the burger and skewers were enough for me. Why don't we save the cooking lesson for another day?"

The amused expression told her Rowan saw right through her excuse.

Rowan stepped forward until she was just a breath away. "I promise, I'll make your time in the kitchen enjoyable." Her voice, low and husky, sent a shiver up Kate's spine.

Kate swallowed. Hard. Able only to nod.

Rowan smiled in victory and started pulling ingredients out of the fridge and cupboards.

"What is it we're making?" Kate asked, apprehensive about this whole endeavor. She was certain Rowan would say some fancy French dessert she wouldn't even be able to pronounce, let alone make.

She was surprised when Rowan answered, "How do chocolate cookies sound?"

Kate tried to hide her relief. Cookies sounded entirely manageable. "You had me at chocolate."

Rowan laughed. "Yeah, I figured I couldn't go wrong with chocolate."

Rowan pulled out a pot, which she handed to Kate. "You can fill this with about two inches of water."

Kate took the pot, already confused. "I'm fairly sure I've never made cookies in a pot of water before."

"You're going to have to trust me." Rowan's eyes shone.

Kate did as instructed, and Rowan pulled a large metal bowl out from one of her cupboards.

Kate watched as Rowan turned on the stove, set the pot of water on it, and then set the metal bowl on top of the pot.

"This is our double boiler," Rowan said. "We're going to melt the chocolate in here. The double boiler helps keep the chocolate from seizing so we can melt it smoothly."

Kate heard a lot of words she did not fully understand, but melted chocolate sounded good to her.

Rowan passed her a spatula and opened a pack of bittersweet chocolate, which she broke into chunks and added to the bowl.

"Your job is to stir the chocolate occasionally as it melts," Rowan said.

She nodded. That seemed easy enough. Nevertheless, she held the spatula tight in her hand and stared at the bowl with an intense focus.

Rowan added a splash of coffee liqueur. "For flavor."

Kate stirred the chocolate as it melted, carefully scraping it from the sides of the bowl, to ensure it all melted at the same time. As she stirred, Rowan stepped behind her, pulling her close and lightly kissing her neck. She let her head fall to the side, and Rowan kissed up her neck to her jaw before lightly biting her earlobe.

She closed her eyes while Rowan's tongue brushed over her ear. She was hyper aware of Rowan's hands as they slid into her pockets, resting against her thighs, which burned beneath the fabric. Rowan's hot breath against her ear sent a shiver of pleasure through her.

"Don't forget to stir," Rowan whispered before stepping back and releasing her.

She groaned. "You're evil, Rowan Barnes."

She bit down on her lower lip as she stirred the chocolate that was starting to melt more rapidly in the bowl.

"You told me you hated cooking. I'm just trying to make the whole experience more enjoyable for you."

She turned to Rowan, who was feigning total innocence. "Uh huh, that's all."

Rowan nodded earnestly.

Kate rolled her eyes and tried to focus on stirring the nearly melted chocolate and *not* on the attraction that coursed through her body.

Once the chocolate was fully melted and smooth Rowan pulled it off of the heat and turned the stove off. She pulled the spatula from the bowl and let a drop of the chocolate hit her finger, which she popped into her mouth, nodding in approval.

Focus, Kate told herself. She took the spatula and did the same thing, surprised at how the coffee liqueur, even such a small amount, shone through.

"God, that's good," Kate said.

"Of course it is," Rowan answered. "Can you ever *really* go wrong with melted chocolate?"

She pretended to think for a moment. "I guess not."

Next Rowan got out her stand mixer, and added eggs and sugar, setting the mixer to whisk the two together.

"We'll just let that whisk for a few minutes before we add the chocolate," Rowan explained. "We want it to get really light and airy. In the meantime, you can help me add the dry ingredients to the food processor, to combine all of those."

Rowan got out measuring cups and spoons and told her how much of each ingredient to add. Then she turned on the food processor, blending all of the ingredients into a fine powder.

"Are you ready for the secret ingredient?" Rowan asked.

"You're going to let me in on the secret ingredient?"

"I am," Rowan nodded with a very serious expression on her face. "But I'm trusting you to keep it a secret."

Kate placed a hand over her heart in vow and said, "I swear, I will protect this secret ingredient with my life."

Rowan laughed and pulled down a small glass bottle of chili powder.

"Okay," Kate said, "now you've lost me. Chili powder in a cookie?"

"Don't knock it till you've tried it."

Kate was skeptical, but said nothing, helping Rowan measure the chili powder into the food processor, and watching as Rowan blended it all together.

"Some of the best combinations are discovered by people mixing two things that shouldn't go together, but somehow perfectly do."

Kate looked at Rowan, the city girl from Portland, who was somehow her perfect match, and she couldn't argue.

Rowan had her scrape the melted chocolate from the bowl into the stand mixer, and once that was all mixed together she added the dry ingredients.

She watched as it all came together. Rowan turned off the stand mixer and used the spatula to scrape the edges and bottom of the bowl, making sure everything was mixed together.

Rowan showed her how to roll the cookies into balls and set them on the baking sheet. Then, once all of the dough was rolled into balls, Rowan slid the tray into the oven and set the timer.

"And now we wait," Rowan said.

"That wasn't so bad," Kate admitted.

"Just wait until you try them," Rowan said. "You won't be able to tell people you can't cook anymore."

"Well, technically this is baking, isn't it?"

Rowan rolled her eyes. "And you say *I'm* the stubborn one. Next time, we will cook a proper meal and not eat hamburgers and skewers beforehand."

Kate laughed, fully aware that her cheekiness had earned her a second cooking lesson. "I should have stopped while I was ahead."

"That's generally good advice," Rowan said with a smirk.

She stepped closer to Rowan. All of the reasons they shouldn't be together seemed so distant to her now. The fears that Rowan was going to go back to Portland were muted. All that was left was the desire.

She traced her fingertips up Rowan's arms. She watched

Rowan's gaze drop to her mouth. The air between them buzzed with anticipation.

She tilted Rowan's chin up with one hand, brushing her thumb over Rowan's lips before capturing those lips with her own. Her hand slid to the back of Rowan's head, her fingers tangling in Rowan's short hair.

Rowan responded by opening her mouth to Kate, letting out a soft groan as Kate claimed her with her tongue.

Kate allowed herself a moment to get lost in the sensation of kissing Rowan and then pulled back just a breath.

"Should I stop now while I'm ahead?" she asked in a whisper.

"Don't stop." Rowan's breath hitched.

The words emboldened Kate, and she leaned down and kissed Rowan's neck, taking her time to trace her tongue across Rowan's skin. She had no intention of stopping this time. She moved slowly. As slowly as she could stand, eager to repay the torture Rowan had inflicted while they were melting the chocolate.

She pressed Rowan against the counter, placing a hand on the counter on either side of her, while she slowly kissed Rowan's throat, pushing aside the collar of her shirt for more skin. It was still not enough. She wanted more.

She eased Rowan's shirt up, and Rowan helped shrug it off.

She took a moment to allow her gaze to trail down the soft expanse of Rowan's chest before leaning down and kissing her collarbone. Rowan's skin was even softer than she had imagined it would be, and her quiet sighs only heightened Kate's need. Slowly, she worked her way down, her lips brushing over the tops of Rowan's breasts.

She gasped as Rowan's hands slipped under her shirt, and danced up her spine, sending a shiver down her back that settled between her legs. She tried to maintain control, but Rowan's hands teased along the bottom of her bra, and before she knew it Rowan was backing her against the counter and pushing her shirt up, gently biting her nipple through her bra.

She groaned and arched her back, only distantly aware of a beeping sound in the background and Rowan pulling away.

162

She reached for Rowan, wanting Rowan's mouth back on her. "Cookies are ready." Rowan laughed, giving Kate a quick kiss and pulling an oven mitt out of the drawer.

Kate ran her hands through her hair, trying to steady her breathing and return to the present. Cookies. There were cookies to focus on.

Cookies were about the furthest thing from her mind.

Rowan would have been content to let the cookies burn. Pulling away from Kate to take them out of the oven had taken all of her willpower. As she set the tray of cookies on top of the stove to cool, Kate slipped her arms around Rowan, hugging her from behind.

"They smell amazing," Kate said with a sultry timbre in her voice and warm breath that hit Rowan's neck and settled low in her body.

"They need to cool before we can eat them." Rowan turned in Kate's arms, so they were face to face a breath apart. A breath too far.

Kate stuck her lower lip out, and Rowan fought the urge to capture it between her own.

"What will we do while we wait?" Kate asked, the question heavy, spoken low.

Rowan ran a hand down Kate's side. "I can think of a few things."

"Is that so?" Kate arched an eyebrow and quirked one corner of her mouth upward. The anticipation, the hope, the *desire* Rowan saw in that gaze knocked the air out of her chest.

God, she wanted Kate. The air between them buzzed with electricity. She had wanted Kate since the day they met, but even once she had learned Kate was gay, even once they'd started dating, she'd known not to push things until she could prove she wasn't going to leave the next morning. Kate wasn't the girl you slept with and never called back. If Rowan was going to make love with her, it had to mean something, and if it was going to mean something, then Rowan needed to be ready.

Standing in the kitchen and meeting Kate's summer-green eyes, which shone beneath the overhead kitchen light, she knew she was ready for it to mean something.

Kate's eyes sobered with understanding as Rowan held her gaze.

"Please," Kate breathed.

Rowan felt the word, as sensuous as any touch. She swallowed hard and took Kate's hand to pull her to the bedroom.

Kate moved to the bed and sat on the edge while Rowan went around the side to turn on the little lamp on her nightstand, illuminating the room in a soft, warm glow. The light caressed Kate, highlighting every curve and angle. She took a moment to memorize the image before she went to Kate, sitting next to her. So close that she could feel the heat of Kate's body, while not yet touching.

Slowly, almost reverently, she tucked a loose strand of Kate's rust-red hair behind her ear. She grazed her fingertips over Kate's jawline before tracing down her shoulder and arm, resting on her thigh. She wanted to touch all of Kate, to explore every dip and hollow.

The want expanded from Rowan's chest, compressing her lungs. She needed Kate like air.

Kate gazed at her, green eyes dark with desire, and that was all she could take. She leaned in and brushed her lips across Kate's, feather light but enough for the spark between them to ignite, burning up any remaining hesitation. Simultaneously they moved into one another, deepening the kiss, lips and hands and bodies fighting for control.

She grabbed Kate's hips, as though she could anchor herself, but Kate arched her body into Rowan, and she felt the room tumbling away.

When Kate took Rowan's lower lip between her teeth, she inhaled sharply before reclaiming control and deepening the kiss. She could hear their ragged breathing, could feel her heart boxing in her chest. Someone let out a guttural moan, but Rowan wasn't sure who it had come from.

164

Kate dug her fingers into Rowan's bare back, sending heat down her spine to her center. She needed more, needed Kate closer, needed to feel Kate's skin against her.

She caught the hem of Kate's tank top in her fingers and tugged upward.

Kate broke the kiss to shrug off her tank top, and Rowan took in her perfect, smooth skin in the soft light. Kate's body was toned, muscles visible from the heavy labor the ranch required.

Rowan grazed her nails across Kate's stomach and marveled at the ripple of muscle in response.

"Rowan," Kate moaned softly. "I need you."

Rowan couldn't have denied Kate anything had she wanted to. She pushed Kate back onto the bed and settled her weight over Kate who clutched at her, bringing their bodies together.

She breathed in Kate's soft scent of strawberry. She felt dizzy with desire as Kate moved beneath her.

She pressed her hips into Kate's, groaning in frustration at the denim barrier still between them. Too many clothes. She needed them gone. She needed to feel Kate—all of her.

With an urgency she was unaccustomed to, she reached between them, searching for the button to Kate's jeans while Kate traced her lips and tongue in distracting trails across her neck.

"Naked," she managed before reaching for the button of her own jeans.

Kate bit her lip and nodded in response before removing her bra and underwear. Rowan removed her own clothes, but hesitated as Kate pulled off her bra, watching as her breasts fell free.

Rowan allowed a moment for her gaze to travel over the length of Kate's body. "You are so incredibly beautiful."

Even in the dim light, she could see the soft flush that rose to Kate's cheeks in response.

Rowan wasn't convinced the moment was, in fact, real. Kate was so much more than she could have ever imagined. She half feared that if she touched her, she'd wake up. And yet at the same time she *needed* to touch Kate, to taste her, to feel their bodies move together.

The need won. She leaned down to kiss Kate's neck, throat, and chest, moving down slowly, taking her time and not wanting to miss even an inch. Kate's fingers knotted in her hair as Rowan's mouth moved over the swell of her breasts, but even Kate's urging couldn't hurry her.

The sharp intake of breath from Kate when Rowan finally took one hard nipple in her mouth told her how badly Kate wanted her there. Kate's fingers tightened on Rowan's hair.

The way Kate moved beneath her, the soft sounds she made with each flick of Rowan's tongue . . . she could drown in Kate, never wanting to resurface. The rest of the world disappeared. There was no Oregon or Texas, just Kate. In that moment, Rowan was home.

"Come here," Kate said, her voice husky. She tugged Rowan up so that they were face to face once more. Kate trailed her fingers over Rowan's jaw, and their eyes locked.

Rowan wanted to live in the endless summers of Kate's eyes forever.

"You're . . . everything," Kate whispered, her gaze dropping to Rowan's lips.

Her heart quickened and she leaned down to capture Kate's lips once more. The words for how she was feeling echoed in her mind, but they were too big to say. She wasn't ready to say them. She could only try to show Kate with tender touches and deep, slow kisses.

Kate's hands traveled over Rowan's body, clutching at her, fingertips into her shoulders, traveling down her back. Kate's touch was fire burning a trail down Rowan's body.

When Kate slipped her fingers between Rowan's legs, her whole body was hit with a shock of arousal. Her eyes squeezed tightly shut, and she gasped hard and fast against Kate's mouth.

She had been the one setting the pace, the one in control, but that control dissolved as Kate began working slow circles with her fingers.

She dropped her head against Kate's shoulder, trying to anchor herself, reminding herself to breathe. She was undone with the strength of her own need. She'd never felt so desperate before.

Kate's fingers continued to guide her closer to the edge, but she needed to touch Kate more than she needed her own release. She shifted just enough to slip her own hand between their bodies, moving through Kate's wetness, finding the spot where Kate needed her most.

She focused on her own breathing as she matched Kate's pace, trying to delay her own orgasm, but Kate's fingers continued to dance over her, bringing her closer and closer to the edge. Despite her efforts, her breathing grew ragged, and her hips rolled faster against Kate's fingers.

When Kate slid one finger inside of her that was all it took to send her tumbling over the edge. She cried out as her body shook with release, so strong she almost didn't hear Kate's cry as her own orgasm overtook her.

When she came down, the aftershocks still coursing through her, she let her weight settle over Kate, grounding herself with the sound of Kate's heart beating a quick drum.

It was a long moment before Rowan's breathing steadied and she felt like she could move again. When she felt she had returned to herself, she slid off of Kate, wrapping herself around Kate's side and pulling a sheet up over the two of them.

"I knew it would be good between us," she said, still breathing heavier than normal. "I had no idea it would be *that* good. I didn't know we'd be magic."

Kate kissed her jaw. "I did."

She closed her eyes and held tight to Kate. From the start, there had been something special between them. Something she'd never experienced with anyone else before. She should have known they'd be magic, but she'd been too scared.

Kate was special.

Sunlight barely filtered into the room when Kate woke. She looked at the clock on Rowan's nightstand and saw it was nearly

167

six. The sun would fully rise soon. Despite having fallen asleep just a couple of hours earlier, she woke refreshed, her body's internal rhythm ready to start the day.

In fact, she felt more refreshed than she had in weeks. For the past month or so she had awakened on her own, and as consciousness had settled in so too did the ever-present stress and uncertainty. She went to sleep tired and stressed and woke the same way. This time, though, she woke to Rowan lying on her back beside her and to the pleasant ache in her body from the previous evening. For the moment things felt just right.

She looked down at Rowan in the dim morning light and smiled. Rowan had one hand tucked back behind her head and the other draped across her stomach. The light sheet covered her only up to her waist, and Kate took a moment to appreciate the view, resisting the urge to wake Rowan by tracing her fingers over Rowan's skin.

Rowan's short hair was tousled across her forehead, and her lips were parted slightly, her chest rising and falling with her slow breaths.

Kate leaned in and brushed Rowan's hair back, placing a kiss on her forehead before quietly slipping from the bed.

She found her clothes and dressed reluctantly, wishing she could climb back into bed, wrap her arms around Rowan, and lie there for a few more hours. Knowing that wasn't a luxury the day would allow, she went to Rowan's kitchen, found the coffee, and set about making a pot before Rowan woke.

As the coffee percolated, she stole one of the cookies that sat abandoned on the stove and popped it into her mouth, moaning at the rich chocolatey flavor with the subtle, earthy heat from the chili powder shining through. The chocolate formed deep brown cracks in the powdered sugar coating, creating a stark visual contrast between the light, sweet exterior and the rich, complex interior. The flavor matched that juxtaposition, with spicy undertones swirling into the sweet chocolate cookie. The powdered sugar provided a lightness to each bite. It was perhaps one of the best things she'd ever eaten.

She chewed the cookie while she walked through Rowan's apartment, looking at all of the framed photos on the wall. In the honest light of morning she saw how connected Rowan was in Portland and felt that familiar concern bubbling within her. She tried to push it away. Rowan hadn't given her any reason to think that she was going to leave. Her fears were unfounded. Rowan was settling in. She'd make friends in Texas, and her apartment would one day have pictures of them hanging on the walls as well.

Kate could appreciate that Texas was a sacrifice for Rowan. She deserved, at least, the benefit of a chance to *try* to settle in. Fear echoed in the hollows of Kate's heart, but she also had a deep admiration for Rowan. It had been brave to move away from everything she'd known for a chance to chase her dream. If the tables were reversed, Kate wasn't sure she could have made such a drastic move. And therein was the fear. She understood how much Rowan was giving up because she couldn't give up her home. She was busy fighting tooth and nail to keep her home.

She finished the cookie and searched Rowan's cupboards for two mugs. She poured the coffee into each and carried the mugs into the bedroom. She set both mugs down on the end table so that she could lean over and kiss Rowan gently on the lips.

"Hey you," she whispered, lightly shaking Rowan awake.

Rowan tossed over onto her side grumpily, pushing Kate off her while she turned.

Kate smiled at the display. "Good morning, sleepyhead."

Rowan opened one gray eye, then the other.

"What time is it?" Rowan asked. "It's still dark out."

"It's just about dawn."

Rowan groaned and snuggled down into her blankets. "This is not an hour anyone should be awake. Talk to me again in a few hours."

Kate laughed but shook Rowan again. "I wish I could," she said. "I have to get going soon, and I wanted to say good-bye first. I made us some coffee, if you want to snuggle me for a few minutes before I have to leave."

"Why do you have to go?" Rowan asked in a tired, pouty voice.

"I've got work to do on the ranch today, and I need to get there reasonably early to get things started. I have customers coming by."

Rowan rubbed her eyes and gave a sleepy smile and a small laugh. She slowly shifted into a sitting position, leaning back against her headboard, her blanket over her lap. "I guess if you *have* to leave, that's as good a reason as any."

Kate nodded and grabbed the two mugs of coffee. She passed Rowan one of them, then slipped into the bed. She leaned against Rowan, who wrapped an arm around her, taking a sip of her own coffee.

"I really do wish I could stay," she said, turning her head to look at Rowan. "Last night was perfect."

Rowan smiled, thinking back to the previous night. "It really was, wasn't it?"

She nodded. "Beyond perfect."

"You sure you can't stay for breakfast?"

She shook her head. "I wish I could. I stole one of the cookies, though, and it was incredible. I have no doubt whatever you'd make for breakfast would also be delicious."

Rowan laughed. "You got into the cookies without me?"

Kate nodded. "I couldn't help myself. They were right there staring at me while I made the coffee, practically begging me to eat one."

"Uh huh," Rowan said. "You simply had no choice."

"None," Kate agreed. She took another long drink of her coffee. "When will I get to see you again?"

Kate looked at her watch and feigned being deep in calculations. "Oh, about three hours from now when you come pick up your beef order."

Rowan poked her in the side. "You know what I mean."

She took Kate's earlobe in her mouth, and Kate felt the air leave her lungs.

"When can I see you, where we can be alone again?" Rowan asked, her voice low and husky.

"Tonight?" Kate asked, feeling like even that was too far away.

"I work," Rowan said.

"Well, darn." She frowned, surprised at the disappointment she felt. "When's your next night off? You could come over. I'll take you out stargazing at the ranch. You can see the Milky Way from out there away from all of the city lights. There's nothing quite like the stars in Texas."

Rowan tilted her head back and gave a contented sigh. "That sounds about perfect. I'm off Sunday."

"Sunday it is," Kate said, feeling like that was six years away instead of six days.

Sunday couldn't come fast enough. She was a little embarrassed to admit, even to herself, how strong her pull toward Rowan was.

She just hoped that it was not a pull like a moth to flame, where she was about to get burned.

Rowan leaned in and breathed her in, pulling her close, and her doubts dimmed.

There was something real between them. She wasn't the only one who felt it, she knew.

She needed to stop worrying. She needed to trust Rowan when she said that she wasn't planning on uprooting herself from Texas.

Kate finished off her coffee and decided it was time to trust Rowan. She was going to choose to be optimistic. Everything was good—beyond good—and she was going to believe it would stay that way.

Chapter Fourteen

Kate was still smiling when she got home, despite the long day ahead of her. The morning sun cast a soft golden glow across the pastures, and the grazing cattle were distant silhouettes in the gentle backlight. She pulled her truck onto the gravel drive to her ranch and stepped out, breathing the fresh country air. It was still relatively cool, with the night having leeched the heat from out of the earth, but the day was beginning to sweat, and Kate could tell it would be a hot and humid afternoon.

Her thoughts immediately went to Rowan. She could practically hear her complaining about the heat already. The thought of Rowan's stubborn grumbling brought a smile to her face. She flashed back to the evening before, and that image of Rowan did decidedly more pleasant things to her. Sex with her had been everything Kate had known it would be and so much more. She could still feel Rowan's skin so soft and warm against her own, and she flushed at the very physical memory.

But while the sex had been phenomenal, that wasn't her favorite memory from the previous evening. What she remembered most fondly was watching Rowan talking and laughing with her neighbors. Rowan had been animated and outgoing, and she'd looked genuinely *happy*.

She'd watched Rowan and realized she could be happy in Texas. That it was possible for Rowan to stay.

In that moment, everything felt *right*. The ranch, Rowan . . . all of it.

She started the day by letting the horses out into the pastures and checking on the pregnant cow she had resting in the barn. She had errands to run, including picking up the day's orders of beef from the processor. There was altogether too much work that had to be finished before her dad's afternoon therapy appointment, but the usual stress never settled in. Dean and Owen would help with the ranch. There would always be more to do. The work would never be entirely done. But whatever they didn't finish could wait until the next day.

She systematically moved through all of the morning's errands. Her mind kept wandering back to Rowan, but she forced herself to keep the daydreaming at bay, indulging only the occasional warm and happy thought or memory.

That became increasingly more difficult as the morning progressed and she watched the time, knowing that Rowan would be by to pick up the beef for On the Range. Her gaze wandered to the road, looking for Rowan's little Honda. When she finally saw Rowan turn into the ranch, she felt like a teenager again, and she forced the grin from her face as she went to greet her.

"That was the longest morning of my life," Rowan said, stepping out of her car.

And the grin was back.

"Yeah?" she asked.

"Definitely," Rowan said. "There were way too many hours spent missing you."

"You're so corny," Kate said. But her heart had quickened at Rowan's words, and her breath caught as Rowan wrapped her arms around Kate's back and kissed her softly.

"Yeah, you're right," Rowan said when she had pulled back. "I should stop. Absolutely no more flattery from me."

Kate shook her head. "Don't stop. I happen to like corny."

Rowan's eyes held her for a long moment before she grinned

playfully and shook her head. "Too late. No more corniness from me."

She gave Rowan a playful shove. "Jerk."

Rowan laughed, a warm, rich sound.

She wanted to stay in that laughter, enveloped in it like a bear hug. She didn't want to move from the gravel drive and back to the day's responsibilities. She wanted to spend the afternoon with Rowan.

But alas, all too aware of the passing time and of her dad's appointment which she needed to get him to, she forced herself to return to the world of responsibilities.

"Let's go get your order." She led the way to the office, gathering the foam coolers of beef for Rowan, collecting the check, and getting Rowan her receipt.

"I won't see you until Friday, will I?" Rowan asked, standing in front of her, the coolers next to her.

She frowned. "I guess not."

Before she knew it Rowan's mouth was on her. She pushed Kate against the desk, kissing her hard, her hands in her hair, her body flush against Kate's.

And then, as quickly as the kiss began, Rowan stepped back with a lazy smile and ran a hand through her thick, dark hair while Kate was left breathless and trying to ground herself.

"I had to do that before I left," Rowan said with an easy shrug as she headed out to her car with the order of beef.

Kate followed and waved while Rowan drove away.

The cheesy grin was still on her face.

She blew out a breath and headed into the house to see if her dad was ready for his appointment.

Warren was waiting in the living room, looking out the large window that overlooked the pastures.

"Ready to go, Daddy?" Kate asked, stepping into the room behind him.

He didn't look over at her and she barely saw the shrug.

She was about to speak when he turned and wheeled past her

174

toward the door. She kept quiet and followed him, opening the door for him, and loading his wheelchair into the truck.

The drive to the rehabilitation hospital was mostly silent. She wanted to speak—the silence was suffocating—but she didn't know what to say. Whenever she offered her dad encouragement, he only seemed to get more upset, so she said nothing. Neither did he, and they drove in discomfort to the city.

As she pulled the truck into the parking lot and turned off the ignition, her dad spoke.

"I don't see why I have to do this. I don't want to be here." His voice was quiet, and he was looking out the passenger-side window.

"These exercises are making you stronger," she said.

"For what?"

The dejection in his voice was palpable.

She looked at her dad, not knowing how to respond. The accident had been devastating, sure, but he was alive. As far as she was concerned, they could figure everything else out. He didn't see it, though, and she didn't know how to help him.

"Let's get this over with," he said, and swung open the truck door.

She made no move to get up. She just looked at him, seeing the utter defeat in his features—her *dad*. She'd always seen him as invincible.

"I was hoping you'd start helping with the ranch soon." She didn't know where the words came from, and the instant she said them she was fairly certain she'd said the wrong thing, but her dad turned to her and closed the door. "Owen and Dean are working on making the barn and the office more accessible. There's no reason you can't help with things like feeding the horses or customer care."

"Kate, it's not worth it," her dad said.

"Why are you so willing to give up?" she asked, feeling the frustration burn within her. Emotion choked her throat and tears threatened.

175

"It's not that I want to give up," he answered. "It's that I want to be realistic. I stopped being a rancher when I fell from that horse. You want us to keep the ranch going. You want me to go back to my life. But it's *different* now. That life isn't waiting for me. I should be moving somewhere small and accessible. I should sell the ranch. You should finish veterinary school. Why can't you let this go?"

"How can you? After everything. After Mom leaving. After all the work we've put in over the years. That ranch has been everything to us. It's everything to *me*. You want to leave me just like she did."

"I'm not *leaving* you, Katie. I didn't choose this. This just happened."

She couldn't look at him anymore. She clenched her jaw and tried to breathe, trying to keep from crying. They sat like that in silence for a long moment until she was sure she could speak without crying. Very quietly she said, "You are choosing to leave me if you give up on this. You're not the first person to be in a wheelchair. The others don't all quit their lives. Things are different. You didn't choose that. But you can either choose to throw away the rest of your life, or you can choose to try to find a new way to be a rancher."

"It's not just about my life." She heard the emotion thick in his voice as well. "My choice affects you, and I don't want my choice to mean you have to give up on your dreams."

"The ranch is my dream." The frustration gripped her tighter. She didn't know how to make her dad see that. "You can make whatever choice you want, but I'm choosing to keep running the ranch regardless of what you decide."

"Katie—"

"No. I don't want to hear it. I'm giving up on being a veterinarian. I was *hoping* we could get the ranch to a more stable place and then I would go back to school. Maybe I'd have to do my courses at night for a while, but you could start helping again, and we could hire more staff if need be."

"I don't want you to put your dreams on hold."

176

She held his gaze. "This ranch is *home*. It's all I've ever known. It's where I fell in love with animals, and it's *why* I want to be a veterinarian. I don't want to give up on it. In fact, I'm *not* going to give up on it. Just don't leave me to carry it on my own. Please?"

He blinked, his eyes misty. "I don't want to leave you to carry it on your own. I just don't know what to do." His voice broke on the last few words.

"That's why we're here," she said. "The therapists here are going to help you. They're going to give you exercises to build your upper body strength and familiarize you with getting around in that wheelchair."

He stared down at his lap, his expression unreadable. Finally, he nodded. "Okay."

"Okay?" Hope blossomed in her chest.

He nodded a little bigger. "Yeah. But we'd better get going. We're already late."

She leaned across the console and wrapped her arms around him, the relief washing over her in a wave of emotion. Kissing the stubble on his cheek, she said, "Thank you."

He grunted gruffly, but she could tell he had softened. She saw her hope mirrored in his eyes.

"We're going to make this work."

"Okay," her dad said again.

She smiled. For the first time since the accident she had her dad with her.

Chapter Fifteen

Rowan had done little else besides daydream about Kate all day. After Kate left she had intended to go back to sleep, but she had wound up lying in bed thinking over the previous evening, happy and sated. She'd have stayed there all day, enjoying the drifting of her thoughts, an amalgamation of memories and new imaginings, had she not needed to work, but work was cushioned by the fact that the first order of business involved going to see Kate.

Kate who was kind, and gentle, and beautiful beyond words.

Rowan had gone to Landreth Ranch, and even after only a few hours apart the sight of Kate had taken her breath away.

She was falling hard. She could feel it in the way her heart expanded at the thought of Kate. When they'd first met, she'd assumed that Kate was a Southern, down-home Christian country girl, who would have run at the thought of even talking to a lesbian. As it turned out, Kate was a Southern, down-home Christian country girl who was also a lesbian and also every bit as into Rowan as Rowan was into her.

Some impressions, she was coming to find, shouldn't be trusted.

She didn't want to go in to work. The kitchen would require focus and that meant finding a way to tear her thoughts off of Kate. Despite not wanting to leave her happy bubble, the afternoon flew past, and before she knew it, it was time to head to On the Range.

She slung her backpack over her shoulder as she left her apartment. Locking her door behind her, she started down the stairs, only to run into Betty from Dave's party as she reached the floor below her.

"Hi, Rowan," Betty said, falling in alongside her. "Headed off to work?"

Rowan smiled, glad for the friendly greeting and familiar face. "The start of another week."

"Hope it's a great one," Betty said. "I'd love to get together and talk more about food and cooking techniques."

"That would be great." She reached her car at the bottom of the stairs. "You have a great day as well."

Betty waved good-bye and Rowan climbed into her car, quickly cranking the AC.

Punk music blasted from the speakers, playing the album she had burned of her favorite Portland bands. She'd been listening to that album pretty much nonstop, but this time as the heavy guitar riffs and blast beats on the drums filled her car she found the sounds loud and jarring. The conversation with Betty, the music, they were all just distractions, and she wanted a few moments before the busy rush of work to think of Kate uninterrupted.

She switched her stereo over to the radio and scrolled through the different stations until she found the local country music station, then pulled out of the parking lot. The music had a Southern twang and was not at all what she would typically listen to, but she could hear Kate in it. The songs conjured images of Kate riding her horse through the open fields to round up her cattle, Kate teaching her to ride, Kate kissing her, back in the rain outside of the barn.

She especially liked that last image.

She was still smiling when she walked into the kitchen, setting her backpack down and pulling out her chef's knives. Energy and excitement hummed through her, and she knew it was going to translate into her food. She always cooked best when she was energized and engaged, when she was *happy*. Daniel wanted clean and precise plates, but more than that he wanted food that was cooked with passion, and she felt like she could deliver on that. She'd had a couple of rough nights over the past couple of weeks. She'd cooked well, but this time she knew she could be perfect.

The dinner rush started off slow but was busier as the night progressed. Sure enough, she maintained her iron focus and sent out food with a meticulous attention to detail. Every steak had deep, even grill marks and the cook was balanced throughout the entire piece of meat. She executed the timing of all of the dishes with flawless precision. As each hour went by with no detail having been overlooked, her confidence grew.

Daniel congratulated her a number of times throughout the evening, and she noticed he was overseeing her less as the night wore on.

Even during the busiest hours of the evening she maintained her composure and kept up with the orders. She finished the meats with precision timing, ensuring that orders were completed together, and she never once fell behind or found herself in the weeds.

When the night wound to a close, she was exhausted, but exhilarated. She'd done it.

She was back on her game.

"Rowan," Daniel said, once the other staff had finished packing up and filtering out of the kitchen. "You did great tonight. I saw a fire in you that I haven't seen before."

His voice was quiet and serious, but the words bolstered Rowan and she found herself standing a little taller in front of him. "Thank you."

Daniel gave a single nod. "You're a good chef, Rowan."

Pride pulled Rowan a little taller. This night was what she'd been working toward. She had been *great*, and Daniel was recognizing her skill. She had almost come to believe she would be incapable of reaching this moment.

"Look," he continued, and something in his expression and his tone of voice caused anxiety to knot in Rowan's stomach. "I think you have a really promising career ahead, but I'm afraid I needed to see that passion and precision in this kitchen far sooner."

The pride burst, leaving a hole of defeat in her chest. She tried to form words to ask what he meant, but the language wouldn't form in her mind. She had spent the evening cooking better than ever before in her life. All she could do was stand there, waiting for Daniel to continue.

"You have an incredible amount of natural talent with food, but you're not quite ready for a kitchen of this level."

Her lungs tightened, and she had to remind herself to breathe. All the while, Daniel kept talking.

"I think you *will* be ready, and based on tonight's performance I think you're very nearly there, but you need to refine your skills a little more before you're really ready for this level."

"With all due respect, I *am* ready. I think I proved that tonight." She somehow managed to keep her voice steady while she felt anything but. Panicky and desperate, she searched for the words to make him reconsider. "I will admit there have been some shaky evenings. This move was hard on me. I lost my focus and passion for a little while. I'm here now. I'm *ready* now."

She didn't want to beg, but this job was *everything* to her. Her focus hadn't been there the way it should have been, but that wasn't a reflection of her skill or readiness. She needed Daniel to see that.

"I'm sorry," he said. "I've already hired a new *grillardin*. I really do wish you all the best in your future endeavors in the kitchen. I will even be happy to provide you with a strong reference. I think you're going to be an amazing chef, but this kitchen at this time isn't the right place for you."

Defeat hit her like a tank, slamming straight into her chest. There was nothing she could do or say that would change Daniel's mind. She'd cooked better than she ever had in her life over the course of the evening, and that hadn't been enough. The writing had been on the wall before she ever stepped in to work that evening. Tears threatened, and she swallowed them, determined not to humiliate herself further by crying in front of Daniel.

"Thank you for the opportunity and the experience," she managed to choke out.

Daniel softened. "Listen, I didn't get to where I am today without getting kicked down a few times. It's part of growing. Keep cooking and you'll get to where you want to be."

The empathy in his voice only made the threat of emotion that much more imminent, so she nodded, picked up her bag, and left the kitchen for the last time, determined to make it to her car before losing the fight against the tears. She made it, but barely.

She had desperately wanted this job—the kind of job she had dreamed of since she'd first thought of working in the food industry. She'd gotten her dream job and she'd lost it. Her pride was hurt. Her heart was hurt.

She sat there, head against the steering wheel, sad and lost. She had no clue what the next step would be.

She started the ignition, but she couldn't stand the thought of going to her empty apartment. Her apartment that was miles away from home where she'd be completely alone.

She found herself headed out of the city into the Texas country-side toward Kate's ranch.

It was the only place she could find some comfort.

Kate woke to the sound of her phone ringing on her nightstand. Groggy, she turned over to see who was calling in the middle of the night, eager to silence the phone and go back to sleep. When she saw Rowan's name, her irritation dissipated.

"Rowan?" she asked as she rubbed sleep from her eyes and checked the time. It was nearly 2 a.m.

"Hi," Rowan said.

She could tell from the single flat word that something wasn't right. "What's wrong?"

There was a long beat of silence before Rowan replied. "I know it's late, but can I come over? I need to see you."

Kate was already climbing out of bed and turning on the lights. She pulled a pair of jeans on underneath her oversized sleep shirt. "Of course. What's going on?"

"I'll be there in a few minutes," Rowan said, and the phone

clicked off, leaving her standing in her dark bedroom, fear swirling low in her belly.

She changed her shirt and went out to the front porch to wait for Rowan as her mind ran through all of the worst-case scenarios that could have Rowan racing out to her ranch in the middle of the night.

She tried to reassure herself that things would be all right, but her mind flashed back to the day she had received the call from Owen that her dad had been in an accident. She knew better than anyone that life could change in an instant, so try as she might to calm her nerves she couldn't help the fear that seeped into her thoughts.

She didn't have to worry long, as it was only a few minutes before the headlights shone into the drive. She realized Rowan had been nearly to the ranch when she called.

Kate went to Rowan as she climbed out of her car, shoulders slumped. Even in the moonlight, she could see that Rowan had been crying. Her eyes were red and puffy.

Kate didn't hesitate. She pulled Rowan into her arms and enveloped her in her embrace. Rowan sank into her, burying her face in Kate's neck.

"Hey," Kate said. "It's okay. Talk to me. What happened?"

Rowan stood for a long moment, breathing deeply, arms tight around Kate's waist and head still buried in her neck. Then she pulled back slightly. "I got fired."

"What?" Kate looked into Rowan's eyes. A wave of relief washed over her, followed by a deep ache. She knew how much Rowan cared about that job. "What happened?"

Rowan gave a small shrug. "Nothing happened. Not tonight. I was completely on my game. I guess I haven't been as focused as I should have been. My work hasn't been bad, but it hasn't been *excellent*. This is a job that requires excellence, and my head wasn't in it like it should have been."

Kate hadn't realized Rowan had been struggling at work, and she felt a flash of hurt that Rowan hadn't talked to her sooner. But Rowan was there now, and needed her support.

"I wanted this so badly," Rowan said. "I really *tried*."

"Oh Rowan." Kate brushed her lips over Rowan's forehead. "I know you did."

Tears welled in Rowan's eyes, and Kate pulled her close again. She gently stroked Rowan's back, reassuring her things would be okay. As she said the words, though, she found herself wondering what Rowan's job loss meant for them. She didn't want to think of herself, but the awareness crept in. Rowan had moved to Texas for the job, and now she no longer had that job.

"Come on." She felt as if she couldn't breathe. "Let's go watch the stars."

Rowan nodded and allowed Kate to lead her out to the field.

She found a clear patch of grass and lay down, pulling Rowan with her. She rested on her back with one arm out, Rowan settling her head on Kate's arm.

"The stars are so bright out here," Rowan said.

"Yeah. You can't see stars like this in the city. This is where I always go when I'm feeling sad or scared."

Rowan didn't say anything; she just looked up at the stars, and Kate did the same. It was a clear night, and the stars speckled the sky in bright clusters. The pale line of the Milky Way could be seen trailing faintly through the night sky.

Kate's problems always felt a little smaller when she looked up at the stars. There was something about the permanence of those little lights that grounded her.

"That's Orion, the hunter," she said after a few minutes, pointing up to the three stars in a straight line that made up his belt. "And those over there are Ursa Major and Ursa Minor— the Big Dipper and Little Dipper."

"All I see are dots," Rowan said.

"The dots connect, I promise."

Rowan studied the sky, breathing steadily, but said nothing.

Kate used to wonder if her mom looked up at the same constellations, and she felt connected even though her mom had left. She wondered if soon those stars would be the only link between herself and Rowan.

"Do you see that star there?" Kate pointed up at one particularly bright star.

Rowan nodded against her arm.

"That's the North Star. It's the only the star in the sky that stays in the same position as the Earth rotates. People use it to find their way home."

"Will it show me where to go?" Rowan asked, her voice barely a whisper.

Kate wondered the same thing. "I'm sorry you lost your job. I know how important it was to you."

"It was."

So many words hung unspoken between the two of them. Kate didn't want to be the one to voice them and was certain that she didn't want to hear the answers to the unspoken questions. Instead, she leaned over and kissed Rowan lightly, tasting the saltiness of tears on her lips.

Rowan kissed her back, slowly but with a palpable urgency. It was the type of kiss that said everything and nothing at the same time, hope and grief all mixed up together.

When they broke apart, Kate lay back down, and they stared at the sky wordlessly for a long while. She looked up at the bright light of the North Star, wondering where it would lead Rowan.

She feared she already knew the answer.

Chapter Sixteen

Sun was just beginning to crack the horizon when Rowan extricated herself from Kate's arms to begin the long drive back to her apartment. They had stayed out under the stars for hours, talking a little, but mostly lying in silence.

There was a lot they needed to talk about. She knew they both felt the weight of the unspoken words pressing down on them, but it didn't seem time to voice them. She didn't think Kate would ask her to stay—she was too proud for that—but Rowan could hear Kate's longing to ask the question. She wanted to be able to tell Kate what she wanted to hear, but she had moved to Texas for a job, and she didn't have that job anymore. She wasn't sure where that left her and what her next steps were.

She watched the sun rise over the pastures, casting the long grass in a soft orange glow. Trees, cattle, and buildings became visible as silhouettes against the bright sepia-toned skyline. On any other morning the visual would have been enough to take her breath away, but this morning she drove in a haze of painful memories and worries for her future.

She replayed every word that she and Daniel had spoken. The rejection of "*not good enough*" replayed on an endless loop. But perhaps worse was the memory of her own response. She burned with embarrassment at the desperation that she'd felt. She was sure it bled through to her words and her face. Losing her job was embarrassing enough without feeling as though she had humiliated herself with her inability to remain professional and accept the loss. She could only imagine what Daniel thought of her.

Worse, she could only imagine what *Kate* thought of her.

Kate was so put together, steady and strong. Rowan was none of those things. She was an emotional mess, terrible at handling change as evidenced by her struggles with the move to Texas, and she had failed at the one thing she had wanted for herself more than anything.

Not good enough.

She had never been fired from a job before, not even as a teenager. It didn't matter what the job was. Whether it was something she was passionate about or not, she didn't half-ass things. When she committed, she gave her all. She'd always prided herself on her work ethic and drive. With cooking, with Daniel Stanford's kitchen, it was more than a job. It was her *dream* job. It was her passion, finally realized. And if she was being truly honest with herself, even though this was the time it really mattered, she *hadn't* given it her all.

As Rowan drove the country roads, she felt farther from home than ever. She missed her parents. She wanted to be able to talk to them face to face where she could see their sympathy and love for her. She wanted her mom to give her a big hug and tell her things would be all right, and her dad to take her mind off the sadness with a cheesy action movie and a big bucket of popcorn. She missed her friends. She wanted to go for drinks with them and drown her embarrassment. She wanted to go to their favorite bar to watch a local band perform. She wanted the familiarity of the city that she grew up in. The place that felt like home. Portland had so much waiting for her.

But it didn't have Kate.

Red and blue lights appeared in her rearview mirror, and the sound of sirens pulled Rowan out of her thoughts and back into the present.

"*Fuck*," she mumbled, glancing down at her speedometer and realizing that she was going a good fifteen miles per hour over the limit.

As if this day could get any worse.

She pulled onto the shoulder of the little country road, and the police officer stopped behind her. She let out a long breath, trying to steady her nerves. She was about to burst into tears, and the last thing she wanted to do was embarrass herself by crying in front of the police officer. She had had enough crying *and* embarrassment in the past twenty-four hours to last a lifetime.

The officer stepped up to the driver's side door, and she rolled down her window.

"Do you know how fast you were going?"

She nodded, exasperated, wanting to get her ticket and go on with her day. "Yes. Sorry."

"You were going sixty-six miles per hour. This stretch here is a fifty zone."

"I know. I'm sorry." She didn't need a lecture. Just the ticket.

"License and registration," the officer requested.

She pulled out both and handed them to the police officer, who looked them over.

"Portland, huh?"

She nodded.

"That's a ways from here. What brought you to Texas?"

"Work. What else?" she answered with a tired sigh.

She just wanted to go home, but the look on the officer's face said her answer wasn't the one she was supposed to give.

"What did you say?" His voice had a hard edge that caused a knot of fear in her stomach.

"I moved here for work," she repeated, nervously this time.

"Did you say 'what else'?"

Embarrassment flared as she realized what had sparked his anger. She bit her cheek, as if she could keep the words in, but they were already out, and the officer was clearly *not* happy with her response.

"How am I supposed to know why you're here?"

"I'm sorry." She hadn't meant the words the way he took them. They had just slipped out, but she certainly hadn't intended to be rude or dismissive. Rowan searched for an explanation to defuse the tension.

188

"It's been a long night," she offered weakly. "I was heading home from my girlfriend's place, and I was so eager to get home that I lost track of how fast I was going." She hoped she could get the conversation back on track, make it about her speeding, not a misconstrued comment.

The officer gave a curt nod and turned to go back to his cruiser to run her license and registration, but as he turned to leave Rowan distinctly heard the clipped, "girlfriend, of course."

Her embarrassment shifted into anger, hot and bright inside of her. It didn't matter what she said or didn't say. From the minute he'd pulled her over he'd had his mind made up about her.

The officer returned a few minutes later. "I have two tickets here for you. One for speeding and one for unsafe driving. I need you to sign here that you've received them. This signature is not an admission of guilt. You may choose to contest the tickets in court if you'd like."

Two fucking tickets? She'd been speeding. She deserved the speeding ticket. But unsafe driving? It was a total bullshit charge.

She had no choice but to sign, though, so she did.

"You have a nice day, ma'am," the officer said, but his words were cold. "And in the future, just a tip, maybe don't take an attitude with police officers."

"Yes, sir." She burned with rage as she rolled up her window, waiting for him to get back in his cruiser and drive away.

She'd lost her dream job. She was tired and embarrassed and her heart hurt. Then, to top it all off, she'd been pulled over by some homophobic Texas Ranger on a power trip.

"This state is the fucking worst," she said aloud.

She wanted to go home.

When she got to her apartment, Rowan slammed her door shut and threw her keys down on the floor. Kate's comfort had been a temporary relief, but any comfort she'd found in Kate's arms had been stolen from her with her encounter with Office Power-Hungry. Her anger at the police officer blended together with her hurt at getting fired into a slow-seething rage, which she directed at the one tangible thing she could find to hate: Texas.

She pulled out her phone and flopped down onto her couch, dialing her parents' number. They were the people she really needed to talk to. They were the ones who had always kept her grounded, comforted her when she was sad, and calmed her when she was angry. She didn't exactly want to tell them that she was a colossal failure, but they were her biggest supporters, and she needed their advice more than ever.

Tears threatened as she listened to the ringing on the other end of the line, and a few spilled over at the first sound of her mom's voice, warm and full of love.

"Hi, Rowan." She sounded so happy to hear from Rowan.

"I hate Texas." She fought to keep her voice from breaking.

"What's wrong?" Her mom's voice was thick with compassion, making Rowan feel more alone than ever. She felt the distance so acutely it hurt. She wanted her mom sitting there, telling her in person that things would be okay. She wanted a big hug from her. She didn't want to be all alone in the apartment.

She wanted to rage about Texas. She wanted to tell her mom that everything was wrong, from the way the people talked and the gross, heavy heat to the tight cinch of the Bible Belt and the guns everywhere. Instead, she took a few deep breaths to steady herself and began to explain what had happened as calmly as possible. "I lost my job. I went in last night, and Daniel Stanford told me that he's found someone to replace me. I wasn't good enough."

Her voice cracked on the last sentence.

"Oh honey," her mom said. "You're *plenty* good enough. I'm so sorry that you lost the job. I know how much you wanted it and how hard you worked for it."

She heard her mom filling her dad in before he picked up the other line.

"I don't understand," her dad said. "You're an amazing chef. It must've been some kind of mistake. Politics I bet. He probably had a friend who wanted a job."

Her dad had always been the one to go into battle for Rowan, willing to defend her no matter what.

"No, Dad." She wanted to be able to agree with him and feel anger and injustice instead of the sharp sting of shame, but she knew the truth. "I had a hard time adjusting to the high-pressure kitchen. It was harder than I'd expected. And I didn't try as hard as I should have."

She hated to admit that. If she had given it everything she had and lost the job, she would have still been hurt, but possibly not as badly. The shame she felt, knowing she had landed her dream job and hadn't worked her absolute hardest to keep it, made her feel like more of a failure than anything.

"This one didn't work out for you," her mom said, "but another one will. You'll get there."

"Most of the greats faced all sorts of rejection at some point in their careers," her dad added.

That was her parents—ever the optimists. They made it all sound simple. Bounce back, try again. She didn't want to bounce back. She wanted to crawl into her bed and stay there. She heard her parents' platitudes, but in the moment they all felt empty. Maybe eventually the words would sink in, but at the moment, her disappointment was too huge.

"I don't know what to do now," Rowan said. "I moved to Texas for this. I hardly know anybody here. I have no friends or family. I have no backup plan. What do I do?" She didn't mention that she *did* have Kate, and her words soured in her throat as though the omission was a betrayal. She didn't want to dismiss how important Kate had become to her, but the pieces of her life were all scattered, and she couldn't see how Kate and Portland and Texas and her career could come together.

"Breathe, first of all," her mom said. "You've got two choices. You can either stay and look for a job there or come back and look for a job here."

She made it sound so simple. All the while the decision swirled in Rowan's mind, clouding all of her thoughts. Everything was too much in motion for her to think.

She felt tears sting in the back of her eyes. She cared for Kate. Maybe more than cared for Kate. But Texas wasn't her home. Her family wasn't in Texas. Her friends weren't in Texas. She didn't want to lose Kate, but her bruised heart hurt so badly, and without her job all she could think about was how badly she missed *home*—her safe place with her people.

"I want to come home," she whispered, the words opening a floodgate to the tears. Then she said a little louder, "I want to come home."

She breathed a sigh of relief. It was not entirely happy relief. It came with its own set of hurt. But it was an answer, and a way to move forward.

A way to move home.

Chapter Seventeen

Kate knew what Rowan had decided before Rowan came to see her. She had tried reaching out to her on numerous occasions in the week after Rowan lost her job. She knew Rowan was hurting and had sent a few texts to check in. She'd called a couple of times as well. But Rowan kept her at arm's length, responding in short texts and not returning the calls. The sudden distance between them told Kate everything she needed to know. She'd known they were over the minute Rowan had told her that she'd lost her job. Really, she'd known this moment was coming all along. Home is where the heart is, and Rowan's heart was in Portland.

Still, when she saw Rowan's car pull in the dusty drive, she felt the bloom of hope in her chest, that maybe Rowan had come to tell her she had chosen to stay. Kate had fallen in love with her. That much she was certain of. She wanted a future with Rowan.

When Rowan pulled in, Kate was out in the pasture sitting atop Stryder, herding the cows. She quickly rode to the edge of the pasture, where she dismounted and tied Stryder to the fence. Fear coiled around her, tight and constricting, but that flicker of hope kept her walking toward Rowan.

"Hi," Kate said. There was so much more she wanted to say. So many words hanging in the space between them. *Don't leave. Choose me. I love you.*

"Hi," Rowan said back, the same single word also speaking volumes. When Rowan spoke the word, it sounded flat. She looked sad and scared, with her hands shoved into the front pockets of her torn jeans.

The flicker of hope Kate had been holding onto was extinguished, and disappointment rose like smoke in its place. She had thought they had something. Rowan had been willing to move to Texas for work. Why wasn't Kate worth just as much?

"I'm sorry to show up like this," Rowan said. "I hope you don't mind. I wanted to talk to you in person."

Suddenly she was six years old again, watching her mom leave and choose a life outside of Texas without her. She'd lived this moment already, but this time she had a lifetime of defenses to protect her. Her walls went up. She felt herself harden.

"You're leaving." She said the words for Rowan.

Rowan's face fell. Kate hated the hurt that she saw etched on Rowan's features, and she hated herself for wanting to take away that hurt while Rowan stood before her, ready to break her heart.

"I'm sorry," Rowan said. "I never meant to hurt you."

"You were never going to stay," Kate said. There was a slight edge of bitterness in her words, but she wasn't sure if it was directed at Rowan or herself. This moment—the heartbreak she felt—she'd known it was coming all along and yet she'd let herself fall in love with Rowan anyway. "I knew you'd leave eventually, and I still got involved with you. It was stupid of me."

This only deepened the look of dejection on Rowan's face. "No."

The word sounded hollow. How could Rowan argue with Kate when she was the one ending things, just as Kate had predicted? They both knew the truth.

Kate swallowed the lump in her throat, but she refused to cry in front of Rowan.

Rowan stepped closer. "Kate, please. I didn't plan for this. At least believe me when I say that."

Kate held up a hand to stop her. She couldn't hear anymore. She couldn't watch the struggle play out on Rowan's face. If it was over, she just wanted it to be over. She wanted the hurt and the embarrassment to end.

"I think you should go."

Rowan let out an audible sigh and brushed away a tear, but she got back in her car.

Kate didn't watch her drive away. She got back onto Stryder and headed out to the field. She had a ranch to run.

Chapter Eighteen

The flight to Portland was the longest of Rowan's life. She had thought she would be excited about returning home. Instead she sat in her seat, staring numbly out the window, her heart heavy with the pain of leaving Kate. She had watched as the plane taxied down the runway and took off, leaving the Dallas-Fort Worth metroplex behind, but instead of relief she felt only grief. She wanted to land in Portland and put Texas in the past. She wanted to hug her mom and dad and retire to the comfortable familiarity of her childhood home for the night. She had always been a bit of a homebody. Moving to Texas had been a bad plan from the start.

Finally, the familiar landmarks of Portland came into view as the plane made its descent. She took in the comforting presence of Mount Hood. She saw trees, so much greener than the dusty dry fields of Texas. She waited to feel like she was home.

She hadn't checked any luggage so she was able to grab her carry-on bag and head directly to where her parents waited with open arms that she sank right into.

"Honey, I missed you so much." Her mom kissed her head.

Her dad had his arms wrapped protectively around both of them.

Rowan held tight to her parents, reveling in the comforting embrace, never wanting to let them go. She had missed her parents too much for words. She choked up, holding onto them as if she were a child again.

She felt like a child—homesick, heartsick, and needing her parents.

"We're so happy to have you back," her dad said. "I know this was your dream job, and I'm really sorry it didn't work out. But, selfishly, I'm glad you're here."

"So am I," Rowan said. "I've missed you both so much."

She followed her parents to their car. As soon as she stepped out of the airport, she relaxed into the cooler, much more temperate, weather.

"God, it feels good here," she said. "In Texas I can't even go outside to get the mail without breaking a sweat. This is perfect."

"It probably feels like winter to you," her mom said. "You're going to have a hard time once it starts getting cold."

The words were spoken innocently enough, but Rowan felt a pang of hurt at the idea that she was somehow, even if only slightly, an outsider in Portland. "Mom, I'm from Portland," she said. "Always have been. Always will be. I don't need to acclimate to the weather here."

She got into the backseat of the car and looked out the window, wordlessly, while her dad drove. She took in the familiar city roads. She'd never thought of herself as having a particular connection to a place before. Home was just home. She'd never given it any thought. But now as they drove past the familiar downtown buildings and turned onto familiar neighborhood streets, Rowan realized the city was as important to her as all of the people in it.

A sense of stability settled into her core. She was home.

Just as quickly as that sense of stability settled within her, so too did the thought of Kate. She couldn't stop picturing the look of heartbreak etched into Kate's gentle features when Rowan had told her she was leaving. Kate had tried to hide the hurt, and eventually she'd slipped on a stony mask, but it had been apparent, and it had broken Rowan's heart right along with Kate's. And then Kate, who was always so warm, had become as cold as winter. Rowan had expected anger, but she hadn't expected the chill. And she hadn't been prepared for the shame she'd felt when Kate pointed out that her leaving had been a given from the start.

And yet, even as that shame and guilt coiled like barbed wire around her heart, she couldn't regret her choice. She'd had to leave.

Hadn't she?

When they pulled up in front of her parents' house, Rowan felt a lump form in her throat. She wanted so badly to get inside and crash on the guest bed, have a good cry, and sleep off Texas.

In the morning she'd be living in Portland again. She could move forward.

When she pushed open the door, however, she was met with a surprise visitor.

Alycia threw herself at Rowan, wrapping her arms around Rowan's waist and kissing her cheek.

"I'm so glad you're back," she said brightly. "Tell me about Texas. I want to know everything. How was your flight? Start with that."

The cloud that had been hanging over Rowan instantly dissipated at the sight of her best friend, and she laughed at the onslaught of questions. Her heartbreak was momentarily forgotten, as was the distance that she'd felt with Alycia over the past couple months. She had her best friend back. Things could go back to the way they'd always been.

She didn't answer any of Alycia's questions, though. Instead she pulled Alycia back into a big hug, holding her close. "How did you know I was back?"

"Your mom called me," Alycia said. "Speaking of which, I'm a little mad that *you* didn't tell me. But that's a conversation for another day. I was thinking we could grab some dinner and drinks and you can fill me in on what's been going on."

She was exhausted—physically, mentally, and emotionally. But Alycia was there, her person, and she'd missed her so damn badly. And Alycia was all excitement and happiness, two emotions she longed to feel. She nodded. "Sure thing."

Rowan tossed down her bag in the bedroom and followed Alycia out the door.

Alycia drove them to one of their favorites, a local pub with a rooftop patio that often played live music. When they stepped inside, the room enveloped her in a sense of *rightness* with its familiarity. Everything from the punk music playing over the speakers to local brews on tap and the gig posters advertising local bands plastering the walls . . . it was all so much more *her* than anything in Texas had ever been. Coming back felt like stepping into a worn-in pair of jeans after spending a long day in a suit.

I wonder what Kate would think of this place? she thought as she followed Alycia upstairs to the patio. She tried in vain to push the thought out of her mind. There was no point in imagining Kate there. She'd never get the chance to show Kate her city. Still, she thought of sitting on the patio with Kate, sipping beer, and listening to music. She wished she could have that moment with Kate. She wished it so much it hurt.

Not that Kate had ever given any indication that she'd have wanted to visit Portland with her. The pressure to adapt had always been on Rowan, with no indication of any sort of reciprocation.

I guess I've reached the anger stage of my grief, Rowan thought bitterly. It felt good to deflect a little of the blame, but ultimately she had been the one to leave.

"I'm so glad you're home." Alycia pulled Rowan back into the present. "I've been dying for you to meet Julie. I wanted to bring her tonight, but I also wanted the chance to catch up, just the two of us. Hopefully in the next couple of days, though!"

Rowan bristled at the mention of Julie. She was glad that Alycia hadn't brought her. The last thing she wanted to do was make small talk with her friend's new girlfriend, especially while her own heart was broken.

Alycia, however, seemed not to notice the way Rowan tensed. She pulled out her phone to show Rowan photos, and Rowan had to swallow her own hurt and try to inject some happiness

199

into her voice to be supportive. She wanted her friend back, and with every happy photo Alycia showed off the fact that they now had separate lives. It didn't matter that Rowan was back in Portland. Their friendship was going to be different than before.

Once Alycia was done showing her photos and filling her in on everything she'd missed in Portland—which really wasn't much, despite how left out she had felt for the past couple of months—she switched the conversation over to Rowan.

"I'm sorry the job didn't work out," Alycia said, her voice gentle.

Rowan gave a small shrug. Everyone expected her to be sad about the job, but the truth was that after her last conversation with Kate she had all but forgotten about getting fired. All she could think about was losing Kate.

"Are you glad to be home from Texas otherwise?"

That was the question, wasn't it?

She had expected to land in Portland and feel nothing but relief. Everything was familiar and comforting. She was back at her favorite bar with her best friend. The climate was warm without the scorching heat, and there were no Biblical billboards preaching at her from the roadside. She could get coffee at Joe's in the morning and then catch up with the rest of her friend group. And yet she didn't feel all that happy to be home. Not when she was there without Kate.

"I won't miss the heat," Rowan managed.

"I bet not," Alycia said. "And probably not your crazy conservative neighbors."

She didn't laugh along with Alycia. "They weren't so bad actually."

Alycia looked at her for a long time as though trying to figure out where Rowan's head was. Rowan shifted uncomfortably under the scrutiny.

"Are you okay?" Alycia asked finally.

"Yeah," she said, automatically. "Of course. It's been a long day."

But she wasn't okay at all.

She was embarrassed about losing her dream job, heartbroken about losing Kate, and haunted by a million nagging "what ifs." But she was home. Eventually that would be all that mattered, so in the meantime she bit back her heartbreak. She didn't have time for it. She had friends and family to catch up with.

There was no use pining for the woman she'd left in Texas.

Kate spent the week after Rowan left working harder than perhaps she had ever worked in her life. As long as she kept busy she could keep the thoughts of Rowan at bay so she didn't stop. She got up at the crack of dawn and worked the ranch until it was dark, hardly stopping even to eat. The to-do list, which had previously seemed to get longer with each item she crossed off, was finally shrinking to a manageable size. She fixed fences, rotated cattle, cleaned stalls in the barn, and tended to the animals, all while helping Owen and Dean with modifications to make the ranch more accessible for her dad. In the evening she went inside to make dinner for her dad and herself, then spent the evenings poring over the budget and client invoices and filing paperwork. She even managed to secure another client, in addition to On the Range, to sell beef to on a regular basis. She worked until she was bone tired and fell asleep the instant her head hit her pillow. It was the only way to keep the thoughts of Rowan from creeping in. There was no point in thinking about Rowan, no sense wasting any more tears.

Nevertheless, as much as Kate tried to move on, she still felt a giant void. Rowan had come during one of the darkest times in Kate's life, bringing joy and levity when Kate needed it most. Suddenly she had been able to see beyond the day-to-day. She'd seen a future with Rowan, a future full of fun and adventure—beyond trips to the hospital and helping her dad with physical therapy and the overwhelming pressure of being the only one left to care for the ranch.

About a week after Rowan left, her dad confronted her about the amount of work she was putting in. Kate woke extra early that morning. It was still a good hour before sunrise. But once she woke, she knew she wouldn't be able to fall back to sleep. Thoughts of Rowan crept in, and rather than allow them to grow she got dressed and went to the front entrance of the house to get her boots on. She was about to go out to the barn to feed the horses when she heard her dad wheel up behind her.

"Where do you think you're going at this hour?" he asked. "It's pitch dark out."

Kate felt as though she'd been busted doing something she shouldn't have been doing, and she was glad the darkened hallway masked the blush that rose to her cheeks.

"I couldn't sleep," she said. "I thought I'd get a jump on some of the day's chores."

Her dad sat in front of her, his arms crossed over his chest, an unreadable expression on his face, and she felt every bit the child again.

"I've heard you get up before the sun every day this past week," he said at last. "And you don't come in until it's dark. Come sit and talk."

She didn't want conversation. She wanted to get to work. She wanted to burn off all of the anxious energy that coursed through her when she thought of Rowan. She wanted to shovel hay until she couldn't lift her arms, and her body was too tired to feel the ache. She wanted to ride Stryder through the fields until the sun burned off the sting of rejection. She couldn't stay inside and dwell.

"I'm busy, Daddy," she said. "I have to go clean stalls and feed the horses and get things going for the day. I'm trying to keep the ranch afloat."

"That's a load of horseshit and you know it." His tone was gentle, but the harsh language pierced her defenses.

"You're trying to keep *yourself* afloat," he continued. "The ranch is doing fine. You've done a fantastic job since my accident. I can't see why all of a sudden, this week, it would be failing. And the horses can wait. You're going to come sit and talk to me."

"I don't suppose there is any point in telling you I'd rather not?" she asked, already knowing the answer.

He shook his head. "No game. Sorry, kid."

When her dad made up his mind, that was that. There was never any other option.

She followed him to the living room and took a seat on the couch while he lifted himself onto the other side. He was getting better at maneuvering in and out of his wheelchair. A month ago he might not have bothered and opted to sit in the wheelchair instead.

"What's going on, Katie?" he asked, bringing her focus back onto herself.

She tried to think of something to tell him other than the truth. The truth made her feel so foolish. She wracked her brain, praying she could come up with *something*. Anything.

"It's about that Rowan?" he asked.

Tears burned behind her eyes, and she hated herself for being so raw. "I was so stupid. I knew she was never going to stay."

He was silent for a long time, and she couldn't look at him. She was scared she'd see confirmation on his face. Instead, she stared down at her hands.

"You know, Katie, over the years I've had the opportunity to work with a lot of horses, and I've trained most of them."

Kate lifted her eyes, not sure how they had got onto the subject of horses. She was about to interject, but her dad held up his hand and kept talking.

"Now some of those horses were gentle mares or geldings," he said. "But that wasn't always the case. I worked with a good number of ornery horses that tried their damnedest to toss me. When I was with your mother, she told me I was crazy and begged me to stay away from those horses, but I never listened."

Kate thought about how Rowan leaving left her feeling upside-down and hurt. "Yeah, and I got bucked off, is that the point? Tossed in the dirt. Like when mom left?"

Her dad shook his head. "No. That's not the point."

Kate closed her mouth, waiting for her dad to continue.

"The point is, there were plenty of times when getting on the horse seemed like the stupid thing to do. And if any one of those horses had resulted in my accident, that would have confirmed how stupid I was. Everyone would be thinking it. I'd probably be thinking it, too. But you know what? It wasn't some stallion that tossed me. I didn't break my back thanks to a bucking bronco. It was my gentle gelding, Pip, who got spooked one day."

Kate sat quietly, processing her dad's words.

"You never know when and how you're going to get hurt," he said. "And the only way to prevent hurt is not getting on the horse—any horse—in the first place. I don't want that for you."

She swallowed hard, trying desperately not to cry. She'd done so much of that already, and she didn't want to cry in front of her dad.

"I'm sorry you got hurt, Katie. But never regret getting on the horse."

She thought back to her time spent with Rowan. She didn't want to regret trying, but *damn* the fall hurt so bad.

Her dad swung his gaze over to his wheelchair. "Even the worst hurt—it's not the end."

This was the first time since the accident that her dad was there for her to lean on instead of the other way around. "Thanks Daddy."

He nodded and lifted himself back into his chair. "I'll let you get back to work if that's what you want to do, but Katie?"

She looked over at him and waited for him to speak.

"Was she a bucking bronco who was always going to toss you, or was she a gentle gelding who got spooked one day?"

"Does it matter?" If she landed in the dirt, wasn't the outcome the same either way?

He shrugged. "I suppose that's for you to decide."

Her dad wheeled himself back to his bedroom, leaving her to get back to the ranch as she'd planned, but she didn't move. She sat on the couch mulling over everything he said to her, his last question playing over and over in her mind.

Chapter Nineteen

Rowan was grateful her dad was willing to go with her to Texas to help her pack her belongings and empty out her apartment. There was no way she would have been able to get through such a task on her own. The thought of going back to Texas filled her with a near panic as the emotions—her dislike for the state, shame about losing her job, guilt about leaving Kate, and desperate longing to see Kate again—were all amplified tenfold within her.

She was so overwhelmed by the barrage of feelings as they left the airport she almost didn't notice the sticky heat until her dad commented.

"God, it's hot. I don't know how you lived here," he said.

"I don't know, either," she answered robotically.

"Maybe while we're here you could show me around a little bit," he suggested as they climbed into the back of the taxi to take them to her apartment where her car was waiting to be driven back to Portland. She'd left quickly, desperate to get home, and now she had to deal with the actual practicalities of the move.

"Yeah," she said. "If we have any time."

If her dad noticed her hesitation, he didn't say anything. He took the hint and they sat quietly for the duration of the drive.

Rowan looked out at the interstate, at the billboards for Whataburger and Six Flags. Those billboards had made her feel like a tourist when she'd first moved to Texas, but now they were familiar and oddly comforting, a fact that was disarming in itself. She didn't want Texas to feel familiar to her, not even if it was familiar to her only in a *place-I-lived-for-a-while* sort of way. She didn't want Texas to leave any kind of imprint. She wanted to move home and erase this chapter of her life.

The taxi turned down the local roads to her apartment, and the familiar feeling was amplified.

She gazed out the window as her dad paid the taxi, and only when he came around to open the door for her was she jarred from her thoughts enough to unbuckle her seatbelt and exit the cab.

"Pro-God. Pro-Gun. Pro-Life?" her dad asked, reading the bumper sticker on her neighbor's truck.

"That's Dave's truck."

Her dad gave her a curious smile, but said nothing, and Rowan offered no explanation as she led the way up the stairs and fished for her keys to unlock her apartment.

She'd only been gone a couple of weeks, but it felt as if she'd been gone for a couple of years and mere seconds, all at once.

"Wow," her dad said, stepping into the apartment. "The place looks good. You really made it your own."

She shrugged, following his gaze as he looked around at her photos and wall art, at her bookshelf and her furniture. She'd tried to make the apartment home even if the state wasn't. Everything she'd hung on the wall, from the photos to the band posters, had a sentimental meaning to her. It all had a story. Her gaze fell on her cowboy hat which rested on the hook by the door. She wistfully picked it up and held it in her hands, thinking back to the spark she'd felt as Kate brushed against her to place it on her head for the first time, and the look of pure delight that had shone on Kate's face.

She set it back on the hook. The hat would stay in Texas, a reminder of Kate that she didn't need.

"I guess we're going to need boxes," she said, looking around the living room.

Her dad was already pulling a Shiner beer out of the fridge, and he stopped to look at her with the bottle in hand.

"We'll get them," he said. "We've only barely landed. Sit. Let's have a beer. Relax for an hour or so. We don't need to have everything packed tonight."

She shook her head. "No. You can sit and have a beer, but I'm going to go get some boxes."

She was already reaching for her keys again when he stepped toward her and handed her the second Shiner Bock that he had in his hands.

"Sit," he said.

She saw that knowing "dad look" on his face. She did as he said, taking a seat on her couch, staring at the label on the beer.

"You know, you don't have to leave Texas," he said.

"Dad, I came for the job, and I lost that. Why would I stay?"

Her dad took a sip of his beer and she could tell he was choosing the right words. "You've been really sad lately. When we packed your things in Portland for you to move to Fort Worth, you were sad to be leaving, but there was also excitement there. Packing up to move home? There's just the sad."

"It's the job," she lied. "I'm upset and embarrassed that I have to move home because I got fired."

He studied her for a long moment, and Rowan shifted under his scrutiny.

"Rowan," he said slowly, "I know getting fired was hard on you. You've always been a perfectionist and harder on yourself than you need to be with any kind of failure. I'm sure you *are* sad about the job. But I know you. This is something more. Being in Portland, you've been listless and quiet. You're never those things."

She couldn't tell him why. If she told him about Kate and how she'd fallen in love, it would only make the heartbreak all the more real. She and Kate were over, and there was no point in wondering if things could have been different. They were from two different worlds and would remain that way.

"Listen," he said "Your mom and I, we love you so much and we've missed you more than you can imagine, but if you decide you want to stay, we will support that decision 100 percent. We can visit you here, and you can *visit* Portland. Moving doesn't have to mean gone forever. We want you to be happy, more than anything. And since you've come back . . . you're not happy."

"I don't have a job here," she said.

"You don't have a job in Portland yet, either."

She frowned and took a long pull from the beer. She didn't know why she was even considering it. She *did* want to move home. Texas had unbearable heat, an abundance of guns, and oppressive religion. She thought of the homophobic state trooper, and the anger rose in her at the memory.

Then she thought of Kate, the sunset bringing out the gold in her rust-red hair, the shine in her eyes that were the green of a summer field. She thought of the way Kate smiled at her, holding her in her gaze in a way that told Rowan that she was *all* Kate saw. She thought of Kate laughing at her when she'd ordered way too much fried food and the sparkle of amusement in Kate's eyes when she'd placed that silly cowboy hat on Rowan's head for the first time.

"I'd be giving up so much," she said, not sure if she meant by staying or by leaving.

Her dad held her gaze. "Maybe think about what you stand to gain, instead."

She didn't know if there was anything left to gain. She didn't know if she could get Kate back. Maybe if they'd had this conversation before she'd ended things with Kate . . . maybe then it would be different. But she'd already lost Kate, and she doubted she would be able to change that. Kate had barely trusted her the first time, and Rowan had left, just as Kate had predicted. Even if she wanted Kate back, there was no way Kate would ever trust her again.

"What if it's too late?" she asked.

"Would you forgive yourself if you didn't try?" her dad countered.

She thought about Kate, hope and fear simultaneously blooming in her chest.

"There's someone I have to talk to." Rowan set the mostly full beer down on the coffee table and stood.

Her dad nodded and, with a knowing grin, said, "Go get the girl."

Kate hammered in the final nail and stood back, taking in the ramp that she'd built with Owen and Dean.

"Is that it?" she asked, not sure she believed they'd actually finished the project.

"That's it," Dean confirmed.

She stepped on the ramp and jumped up and down a couple of times, as if not believing it could actually bear weight. Then she grinned and high-fived both of her ranch hands. "I can't wait to show him!"

Kate went into the barn and took in all of the changes that had been made. They'd lowered hooks and shelves so feed buckets, brushes and other horse-care accessories were within arm's reach for her dad, and he'd be able to wheel himself in and out. She'd also ordered a front-wheel wheelchair attachment, which would allow him to navigate over the rougher terrain on the farm, giving him a lot more mobility and freedom at home.

She didn't expect him to be able to leap in and take over any of the ranch work, but at least now he'd be able to be involved. He could be around the animals again. She knew that just getting to be in the barn with the horses would lift her dad's spirits. He didn't belong in the house.

She walked through the barn, peering into the stalls where the horses rested, stopping when she reached the second-to-last stall at the end. Pip stood in his stall, sleepy, eyes lidded. After her dad's accident, Kate had wanted to sell the old horse. He was a good horse, and it hadn't been his fault, but still, she didn't see the need to keep Pip on the ranch. Her dad, however refused to let her sell the horse, and so she'd had Owen and Dean care for Pip and take him out riding.

Kate stuck her hand into the stall, and Pip pressed his nose against her palm. He wasn't a violent or reactive horse. He just got frightened one day.

She thought, once more, about the conversation she'd had with her dad about Rowan.

"Was she the bucking bronco who was always going to toss you, or was she the gentle gelding who got spooked one day?"

Truthfully, Kate didn't know. Maybe, no matter what she did, Rowan would never be happy in Texas. Rowan had made it plenty clear how little she thought of the state. And Kate *couldn't* leave Texas. She had her dad and the ranch to take care of. Maybe she and Rowan were simply not meant to be.

But maybe Rowan was frightened. Texas was a sacrifice for her and a bit of a gamble. She'd risked everything for a job that hadn't worked out, and Kate had expected her to risk it all for a relationship without even offering Rowan the reassurance of her own investment in the two of them. Rather than help calm Rowan's fears, Kate had responded with her own.

It was no wonder she'd landed in the dirt.

She scratched behind Pip's ears. She knew what she needed to do now.

Chapter Twenty

Rowan drove the now-familiar dusty road toward Landreth Ranch. With its rolling hills and wide-open fields, she found the drive every bit as pretty as that first morning when she'd first headed out to a Texas cattle ranch, nervous and excited and having no idea what course that drive would set her on. She'd had no idea that the drive would come to feel like her drive home.

She turned the car into the ranch, so scared she could hardly breathe. The setting sun cast a wildfire blaze of reds and oranges across the sky over the pastures. She saw Kate silhouetted in one of the fields and got out of her car to head in that direction.

Please let her forgive me, Rowan thought desperately. She'd had nearly an hour's drive to try to formulate words, but the perfect eloquent apology hadn't come to her, and she prayed the words would find her once she saw Kate.

As she neared the field, she slid the cowboy hat Kate had insisted she buy onto her head.

Kate didn't see her approaching. She had her back to Rowan, tending to one of the cows.

"Kate Landreth, I need to talk to you," Rowan called as she approached.

Kate turned at the sound of her voice and met her gaze. Rowan desperately searched her face for a clue as to whether or not she would be willing to speak to her, but Kate's expression remained unreadable.

Rowan swallowed the fresh wave of fear that bubbled up her throat. She climbed through the large slats in the metal gate separating her from Kate.

"I need to talk to you," she said again, softly this time, pleading.

"What are you doing here?" Kate asked. "You're supposed to be in Portland."

"Kate—"

"And take that thing off your head," Kate added, gesturing to the cowboy hat. "You and I both know it's not you."

Kate's tone wasn't harsh, but the words sent an icy chill through Rowan anyway, even in the sweltering heat.

"What if I want it to be me?" she asked. She ran her fingers over the brim of the hat.

Kate stepped closer. "You don't have to change for me, Rowan. That's not what I want."

"What about what I want?" she asked. "What if I want to wear cowboy hats and ride horses and do all of those Texas things? What if I want to do it all with you?"

Kate shook her head, but her gaze was gentle and her body language warm. She didn't seem like she was trying to push Rowan away, and yet she wasn't exactly letting Rowan in, either.

Rowan took a chance and continued. "No. Not 'what if.' Kate, I want all of that. I want to watch sunsets with you. Sunrises even—since you'd be able to wake me up in time to see them. I want to cook you fancy dinners, and I want you to force me to try ridiculous cowboy things. I want to go to the state fair with you and ride every ride until we're sick. I want to learn to milk cows and two-step."

"I understand why you had to leave," Kate said. "I—"

Rowan interrupted her. She didn't want to hear Kate's arguments. She needed her to know how serious she was. "I went back to Portland, and I was empty without you. I spent *months* missing Portland. I missed my friends and my family. But when I got there, I felt more homesick than ever. You're home to me, Kate, everything I thought I needed. I was wrong. It's all here, standing in front of me. Maybe Texas isn't everything I dreamed of, but *you are.*"

"Rowan." Kate teared up.

This time she waited for Kate to say more, unable to tell if she wanted her to stay or go.

"I bought a plane ticket to Portland," Kate said at last.

Of all the words Rowan had expected to hear, she never would have anticipated those, and her head spun as she tried to make sure she'd heard Kate correctly.

"I can't move to Portland," Kate said. "I know I'm asking more from you than I can offer myself. But I want a life with you, Rowan. Stay here in Texas with me, but show me Portland. Take me with you to visit. Introduce me to your parents. And take off the cowboy hat. You don't need it. Be you. We can find things you love in Texas. This state isn't all country music and rodeos. We can go see bands that *you* love and taste-test all of the local food trucks, and you can teach me to cook."

Kate took Rowan's hands, and traced her fingers over Rowan's, gazing at her with a pleading look in her eyes.

Rowan's heart was so full it hurt, and she struggled to find words around the lump in her throat. "You'd really come to Portland with me?"

"I told you, I already bought the ticket," Kate said. "I was planning to come try to win you back. You just had to upstage my grand gesture."

Rowan gave a nonchalant shrug. "You should have figured out your feelings a little sooner then."

Kate laughed, a warm, rich sound Rowan wanted to hear for years to come.

"I couldn't wait for you to come win me back," Rowan said. "I love you and missed you too much."

"Say that again." There was no longer laughter in Kate's green eyes, which were wide with emotion.

"I love you," Rowan said.

She took Kate's chin in her hand to hold her gaze before saying it once more. "I *love* you, Kate."

Kate leaned in and kissed her—a light, sweet kiss that carried the promise of so much more, the answer to all of Rowan's hopes.

"I love you, too," Kate said against Rowan's mouth.

She wrapped her arms around Kate and pulled her close, deepening the kiss.

Kate smelled of sunshine and hay and strawberries, and Rowan breathed in, feeling the hole in her heart mend itself.

When they finally broke apart, Rowan pulled the hat off her head and looked down at it.

"Do you really think it's not me?" she asked. "I thought I looked quite dashing in it."

"You do," Kate agreed, and she took the hat and placed it back atop Rowan's head. "You look incredible."

Rowan smiled. "Good. Because it's kinda growing on me. A little like Texas."

Epilogue

The server called out orders, and Rowan worked diligently to fill them. She had been in the new kitchen for a couple of weeks, and while she no longer felt the intense *need* to prove herself, she remained determined to make a good impression. Her neighbors, Betty and Randall, had been gracious enough to offer her a job at their largely family-run restaurant, serving good old-fashioned Texas cuisine and comfort food. The restaurant didn't have the glamour of working at On the Range. She wouldn't be a celebrity chef, making waves in the culinary community, but Rowan was learning the secret to cooking the creamiest mashed potatoes she'd ever had in her life and perfectly crispy buttermilk fried chicken, which had the most satisfying crunch when she bit into it. She was learning how to season catfish to perfection and how to make true Southern grits. More importantly, she felt like she was a part of the team, and she was able to cook food she was passionate about.

"You're doing great," Betty called, dipping a spoon into Rowan's sausage gravy to taste it. "Mmm. Yes. That tastes just like my mama used to make it."

Rowan smiled and kept whisking the gravy as it thickened.

She was working the Saturday morning brunch shift. Bacon sizzled from the cooktop beside her, and she heard the satisfying sizzle of eggs hitting the hot pan at the station behind her. Betty was teaching her everything there was to know about Southern cuisine, and she brought with her all of her grill knowledge and her connection to locally sourced beef through Landreth Ranch. The Down Home Diner had been popular before, but was suddenly earning new accolades for their *perfect* steak and eggs and grits.

"You know," Rowan said to Betty as she worked, "until I moved to Texas, I had never had biscuits and gravy in my life."

"Well now, that's just a damn shame," Betty answered. "Biscuits and gravy are one of God's greatest gifts. I swear nothing warms the soul more than a good breakfast of biscuits and gravy. It's my favorite dish to have on a cold winter day."

Rowan laughed. "I'm still not convinced Texans actually know the meaning of the word 'cold.'"

"Just you wait, darlin'. Come January, you'll be eating those words. Now, we're never going to get feet of snow or anything, but it gets cold here."

"I'll believe it when I see it," Rowan answered, although she had to admit the temperature had started dropping ever so slightly.

The timer went off on the oven and she pulled out the tray of fluffy biscuits. She cut the biscuits in half and set them onto plates before spooning the sausage gravy over them and passing them down the line for bacon, eggs, and fruit to be added.

The morning went by quickly. She talked and laughed with her coworkers as she filled orders. She was almost sad when her shift came to an end.

Six months ago if Rowan had been told she would be working in this small family-run diner, she'd probably have turned her nose up. She wanted a high-pressure, high-stakes kitchen. She wanted to work with the best in the industry. She wanted to *be* the best in the industry. It wasn't until she was working in this comfortable kitchen that she realized how unhappy the other kitchen made her. This job challenged her. She was learning new food she'd never cooked before. She was given more autonomy than she'd ever had in a kitchen. More importantly, cooking was *fun* again.

She had a smile on her face as she packed up to go home at the end of the day.

"Keep up the great work," Betty called as Rowan headed out for the day. "Will we be seeing you and Kate tomorrow evening?"

"We wouldn't miss it," Rowan said. Sunday evening grilling by the pool with Betty, Randall, Dave, and Cindy had become a weekly tradition.

She waved good-bye and headed out to her car, eager to see Kate. She had promised she'd get to the ranch as soon as possible once her shift ended. It was a big day for Kate and her dad, and Rowan needed to be there.

She drove out to the ranch, singing along with the country song that played on the radio, her windows rolled down so she could enjoy the warm breeze.

When she got to the ranch, she found Kate tying Mickey to the fence inside of the small riding pasture.

Rowan parked her car and went to her.

"Hi you." Kate smiled as Rowan stepped into the pasture and slid her arms around Kate's back.

"Hi," Rowan said with a slow smile before she leaned in to kiss Kate.

It didn't matter how many times they kissed. She still felt her stomach tighten at the feel of Kate's lips on her own.

"Are you ready for today?" Rowan asked.

A smile lit up Kate's face as she nodded. "I can't wait. This is huge, Rowan. I can't believe you were able to make this work."

Rowan gave a shrug. She hadn't done much. She'd made a few phone calls. That was it.

"Don't downplay this," Kate said. "What you did for us was amazing and thoughtful."

Rowan didn't have to answer because another car drove into the lot and parked.

A minute later a woman joined her and Kate out in the pasture where Mickey stood. She introduced herself as Sandy, the equine therapist Rowan had contacted a couple weeks earlier. Kate had been so excited when Rowan told her she'd found someone who used horses as a form of physical rehabilitation. Rowan had called to ensure that the treatment was appropriate for patients in wheelchairs, and Sandy had excitedly told her about all of the physical benefits of equine therapy in developing core strength and balance in patients with paralysis. Rowan had passed on the information to Kate, but she knew the physical benefits didn't matter to Kate nearly as much as the possibility of her dad being on a horse again.

Owen joined them all in the field while Dean helped Warren maneuver his wheelchair over the gravel path to the pasture, which they were looking into getting paved for him.

"Today's the big day, Daddy," Kate said.

Rowan could see the apprehension on his face, but there was excitement there as well.

She held Kate while Sandy talked with Warren, explaining the process to him. Kate leaned back in Rowan's arms, and Rowan breathed in her soft scent. She couldn't believe how lucky she was that Kate had given her a second chance.

"I love you," Kate whispered.

Rowan kissed her ear. "I love you, too."

Then it was time. Owen and Dean helped Warren up onto Mickey and spotted him as Kate and Sandy led the horse through the field. Rowan leaned against the fence and took in the happiness that radiated from Kate, who beamed with pride as they led her dad, who was on a horse for the first time since his accident, around the pasture.

Rowan's emotions caught in her throat. It would be a long road for Warren, and he was far from being able to ride on his own. But he had started taking over some simple tasks around the ranch, and the possibility of riding horses again, even if way down the line, would open a number of doors for them. Kate was considering picking up an evening class or two in the fall. Rowan couldn't have been prouder of both of them.

She watched as they reached the far end of the pasture and turned back toward where she stood. Kate smiled and waved.

Her heart warmed as she waved back.

There was no longer a doubt in her mind about where she belonged.

She was home.

Acknowledgments

When I moved to Texas for graduate school, I was unprepared for how homesick I would be, and I am forever grateful to my friends who welcomed me, showed me their state, and made me feel at home there. A part of my heart will always live in Texas with y'all.

Thank you, Salem West and the team at Bywater Books, for helping bring this book to life, not just by taking my words and putting them in print, but by providing such incredible care and dedication to quality. I feel so blessed to have had Rachel Spangler as the content editor for this book. Rachel, you were once again a wonderful editor to work with, and your feedback reined me in every time I started thinking that I needed to delete the entire draft and start from scratch.

Thank you, Susan X Meagher, for your mentorship and feedback on the very first drafts of this book. You helped me take my initial idea and shape it into a real book with your sharp eye for character, motivation, and story arcs.

Mom, the only reason this book was finished on time was because you helped me with Addison so that

I could sneak off for a couple of hours here and there to work on my edits. Thank you for your unending support and love for both myself and for Addison. We love you.

Sandra, if you ever get tired of being a paramedic, I suspect you could have a career in editing. Thank you for reading drafts of this book over and over again, and pushing me each time to add details and character motivation. You've been so incredibly supportive of my writing, and I consider myself lucky to have you in my corner.

And last, but definitely not least, a big thank you to my Addison for teaching me the true meaning of love. You've mostly been a distraction when it comes to my writing, but I can't imagine my life without your big grin and happy babbles. My life is so much brighter with you in it.

About the Author

Jenn Alexander was born and raised in Edmonton, Canada. She lived in Texas for three years while completing her MS in Counseling, and is currently living back in Edmonton, where she works as a play therapist. When she's not writing, she spends her time playing drums, traveling, and spending time with her family. She lives with her daughter, Addison; her girlfriend, Sandra; and their two troublemaker pets.

At Bywater Books we love good books about lesbians just like you do, and we're committed to bringing the best of contemporary lesbian writing to our avid readers. Our editorial team is dedicated to finding and developing outstanding writers who create books you won't want to put down.

We sponsor the Bywater Prize for Fiction to help with this quest. Each prizewinner receives $1,000 and publication of their novel. We have already discovered amazing writers like Jill Malone, Sally Bellerose, and Hilary Sloin through the Bywater Prize. Which exciting new writer will we find next?

For more information about Bywater Books and the annual Bywater Prize for Fiction, please visit our website.

www.bywaterbooks.com